Departures

Departures

LORNA J. COOK

St. Martin's Press ⚓ New York

www.stmartins.com

Library of Congress Cataloging-in-Publication Data

Cook, Lorna J.
    Departures / Lorna J. Cook.—1st ed.
      p. cm.
    ISBN 0-312-32128-7
    1. Brothers and sisters—Fiction. 2. Teenage girls—Fiction. 3. Teenage boys—Fiction. I. Title.

PS3603.O68227D47   2004
813'.6—dc22

                                                     2003058183

First Edition: February 2004

10 9 8 7 6 5 4 3 2 1

For my family but especially and always, Christopher

acknowledgments

I wish to thank Lisa Bankoff, my agent, and Dori Weintraub, my editor, for their enthusiastic and honest guidance along the way; Carla Vissers for careful reading and writerly support; and my friends for cheering. I am also grateful to my parents, sisters (natural and acquired), and sons for their influence on my notion of family life—that it is complicated and priceless. And I am indebted to my husband, Chris, for always valuing my writing life, making it possible in so many ways, and never doubting that it would be worthwhile.

Surely whoever speaks to me in the right voice,
him or her I shall follow,
As the water follows the moon, silently,
with fluid steps, anywhere around the globe.

—Walt Whitman, "Vocalism"

Departures

Suzen VanderZee is in love, or nearly. She feels herself on the verge of it, the way she can tell when a flu is coming on, by the strange roaring in the back of her head, the hint of wooziness, the loss of appetite. At the same time, she is lit with a kind of swoony anticipation, as if waiting for a phone call, or a telegram sliding through the mail slot, announcing that this is it, this is the One. She doesn't know yet whom she is in love with, but she senses that she will be sure, soon.

She is only seventeen, but she has always had premonitions. Like her mother, Esme, from whom she inherited blond hair straight as straw and a long, lean frame, Suzen has a touch of clairvoyance—or perhaps she is simply observant, as quiet people tend to be. The eldest of four children, Suzen doesn't know why she is so reserved; sometimes she considers it a lost opportunity that she isn't bossier. Though she often is left in charge of her siblings, she prefers to be alone, separate. She can hardly wait until she truly flees, rises out of the familial nest like a strong, sleek heron.

Meanwhile, she closes herself off in her corner of the house, at the far end of the upstairs hallway, whenever she can. With her eyes closed and nothing but the sound of wind and rain outside her bedroom window, Suzen transports herself to another place and time. Her bed is pressed all the way against the wall beside the screen, which faces north, so she can inhale the night air thick with wet grass and turned soil, leaves just beginning to curl and spoil. The shush of passing cars on the distant highway sounds like crashing waves. Concentrating hard, she rests her head on her arm and lets her hair fall over her face, and imagines she is in a house on a hillside in England, the blankets wrapped around her waist like a gathering of bustle and skirts. Admittedly, she is a little obsessed with the Brontës at the moment, along with Thomas Hardy and anything moorish, boggish, foggy, and romantic. She associates bone-chilling dampness with romance; she also conjures couples before raging hearth fires, covered laps in carriages, and the dark sky over choppy seas. A very alluring picture, very unlike her real world.

In that life, she is a high school senior in a western Michigan town whose sole claims to fame are a visit by a Dutch queen in the 1950s, and a successful furniture factory that churns out armoires with such pride you'd think the nation depended on cherry-stained wardrobes with movable shelves. Suzen's father, Malcolm, is an English professor at the local liberal arts college, Field, which might explain her literary interests, her Anglophilic tendencies. For one semester, when Suzen was seven, the family lived in Wales while Malcolm researched and wrote; Suzen remembers those months vividly, has woven the landscape into her mind like a blanket under which she likes to hide, to burrow away from the world. Sometimes she wishes she were seven still, and not seventeen, not faced with the affairs of adulthood—especially when she observes her parents, sloshing about in their respective routines.

While her father is consumed with books and long dead poets, teaching students who probably sleep through half his lectures, Suzen's mother is a lapsed painter who has given up her talent to toil away at household duties and the concerns of her offspring. Some of her canvases, half-completed abstracts, remain propped along the guest room walls, and Suzen derisively thinks it's probably a good thing her mother gave up. They look to her like poor imitations of Picasso, too splashy and blocky, random swirls and soulless faces. Suzen imagines her mother standing with a brush poised, thinking hard, trying to make something profound; the finished products are transparent with self-conscious effort. But then, she was young.

Esme was only nineteen, two years older than Suzen, when she first got pregnant. A sophomore in college, her long hair swept over one shoulder, Esme had met Malcolm when they lived in the same coed dorm. According to their how-we-met fable, Esme had wandered down the hall to Malcolm's room to ask if he would mind turning down his stereo so she could study.

"Or are you a music major?" she asked sweetly. Like an idiot, Malcolm had missed the facetious lilt in her voice, and sheepishly shook his head no. "I didn't think so," Esme said, before turning around and leaving.

Suzen used to think the story funny, but now she finds it a little sad, so representative of how her parents continue to grate against one another. She thinks of their marriage as the cycles of a washing machine: agitate, rinse, spin. It's no wonder, she muses, living in a house full of children and rodents, papers taking over the kitchen countertops like kudzu. Apparently it all happened so fast, they had no time to think; they just coped. Suzen imagines her mother, a mere kid herself, pulling a plastic wand from a kit and finding herself about to be someone's mother. Suzen's, to be exact. Yet, Esme abandoned college without apparent protest, and planned a small tasteful wedding, as Malcolm graduated and prepared for graduate school. Esme painted then, apparently prolific during her pregnancy, and in the first few years of motherhood. She even sold some of her early artwork, astoundingly, enough to keep them afloat while Malcolm studied.

Now that there is some money in the bank, and all four of her children are in school, Esme never paints. Suzen wonders what she does all day to stay so busy that she seems harried and exhausted. After all, it's not like they need to be cleaned and fed anymore; Evan is fifteen, Hallie nine, and even Aimee, who is in kindergarten, is fairly self-sufficient. Esme does some volunteer work at an agency called the Phoenix Center, mentoring women recovering from divorce, abuse, or welfare dependency, but Suzen knows little more about them. They remain invisible, peripheral creatures on the other end of the phone line. Once, when Esme was leaving to go see one of them, Suzen asked her about it. Her mother gave an offhand answer, laced with self-importance: "I can't really say—it's supposed to be confidential." Suzen thought it probably amounted to nothing more than a car ride to a bus station.

She suspects that her parents' lives are sorely lacking adventure and meaning, which is why her mother fancies herself a saint and her father routinely talks about going overseas. Every two years or so, he plots an escape, a trip that never materializes due to financial or professional constraints. She knows, too, that her mother yearns for freedom, but would never dare admit it. She is the classic martyr, taking her medicine standing up, gamely shouldering the burdens life has bestowed on her, thanks to her own choices—or mistakes. Suzen loathes her for it. She wishes Esme would just go ahead and say, "Damn it, I was going to be an artist!" But she never will. Esme, who is beautiful (and knows it), probably can't believe she is already thirty-seven with four kids and no life to speak of, though she goes on with it, irritable and put-upon, pent up with creativity while she performs endless, mindless tasks. Once, Suzen saw her mother unloading the dishwasher with such force, she broke three glasses, dropping them into the trash can one after the other without missing a beat.

Suzen, people say, looks just like her mother, but she will never be like her. For one thing, she has no interest in children, or marriage, and she plans to take care of herself—soon. Already she has begun a part-time apprenticeship at the local nursery, biding her time in between until she can return, rushing through the fog-painted glass doors to the damp green paradise on the other side. Like her romantic fantasies, the botanical one took root early, through her childhood reading (and rereading) of *The Secret Garden*. She has been drawn, ever since, to the tactile joys of soggy soil, fragrant blossoms, dripping petals, and low-slung bowers. She spent a large portion of her summers poking around in the backyard, her wrists ringed with bracelets of dirt, taking over where her mother had given up on weeding and snipping errant branches. Sometimes she limply lay on the lawn for hours, inhaling, dreaming.

Nowadays she follows another Mary; like the fictional one in her little walled garden, she tends to growing things, watching with delight as they evolve out of seemingly nothing but sun and air and water. Mary Strohman, the owner of the nursery, is Suzen's mentor and new-found idol. When she offers Suzen simple instructions on the care of seedlings, shrubs, and roses, Suzen listens, enthralled, as if memorizing poetry. After school, Mary sometimes takes Suzen along with her on landscaping jobs, where they mark off small gardens and plan berms. They drive down the road in Mary's pockmarked pickup, carrying a moving forest of red maples balled in burlap, their leaves fluttering in the wind like a thousand little flags. Men and machinery take over some of the work from there, but Suzen, watching, has learned that Mary is the genius, the architect without whom there would be nothing but dirt and spotty lawns.

After merely four weeks traipsing after Mary, Suzen believes that she wants nothing more than to dig and plant for the rest of her life. Although she knows that her parents—especially her father—would be disappointed to know that she is reconsidering college, lately she hasn't even been reading her homework assignments, eschewing them for seed catalogues and gardening magazines. She hides them under her bed like contraband, so no one knows her fantasies. She doubts anyone even takes note of the dirt beneath her fingernails, the fact that she rises before dawn to put in extra time at Strohman's.

She loves it best then, dewy and quiet, when there aren't any customers, and she can be alone with Mary, the potted plants around them bobbing, as if eavesdropping on their hushed conversations. It is the only thing that keeps her grounded these days—or rather, aloft. Sometimes she feels the combination of anticipation and longing are going to collect inside her like water in a clogged fountain spout and, when finally released, she will shoot through the ceiling. She is torn between wanting to stay put and learn, and running away to the unknown—between being herself and someone else altogether, someone like Tess of the d'Urbervilles.

Along with her gardening books she keeps a stack of travel magazines underneath her bed, and she pulls one out now, turning to the back pages, thick with advertisements. She inspects the airfares for Great Britain, package deals that include lodging and train rides to the countryside, to places with charming names like the Cotswolds and Nottingham and Stoke-on-Trent. She would pack a single bag and board a flight. Press her face to the tiny windowpane and watch her familiar world recede to pinpoints, then be lost in a film of clouds until the green moors appeared below, dotted with sheep, laced with rivers, and dark patches of woods and heath.

Evan VanderZee hunches over a map, memorizing the wheat-colored peninsula pressed like a Colorform into pale blue seas. He knows the exact distance between Rome and Naples—half his thumbnail—and that Italy's longest river is the Po (418 miles), and Lake Garda its largest lake (143 square miles). He is using his nine-year-old sister's atlas, an oversized picture book with handy little facts lining the margins, and bold typeface naming the countries. Evan likes to sit at his desk and run his fingers over the smooth terrain, claiming it. When he has the details worked out, he plans to flee the country. It is not an act of lawlessness nor treason. It is simply—a feeling. He is sure there is a word for his particular combination of yearning and angst, though he hasn't found it yet—it is likely in another language, a perfect *expresión*.

When Evan's father Malcolm was eighteen, he and a friend hiked their way halfway across Europe, growing their first beards and flirting with local girls, until they ran out of money and their zeal for hostels. At least, that is how he tells it. Evan suspects it was not so romantic, and he doubts his father ever got "lucky." Malcolm VanderZee is a professional nerd, a tenured English literature professor and the co-chair of his department at Field College in Whitesburg, Michigan, who dreams of moving the entire family to Italy.

Evan doesn't think there is a chance that his father will succeed in his endeavor. He is forever proclaiming great ideas, ways for them to see the world, while the only place they ever go is to Chicago for long weekends, wandering the same museums, eating sloppy gyros. Evan continues to hope, however. He knows that Malcolm is overdue for a sabbatical; his last one was nearly ten years ago in Wales. For a semester the family lived in a drafty cottage while Malcolm wrote an anemic, forgettable book about Dylan Thomas. It was published by some microscopic university press and twelve copies of it remain perched proudly on the family room bookshelf. No one has ever requested a copy, as far as Evan knows. One Christmas he received one as a stocking stuffer, but Malcolm took it back, laughing and pretending it was a joke when he saw his son's baffled reaction. Looking back on those six months in Wales, however, Evan has fond memories. Instead of homesick, he felt exuberant, alive. He was barely six, but he suspected even then that it was preferable to be an American outside of America; he stood out, and he was admired. Ever since, the foreign seed has nestled deep within him, waiting for another opportunity to sprout.

Though he speaks but a word of Italian—*Buongiorno!*—he would go in a heartbeat. He believes his life will only truly begin when he escapes the intolerable conditions of his current existence, which is being a sophomore in a bland Midwestern high school, a place completely lacking exoticism and romance. A place where a big day means a food fight in the cafeteria; recently Evan watched one in progress, the macaroni flying toward the ceiling tiles, missiles of green beans assaulting the heads of screaming girls, and he thought he had landed on an alien planet, he the only sign of intelligent life.

Evan is fifteen years old, the second of four children, including his angst-ridden sister, Suzen, who lives in her room like the madwoman in the attic of some old English novel, and his younger siblings Hallie and Aimee, to whom Evan is a hero. Or so he likes to think. Much of Evan's inner life revolves around an ever evolving movie script in which he is the star, the central figure riding into the foreground, or appearing around the doorway, up the back steps (always at just the right moment) as the drama unfolds, as the music soars. He imagines that something *is* just around the corner, something great, something life-altering. He is nearly a man, tipping from one stage to the next, growing and looming ever larger in the scheme of things. He is here for a reason, he thinks, destined for great things. He just has to find out what they are.

And lately, he feels certain he stands firmly on the cusp of change; it's in the air, it's in the tension in his household. He suspects that sooner or later, his mother is going to cave into his father's longings, and they will pack up their belongings and go. He is more than ready. Esme, however, is not.

Evan stood in the hallway outside his parents' bedroom one night recently while Malcolm futiley tried to make a case for Tuscany. His mother interrupted.

"We need a snake," she said.

"A snake?"

Esme sighed. "For the girls' hair."

Evan inched closer to the door, stumped and curious. A snake for his sisters' *hair*. He wondered if his mother had lost her head over the proliferation of pets in the household, particularly those of the rodent family. In addition to their aging Labrador retriever, Edgar, there were (at last count) two gerbils, two guinea pigs the size of groundhogs, and an albino mouse—all of them living in Hallie's room in a row of glass and screened cages—and a rat named Cupcake, who somehow had earned a place of honor in a corner of the kitchen.

"Okay, I'm lost," Malcolm said. "What are you talking about?"

"The bathtub *drain*. I've been telling you this for weeks. Their hair keeps clogging the drain and we have to call a plumber every other month. I figure we should just get our own metal snake and do it ourselves." She slammed a drawer and said, "I don't know why I keep bugging you about it, like it's 'the man's job.' Forget it. I'll do it myself. Anyway, I can't think about Italy when the house is falling apart, *okay?*"

Before his father could respond, Evan heard his mother stomping across the floor to the door. He stepped out of the way in time to avoid being caught in the act. Esme brushed past him without seeing him. Or so he thought.

"Evan," she said on the way down the stairs without turning around, "see if you can round up some dinner. Call Mr. Cheese and order pizza, I don't care what. I have too much to do."

Evan considered going into his parents' room to encourage the home team, but thought better of it. Malcolm would be brooding, like a spurned child. *I want to move to Italy* probably sounded to Esme like *I want a pony*. Not only did she likely think it another fantasy, she couldn't be bothered with the hassle.

He believes that his father may be serious this time, and that if only he can work out the details and get the family to Italy, everything will be fine. Things will change. Malcolm will change. He will learn to live in the moment, dancing around a golden field, underneath the olive trees, while his wife and children look on. He'll be a different sort of man, he'll be—Zorba the Geek. Evan leans back into his squeaky desk chair and smiles to himself. Even though he disparages his father (such an easy target) this time he wants to be his ally. He wants this trip—he wants *anything*—to happen.

When he closes the atlas and crawls into bed, he lies there awake, staring at the lace shadows of trees on the wall, brooding himself. He feels the longing press against his chest like a small heart attack. And it isn't just the trip he wants; more than anything else he wants a girl called Soci Andersson.

So-see. In fourth-period homeroom. With that boyishly short hair poking up in dark little tufts, the curve of her long neck arched in front of him, so close he could touch the smooth skin if he dared. With black sweaters and short skirts and black tights with holes in them. Evan can't help staring at those holes, windows to the smooth skin of her thighs.

Though there really is no resemblance, she is Jean Seberg come to life from the black-and-white world of 1960 Paris. And Evan, of course, imagines himself the renegade, Jean-Paul Belmondo, slouching and flirting through *Breathless (A Bout de Souffle): "I can't do without you." "Yes, you can." "I don't want to."* Evan has seen the film in a theater twice, and rented it from the library nine times. He is certain the librarians laugh at him when he comes through the door.

He cannot concentrate in homeroom anymore. He slouches in his seat with his eyes boring loving holes into Soci's swanlike neck. He wonders if she can feel it. His teacher calls his name and he hears it sometimes, but usually only after the laughter of his peers, their faces peering at him, bemused, snapping gum, watchful. No one knows what he is thinking, and that is the only thing that saves him. He can feign fatigue or boredom; lust is easily hidden under half-lidded eyes.

Soci is the only thing that keeps him going to school at all, though he has begun to skip the last period of the day on occasion. Then Evan wanders the town, the record shops, the Esquire Theatre that runs only old classic or foreign films. He can lose himself there, in the front rows, away from the strange single men doing who knows what in the back rows or balcony. Evan stretches out, making himself appear larger and slightly more menacing, just in case. No one has ever approached him, though, and he has come to feel a kind of camaraderie with the other moviegoers; maybe they all just want to be left alone, to sink into a soft mohair seat in the dark, to slip into another world for a couple of hours on an otherwise interminable afternoon. Strangely, not even the Esquire proprietor, Eddie, a lanky man of around thirty, has inquired why Evan is there, obviously truant. Perhaps Eddie was just like Evan at fifteen, and that is why he now owns a movie house, so he can continue to do what he loves best escape from real life. Eddie always greets Evan cheerfully, tearing off the red ticket stub, sifting popcorn into a large cardboard tub. He even knows by now that Evan prefers extra salt, no butter, and that he likes lots of ice in his Coke.

Tomorrow, Evan hopes to find the nerve to ask Soci to join him. She looks like someone who wouldn't mind flouting authority. She recently relocated to Whitesburg, from just outside New York City, with an air of knowing more than anyone else in the tenth grade. For the past two weeks, Evan has imagined sitting in the dark beside her, watching the light of the projector flicker across her smooth cheeks, watching her smile as the French girl knocks on a door, murmuring, "*C'est moi,*" in her sweet lilt; Evan has seen this film four times now, and is learning to anticipate the dialogue without reading the subtitles.

He drifts to sleep with images of large-screen faces and moving lips, words he cannot understand and laughter that sounds like it is coming from another world. When he wakes, he is disoriented, as if he really has been somewhere else, and it is within a lingering cloud of culture shock that he rises and absorbs his surroundings, feels his way across his own room and into another mundane day.

But when he thinks of Soci—and always, somehow, he is thinking of Soci—suddenly he grows alert, forms a plan. He pulls on jeans, wrinkled, still bearing the shape of his knees from the day before, and a shirt that seems clean. His mother has been attempting to train her children to tend to their own laundry—everyone but Aimee, who is only five—but Evan has found a way around this chore. When he gets behind, he simply recycles, plucking shirts and pants from the top of the heap first, working his way down. It is efficient, and no one at school notices or cares anyway. However, lately, because of Soci Andersson, he has begun to groom. He showers daily now, fluffing his unruly hair with a towel, and checking his teeth. Though he still believes that wrinkled clothing holds some charm—giving the appearance of nonchalance and devil-may-care diffidence—he makes sure everything smells clean.

He stands taller, profile to the mirror, and places his hands on his hips, noting—not with pride, but just self-observation—that his biceps are a shade thicker, more carved than a week ago. His torso is lean, his front almost completely flat, top to bottom; he considers this wall that his body forms and thinks of Soci leaning against it, pressed to it like warm stone. He closes his eyes and sways a little, thinks of her softness, her breasts melting against him.

Suzen wakes with a pain in her chest. She sits up, pressing her palm to her breast. *Oh Lord*, she thinks, *not again*. Every month, for the past six months, her breasts have continued to grow incrementally, yet notably. She fears they will never stop and one day she will simply topple from the weight. Unlike most girls her age, Suzen does not welcome the hormonal changes in her body. The height, yes—she aspires to five foot ten—but not the curves. If she could, Suzen would remain boyishly slender, lean and fast, as she has always been, able to outrun almost anyone in her class. Now she feels herself growing slow and plodding, her hips swaying without her permission.

Her mother recently complimented her on her shapeliness. "What I wouldn't give to look like that again," she'd said, patting her own small belly that was permanently pouched from four pregnancies. Suzen said nothing, just walked out of the room, chagrined. She hates not only the resemblance between them, but the proprietary nature of her mother's comments, as if she used to *be* Suzen, as if she has already lived the life Suzen has yet to discover, and thus, is depriving her of its inherent sweetness, its surprise. She wishes Esme would leave her alone, would acknowledge that they are separate people and that Suzen is not merely a younger version of herself, or worse, a clone designed to carry on the work that Esme, as one woman, cannot possibly do by herself—namely look after the younger VanderZees.

Wrapping herself in a flannel shirt, braiding her hair loosely with her fingers, Suzen trudges reluctantly to the kitchen where she finds that, of course, no one is in charge. Evan is sifting cornflakes from the box directly into his mouth while Hallie attempts to make pancakes from a mix. Aimee is calmly eating a frosted Pop-Tart, sitting cross-legged on the floor next to Edgar, the aged mutt. Esme walks in a moment later, dressed but still damp from a shower. She runs her fingers through her hair, loosening the knots and then shaking it out, like a teenager. Suzen notices that she is wearing lipstick today, and even mascara. Though she has taken more time than usual with her appearance, she cannot hide the fact that she is first, and foremost, a mother. And she is clearly peeved by the scene that awaits her.

She glances meaningfully at Suzen, who is not sure if the look is an accusation or a plea for commiseration. Suzen turns away and busies herself with fixing her own breakfast, as if she is alone. She shuts out the noise and commotion of her family until there is nothing but the sensation of the cold rush of refrigerator air on her skin, and her fingers reaching for the juice, clasping the bottle, then pouring it, and the momentary thrill of drinking it, fast, thinking only of the cold tangy liquid on her tongue, the faraway orange groves crossed by ladders and dotted with hatted workers plucking fruit. But then Edgar noses her shins and she has to reach down and pet him, gently move him away from the open refrigerator, snap back to the reality she cannot escape.

"Why didn't you wait for me, Hal?" Esme is asking, exasperated, surveying the batter scattered over the countertop and the phlegmy egg whites dripping onto the floor. "Look at this mess."

"That *is* gross," Evan agrees, pausing to brush dry cereal from his shirtfront. "We're almost out of everything, by the way," he tells Esme.

"I know. Get a bowl, for Pete's sake," Esme scolds him.

"Who is Pete, anyway?" Hallie asks, smirking at Evan, awaiting his punch line.

Suzen rolls her eyes. It is always the same. She reaches for a bagel and swipes butter across it, saying nothing to anyone. She hates the morning routine, the banter.

"Repeat's brother," Evan says, sitting behind the fortress of cereal boxes on the table. "Pete and Repeat were sitting in a boat. Pete fell out and who was left?"

"Repeat," Hallie says on cue. Aimee laughs, too, belatedly, always slow to catch jokes.

"Pete and Repeat were sitting in a boat—"

"Very funny, as always," Esme says, whacking Evan on the head lightly. "A bowl," she says again. She turns to the griddle and begins ladling batter.

"Okay, okay," Evan says, jumping up to get a bowl from the cupboard. He pulls out a plastic one, a remnant from high-chair days, and proceeds to spin it on one finger, like a top. Aimee hops up and tries to grab it from him.

"Let me try it, Ev," she whines. He turns his back and keeps spinning, then sits down, ignoring her and filling the bowl with cereal. Esme continues pouring and flipping, like a short-order cook, while Hallie launches into retelling the story line of a book she is reading, chapter by chapter. Esme responds by turning to Suzen and asking brightly if she remembers reading the same book when she was Hallie's age. Suzen shrugs, aware that her mother is simply trying to engage her, futilely throwing out her line to reel her in, be her pal, find some common ground. They both know Suzen is living in another world altogether, that their blissful mother/daughter days are over. Suzen wonders why Esme doesn't just give up, transfer her motherliness onto the other girls, who so obviously *want* her attention. Suzen blatantly ignores Esme, as if she hasn't heard her, or more important, doesn't care.

"Mom, you look pretty," Aimee suddenly says. "Where are you going?"

"Nowhere."

"I was talking," Hallie says, irritated. "So, the neighbor with the horse . . ." she goes on, unheard by her audience, who has turned back to the stove, spurned and wounded. Suzen knows; she can tell by the tilt of her mother's head. She feels a shade of regret, she almost relents and tries to make it up to her, but instead she stands to leave.

Suddenly Esme turns to her, making one more pitch. "Are you working after school today?"

"No, I'm not scheduled. But I might stop by there if—" She stops. She doesn't want to talk about Strohman's with her mother, with anyone, for some reason.

Aimee intervenes, yanking on Esme's sleeve and begging her to let her wear her raincoat, which she loves. Usually Esme doesn't care, allows her children to express themselves however they choose, but lately she seems annoyed by Aimee's quirks, her strange demands. "No" is all she says, while Aimee goes on to make her case.

"It might rain. Hard."

"It's sunny. Forget it."

"But I need it," Aimee says plaintively. On and on it goes.

Suzen notices Evan, still eating, apparently oblivious to his surroundings. But unlike Suzen, who tunes everyone out in order to think, Evan seems not to have an inner life, at least not as rich as hers.

Suzen cannot imagine what a boy would dream about, care about, other than the thudding, tangible pleasures of food and strength and sleep. He seems like an oversized mutt, bounding in and out of the house, running to soccer practice, returning home to eat twice his share of food, leaving a trail of clothes and books for someone else to trip over before he collapses, sometimes actually panting, on the sofa, half asleep. Yet, Suzen can't help but admire his careless happiness. She wonders what it's like to live so viscerally, unconcerned with familial chaos, with secret dreams and longings.

Evan pours more cereal into his little bowl and eats it noisily as there is no milk to soften the flakes, the crunch. His sisters and mother move about the room, up and down from chairs, back and forth to the sink and table, talking, talking, talking. He has found that there is no way for him to push through into their feminine world, though it is clearly visible, as through strings of beads, or water. He has watched and listened his whole life, and still he is not really part of them. The only way he can enter, it seems, is through jocular diversion, inane routines, familiar jokes, and sometimes, with Hallie and Aimee, roughhousing and sport. With Suzen, there is no contest. She is older, probably smarter—though he'd never admit it—and decidedly more aloof. They don't talk to each other, they react. Most often, they stay away from each other like cohabiting inmates, just biding their time. Sometimes Evan imagines asking Suzen her opinion on male behavior; she could be a valuable resource, and he really would like to know— from the other side—how to act, what to do. He wonders what she would think of Soci (not that he needs her approval) and how he might likely proceed. Would Suzen tell him whether girls prefer to be pursued, or like to start as friends, and is there any right way, or is it different with each one? And how does he know if someone is the One? He looks over at Suzen, whose long hair is skimming her bagel, who is ignoring everyone around her, and he knows that, of course, there is no way he could ever ask her anything.

"Evan," his mother is saying, faroff like his teacher, and finally he looks up. "I think we need to talk about something."

He knows she knows. He has been missing classes, disappearing so successfully for a few weeks now, he'd thought he was getting away with it. Obviously, his absence has been noted. He stalls by digging at clotted cereal in the back of a molar with one finger. Hallie arranges Lucky Charms around her pancake, lining marshmallow stars along the rim of her plate, waiting to come to Evan's aid if necessary. She is an expert at distraction methods, placating the adults, running interference. Hallie hates discord. If she could, she would make everyone hold hands and sing "We are the World." Evan laughs out loud, picturing it.

"I don't think it's funny," his mother says sternly. "I got a call from Mrs. Barnes yesterday, you know. She is concerned about your 'indifference,' as she called it. She says you barely passed two quizzes this month—easy ones. And that you have been AWOL more than once. What is going on here?"

What can he tell her? That he is in love with a girl's neck? That he never before noticed that particular part of the female anatomy? That as soon as he sits in his desk behind her, the entire world shrinks down to the singular focus of brownish feathers of hair on a silken slope of nape? That he lives in desperate hope—and dread—that she might actually turn around and look him in the eyes or smile, and then he would surely explode (explode, from the Latin word *explodere*, originally meaning "to drive off the stage with hisses and boos")? Everyone would know. He would be doomed.

"Um," he says to his mother. "Nothing. Nothing's going on." Clearing his throat, he tries for a more satisfactory answer. "It's just that by sixth hour, I'm kind of really tired, you know. I hit my afternoon lull; I think it's a drop in my blood sugar. Sometimes I go outside to get some air. That's all." Out of the corner of his eye he can see that Hallie, at least, is impressed.

Esme is not. "A lull? I see." She pauses, waits for further explanation, as she is not buying it.

"Yeah," Evan persists. "It's actually pretty common, particularly among adolescents, according to four out of five doctors surveyed."

She cannot help smirking. Evan has always been able to mollify his mother with his intellect and wit. Which is why she and his eldest sister fight so much. Suzen completely lacks a sense of humor. Their mother's most common words to her are, "Lighten up." In fact, Suzen has already left the room, fed up with the lot of them.

Esme, however, is not finished with him. "Evan, you're too smart to blow it with one class, you know. Just pay attention, okay? Have a candy bar before sixth hour if it will help. For Pete's sake."

"Who's Pete?" Evan asks. Hallie spews her Lucky Charms in another fit of laughter. They are all laughing so hard now, it draws Malcolm into the room.

"What's so funny?" he asks.

"Nothing," says Esme, smiling. "You had to be there." She wipes the table with a matted dish towel and straightens up, back to work.

"Well, I'm here now," he says, trying to get the joke, but it's hopeless.

Evan looks at his dad, the absentminded professor, and wonders how he gets through the day. He always looks a little tired, preoccupied, like he has been on a long trip and is struggling with jet lag. Even his hair, a little bushy (hippies' era), looks bewildered. Evan thinks about how hard his father tries to fit in—at work, in social circles, in his own family—and fails, ever the new kid at school. It probably would do him good to get away for awhile; Evan wonders if he has even applied for a sabbatical, if he has remembered such details. Try as he may, he is not like normal men, like the other dads Evan knows.

Sometimes Malcolm invites Evan out to a movie, or into the den to watch college basketball on TV, just the two of them, the guys. But it occurs to Evan that they never actually talk much; there is always another focus—the screen or the game, even the commercials, and that is what connects them. *Nice pass. Whoa, did you see that? Do you think that's real dandruff, 'cause it looks like snow. Wouldn't you hate it if your name was Butkus?* After awhile, Malcolm can't resist switching channels, and then it is all over; he always gets hung up on the History Channel or *Masterpiece Theatre*. Evan has to sneak away and find the score on the radio.

Evan kisses his mother on the cheek like a gentleman. "I promise I'll be good today." He waves at his dad, who is walking toward his study, and heads out the door.

On his way down the driveway, Evan is watching himself strut. The drive curves at the end, where it joins the brick sidewalk, a charming old-fashioned touch, an effort on the part of the Historic District Association to maintain a connection to ye olden days. While pretty, it's a hassle; children are forever tripping on upended bricks, lodging bicycle tires between grooves. And residents are expected to weed the inevitable tufts of grass that rise up like untrimmed sideburns along the borders. But what Evan likes about the brick walk, lumpy and unstable, is that if he pretends hard (a talent he clings to even at fifteen), he can picture himself not in Michigan but on a Roman side street. He wishes he were Italian. Or even Peruvian, like the exchange student Eduardo at school who turns heads simply because he is from Somewhere Else. It's as if he's landed in Oz—girls gather around like Munchkins, eager to show him the way. And he can break all social rules without offending anyone (*He doesn't know any better*), wear the oddest combination of clothing—even childish knit caps no one else would be caught dead in—and appear *au courant*. When he talks, he misses critical parts of speech and people think it adorable. Evan would like nothing more than to be like that, the foreigner, the outsider.

He is at the sidewalk now. *The police behind the parked cars are waiting for him. He will saunter toward them, unafraid—'How you say?'*—*audacious. He will grin at the cameras, go out in a blaze of glory. Look, here comes a girl out of the morning fog, running to intervene, to embrace him one more time before the bullets fly.*

Evan squints and sees that the girl running toward him is his sister, Suzen. He is horrified to have mistaken her for an apparition of beauty. She is flushed and breathless, shirttails flapping.

"Where have you been, Suzy-Q?" Evan asks, blocking her path.

"Nowhere," she says. "Move it, I'm gonna be late. I forgot my backpack."

"You can run but you can't hide," Evan says for no reason, grinning as she pushes past him. He likes to grate against his sister whenever opportunity arises.

"Bugger off," she calls back in a bad English accent, before opening the door.

The domestic tedium continues in the kitchen and Suzen tries to slip through it unnoticed but it is too late. Her mother catches her in her disorganized net; "Suzen," she says, "I need you to help Aimee get ready. Dad's on the phone with somebody from the college and I'm running late here—" Before Suzen can utter protest, Esme is gone. Suzen looks at her sister trying to tug her sneakers on her feet, and sighs.

"Come here, brainless," she says to Aimee, who shuffles across the floor on her rump. "I'll tie if you at least put them on yourself."

"She should know how to tie already," Hallie notes derisively. "I mean, they're supposed to know that by kindergarten."

"I'm in kindergarten," Aimee says defensively.

"Duh. I mean you should have learned *before.*"

"Before what?"

"Forget it," Hallie says, rolling her eyes. "You should just wear Velcro."

"Velcro is for babies."

"I know."

"Just drop it, Hal," Suzen says, like a mother, but she is trying not to laugh. She yanks the shoelaces and ties them, then pulls Aimee to her feet. Her sister becomes a rag doll, floppy and compliant. Sometimes Suzen wonders if she was a mistake, coming late in the family; perhaps their parents neglected birth control. She has noticed that Esme has never paid unusual attention to Aimee, treating her like one of the pets, another creature to feed and bathe, sending her out to play. Esme is distracted more and more lately, and Suzen wonders if her mother is suffering a midlife crisis. She's frequently away, tending to other women, attending seminars and who knows what. Suzen senses they are all becoming peripheral to her, and in a way, she is relieved. It means Esme doesn't notice or care what Suzen does herself.

"Come on," Suzen orders her sister. "We're all going to be late if you don't get moving."

"I hate school," Aimee moans.

"At least you only have to go half a day," Hallie says. She turns and taps the glass cage that holds Cupcake, her favorite pet, a sleek white rat who stands upright, star-shaped paws pressed to the glass, staring with beady black eyes. Suzen thinks it uncouth to keep animals in the kitchen, yet she has a tender spot for Hallie. She is such a serious child, a loner for the most part, who seems to slouch around with tiny burdens bowing her shoulders. Her rodents somehow calm her; Suzen knows Hallie whispers to them, whiplash tails curled around her wrist. It's this quiet slipping into a private place that Suzen understands, and thus, admittedly favors Hallie. Aimee, like Evan, seems all surface angles and temporal needs, lacking a dreamy disposition, or even imagination.

Esme rushes in then, keys jingling. "Okay, girls, let's go, we're going to be late." She looks at Suzen, apparently surprised. "I thought you'd left."

"You told me to help," Suzen says, exasperated. "I *was* leaving."

"Oh. Do you need a ride?"

"I'm walking," Suzen tells her, her tone defiant.

"Fine."

Suzen watches them leave, her mother not looking back as she backs out of the driveway; she could run over someone. Standing alone at the curb, it occurs to Suzen that if no one cares what she does, she is free to choose. At school she will be marked *absent, unexcused*, but it has rarely happened before. It won't affect anything in the long run.

She turns in the other direction and starts to run, feeling the wind in her long hair, giddy with her rebellion. When she nears Strohman's Nursery, the sun is just skimming the tops of trees, the edges of aluminum siding. She slows down. The air is quiet and cool, and the only sound comes from her own footsteps and geese honking overhead, heading south. She looks up and smiles, happy to be a witness to something so primitive and eternal as the migratory cycle of birds. Opening the glass door of the nursery, she is struck anew by the sweet earthy aroma, the humid, greeny air.

She finds Mary in the wooden shed that holds tools and wheelbarrows, bending over a crate, writing on a legal pad. She turns when she hears Suzen come in, and smiles. "Hey, Suzy, how are you?"

"Fine, thanks," Suzen says, smiling shyly. She is still getting used to being part of this adult world of work, longs to be a real part of it. If she could, she would skip school every day and stay here, dirt crusting the knees of her jeans, her hands busy in soil.

"No school?" Mary asks.

"No. My morning classes were canceled," Suzen says. It is not exactly a lie; she simply doesn't admit who canceled them. She walks toward the large greenhouse, and finds it still locked. "Mind if I go in?" she asks.

"Go ahead," Mary says, and moves to unlock the door. When

Suzen steps inside, Mary warns her that the overhead sprinklers are on. "I'm afraid you might get wet," she says.

"That's okay," Suzen says. She doesn't say that she loves it, that she wants to be drenched, soaking, that she could stand there all day, underneath the rainy ceiling, the green around her pulsing. When Mary leaves her alone, Suzen looks around her, unmoving like a quiet creature awakening in a new forest. It seems she can see the leaves actually breathing, trembling as if in heat—the lobelia reaching for the slender hand of the ficus. Even their names sound sexy: *climatis, euphorbia, phlox, cockscomb*—all of them clean and wet and brilliant.

She thinks about sex a lot these days, even while standing all alone beneath the virginal mist of Strohman's Nursery. She thinks mostly about kissing. Sometimes her lips burn with longing and she licks them, presses the back of her hand to her mouth to stop the feeling. At seventeen, however, Suzen has only ever kissed four boys, all forgettable, except Tom from chemistry class, who teased her into experimenting. The kiss—deep, lingering—was as far as she let him go, though his hands began to wander. Suzen pulled away, making excuses. She has not visited even one of the bases her peers have run through again and again. She knows girls who discuss the act of fellatio as if it were a new hobby, like beading bracelets or glazing pottery. "It's not that hard to do," they say over lunch, "once you get the technique down." They offer tips for the uninitiated, then collapse in laughter. Suzen just listens, amazed and horrified. Do boys *expect* this? Unlike the other girls, she is not the least bit interested in male genitalia, tries hard, in fact, *not* to think about it. What if all you want to do is kiss someone, she wonders, kiss and kiss until your stomach is in knots and you could faint from the lightness of air?

She daydreams and drifts around the nursery the rest of the morning, working but not working. When employees or customers approach her, she pretends to study the label tucked into the dirt of a plant, as if she truly needs to know whether a Persian violet prefers sun or partial shade, if the soil requirements for hibiscus are moist, sandy, or acidic, or how far apart to space impatiens. When she is loping after Mary, mentally gathering the facts Mary drops along the way like flower petals, like crumbs leaving a trail in the woods, Suzen thinks about her—what Mary's life is like, who she loves.

There have been quiet rumors that the reason Mary and her husband Philip, the divorce lawyer, got divorced was because Mary allegedly had a brief affair with a designer from Chicago. A woman. Mary hired her own attorney and they settled things quickly, fairly equitably. Philip kept the house, Mary the cottage at the lake where she now lives alone, commuting twenty-five minutes each day in her rusty pickup. Mary insists to friends that she prefers the old trusty truck to her ex-husband's chocolate brown BMW. Mary has not appeared the least bit spiteful about the divorce, nor the hints that she is, *you know, from the other team.*

Suzen knows all of these things from conversations overheard in the nursery parking lot when she carries plants to customer's trunks. She doesn't care what they say; they don't know Mary the way she does. Though Mary is twelve years older than Suzen, and nearly half a foot shorter, it doesn't seem to matter. Suzen treasures their unique camaraderie. And she admires everything about Mary, how she is kind and funny and self-deprecating but also fiercely self-confident. How she is tiny and lithe, though also curvy, her small full breasts shifting softly when she bends over. How her hair, burnished white blond, cut short and a little messy, is like that of a movie star off duty.

A friend from school, recently shopping at Strohman's for a plant mister for her mother, remarked to Suzen, "So, it must be weird working with her." She looked pointedly in the direction of Mary, behind the cash register.

"No. Why? Mary's really cool," Suzen said defensively.

The friend regarded her with a bemused, half-mocking expression and said, "Don't tell me you're one of them."

"Them?"

"A *lesbo*." The friend laughed. "Suzy the lezzie."

Suzen stared, balked. She shook her head and refused to answer, making it clear by her exasperation how wrong her friend was. The friend who suddenly was falling off her friendship roster.

By late morning, when there is a lull in business, Mary motions Suzen to the rose greenhouse. Suzen follows, wiping her brow with the back of her hand, where there is no dirt clinging. It's a bright, blue September day. School is going on across town without her, and for a moment Suzen feels like another person altogether, as if she is no longer a student, as if she has slipped through a secret turnstile into adulthood without a ticket. It thrills her, this escape. What if she never went back?

When she reaches the entrance of the greenhouse, the scent is overwhelming. It is like coffee hour at church, when the old women gather and their combined perfumes and hand lotions fill the air. It is like church in other ways, too. The ceiling is lofty and sunlit, and shadows fall in delicate splinters across the floor. The air is hushed and reverent, and Suzen always feels she should whisper when she is inside.

"I'm just moving things around, for fall," Mary tells her. "It's hard to imagine, with the temperature like this, but the weather is unpredictable. I'll need help moving some things inside, if you want to go start on the tables on the south side."

"Okay," Suzen says. For some reason, she moves slowly, reluctant to leave. She wants to be near Mary, close enough to watch her talk, her lips curled in a smile, to see the perfect pores of her skin, the soft glow of sweat on her forehead in the sunlight now pouring through the glass. When Mary takes off her shirt and wraps it around her waist, Suzen sees that underneath she is wearing only a white tank top, no bra. Her small arms are sculpted like little plums, from carrying heavy clay pots and moving stone benches around the grounds to make room for more trees. She can lift those trees, too, the young ones balled in burlap. The men who work at the nursery no longer rush to her aid; they have seen her work and respectfully let her do it herself. The men are the only ones who do not gossip about Mary. It is the women who talk, eyebrows raised, breathy *You're kiddings* spoken over and over.

Walking to the far tables covered with potted geraniums and rust-colored mums, Suzen thinks how she wishes she were more like Mary, lovely and content, not growing gawkier and full of longing. She wants to be that comfortable in her own skin, letting what others say about her simply brush off like pine needles. Working happily, driving home alone.

Suzen imagines her little house at the lake, Mary sitting on a flag-stone patio with a glass of red wine and a book, her fingernails scrubbed clean, her feet in thick socks. Sitting and staring at the pewter water, curling up to read. She wonders if she reads the Brontës and Hardy. If she looks over the dark lake and thinks she could be any-where, in another time. Perhaps she sits atop her windswept hillside watching tiny ships curve over the lip of the horizon, wraps herself in yards of wool, and waits for someone to appear. Perhaps she has a lover.

Whenever Suzen tries to conjure a lover for herself, she thinks of Eduardo, the Peruvian exchange student she has a mild crush on (who doesn't?). She lifts a heavy clay pot filled with drooping Chinese lanterns, and carries it toward the greenhouse. She moves, lost in her thoughts, lost in the vision of Eduardo pulling off his T-shirt and press-ing his smooth chest against her breasts, pulling her close and kissing her softly. They are standing next to a window in a little cottage, the waves churning outside. She waits for the familiar thump of excitement but it isn't there, as if she isn't trying hard enough. Suddenly she can't even picture Eduardo's face. It is someone else taking his place, though Suzen cannot see who it is, who she wishes it to be.

"Suzy," Mary says, coming up behind her and startling Suzen. "Do you think you can come early, before school, tomorrow? I have some things I could really use help with. Plus, I'll give you free coffee."

"Sure," Suzen says quickly, without considering, setting down the plant. "I can come." She smiles.

"You have the prettiest teeth, did you know that?" Mary says. "Did you ever have braces?"

Suzen shakes her head no. But she retains the compliment, holds it inside like a bouquet of flowers as a strange feeling pulses through her.

You have really pretty hair, Evan thinks. No, *You have a great smile.* Too obvious. Clichéd. He tries again, silently. *You are the best thing that ever walked into my life.* He moans, puts his head down on his desk. He has arrived ten minutes early to wait for Soci to take her seat in front of him. He wants to be ready.

He hasn't seen her in the hallways all morning and worries that she is sick—or suddenly relocated. In a strange way, it would be a relief. He had no idea love could turn a person inside out. Raw, like the hunger after the flu, desperate to be filled, but not sure with what. Evan doesn't know how to be in love, nor what to do or say to make it happen. He keeps waiting, as if it might come to him in a glimmer of inspiration. But each time Soci walks into the classroom, head bowed, lost in her mysterious thoughts, sometimes tugging on her tights at her knees (an endearing habit), Evan is at a loss. She seems not to see him at all, but once, her eyes lifted for a moment in his direction, and he felt himself flush. Then she sat down and opened a book, never looking up again.

Evan sits up and stares at the doorway. A few other students are coming in, talking, laughing. He doesn't hear what they are saying and he doesn't care. He was hoping, crazily, that *she* would be the first to arrive, so they would be alone.

The others take their seats in the back row, still talking, unaware of the electricity in the room as Soci enters. Evan, however, cannot take his eyes away. She is not wearing disheveled black today, but is sauntering into the classroom as if it were a Parisian runway, wearing a tight red dress that stops halfway down her thighs.

"Whoa," one of the guys in the back calls out unself-consciously, another just whistles. Soci smiles in their direction as she slips into her seat in front of Evan.

Evan is speechless. In his head a tape plays round and round, Eric Clapton crooning, "Layla." Evan has a gift for hearing music exactly as if it were being channeled through him and he is surprised that no one else hears it.

Soci is looking at him now, half turned around, apparently waiting for him to speak. The music is reduced to a quiet, thumping hum in the background.

"You look great," Evan finally manages to squeak. He clears his throat and tries again. "It's a nice, um, dress."

"Thanks," she says, smiling. "I didn't think you'd notice."

"Me?" he says, grinning shyly. "I notice every day."

Soci tilts her head and regards him appreciably. "That's really nice to know," she says. She turns around to face him fully, arms crossed over the back of her chair, studying him as if he were a specimen brought into the room for just such a purpose. Then she gazes so directly into Evan's eyes he cannot blink, or look away.

"You want to get out of here?" she asks in a low soft whisper. She is already getting up from her desk. So is he, without realizing it. "Come on," she says, still quietly. "Let's go." She is Ariadne and he Theseus, following her voice like an enchanted red thread winding through the labyrinth. It is the opposite of what he'd imagined and planned—that he would ask her, and she would follow.

Outside, the bell is ringing, and the final stampede of late-comers are rushing off to afternoon classrooms. No one sees or notices the two of them, renegades who have walked calmly out of the building. Evan has done this by himself at least six times in the past month, each time feeling as if he were using up stolen currency, or poker chips, expecting any moment to be caught. After his mother's warning this morning, he fully intended to change his ways, amending his plans to invite Soci to go out after school instead. But here they are; there is no turning back.

Fifty yards into the parking lot Soci pauses and pulls a pack of cigarettes from her black shoulder bag. She shakes one out expertly, then holds it toward Evan.

"Want one?" she asks.

He thinks for a long moment, during which he recalls drug prevention month in fifth grade, the teacher waving around a photograph of blackened lungs. She wore a too-tight gray suit and had a bad perm and paced the room as she warned of the dangers of cigarettes. Evan thinks about black lungs while he looks at the beautiful girl before him, her skin porcelain, her eyes clear and bright. She is smiling, her teeth impossibly white, unstained. And she is lighting up, blowing her smoke off to one side, considerately.

"You don't have to, you know," she says, her tone amused. "You don't look like the smoking type to me, anyway."

"Yeah, well," he starts, considering a denial, then surprising himself with his own honesty, "that's because I'm not."

"Do you mind if I do?"

"No." He doesn't care what she does or doesn't do, as long as she is with him. The girl with her waifish hair, her beautiful curved neck, smoke trailing like a halo around her head. He still can hardly believe she left the building with him, that she asked him. Somewhere, someone is playing Bruce Springsteen. Evan hears the familiar harmonica, the saxophone wailing.

"Come on," Soci says grinning. "Let's get lost."

Evan, hypnotized, nods. *Baby, we were born to run.* They begin to walk away from the school grounds, aimless, but moving quickly. Suddenly Evan stops, remembering his original plan, and blurts, "Do you like foreign films?"

Soci nods. *"Mais oui!"*

Evan smiles, impressed. He takes her hand and pulls her with him. It is fifteen blocks to the Esquire, but he knows it won't matter. He can feel the warmth of her slender fingers in his, fusing together.

When they arrive, Soci drops her cigarette butt outside the Esquire doors and grinds it with her heel. Evan sees that the matinee crowd today is thinner than usual; in fact, the lobby is empty except for one man heading to the balcony steps and Eddie slouching over the concession counter, propped on one elbow and reading a newspaper. He looks up and smiles when he spots Evan, stops smiling when he sees Soci with him. For a moment, it seems there is some flicker of recognition, but Soci, who also has seen Eddie, stares at him blankly. Perhaps he thought she was someone else, or he is just stunned by her beauty. Perhaps he, too, notes the resemblance between her and Jean Seberg.

"Two, please," Evan says, handing over his money.

"I can see that," Eddie says, wryly. "Anything to eat or drink?"

Soci points to the glass case. "Junior Mints," she says. Evan pays for them, and a Coke for himself, forgoing the popcorn, which he suspects might prove too loud and messy. He walks toward the velvet curtain separating the lobby from the theater doors, pushing his way through, Soci close behind. She is opening her little box and already eating a piece of the candy, which Evan realizes she is doing to mask the cigarette scent. Though it clings to her clothes, when she leans in to say something to him, her breath is now chocolate-minty. They sit midway down, in the very center seats, a sea of faded cranberry mohair around them, completely empty. Evan sighs with relief. He glances at his companion, hoping not to appear nervous.

Soci's skirt has ridden up; Evan can see the firm muscles of her thighs in black tights. She makes no move to tug the hem down. Evan shifts in his seat, slowly letting his legs go slack, so that his right knee nearly grazes her left. She smiles, nudges him. Whispers, "Hey."

"Hey." He smiles back. "We don't have to whisper, you know. There's no one else here."

"I know," she says even more softly, her words blowing into his ear. "But I like to whisper."

The film begins, and Evan holds his breath, not sure why. There isn't a great deal of suspense in the story and he already knows every reel by heart, every word of dialogue. He recognizes the music, anticipates the expressions on the actors' faces. What he doesn't expect, though, is Soci whispering along with the beautiful dark-haired star, line by line, in flawless French. He turns to look at her. Her soft profile, dark short hair tucked behind her curved ear, the long curled eyelashes. When the girl in the movie knocks softly on the door and says once again, "*C'est moi*," the words come out of Soci's mouth.

At that moment, as if keenly aware he has been watching her, she turns, leans over, and kisses Evan fully on the lips. His paper cup full of ice and cola slip to the floor in a slushy crash; he can hear the liquid gurgling out of the bent plastic lid and streaming down the sticky concrete floor. He doesn't care. He reaches out his now free hands and pulls her face even closer. It happens so easily, in spite of the fact that he has never done it, not like this. He forgets all the girls he's kissed since he was thirteen, a mere handful of unmemorable events. Soci's tongue dips into his mouth; he feels her lips spreading open into his, surrounding his. Though he has watched it a thousand times in movies, he had no idea it would feel like this. He always thought kissing was just a brief precursor to intimacy, that one did it to get things started; he did not know it could be so deeply intimate in itself. Now, he thinks it is more than enough in itself. At the same time, Evan is aware of other sensations ricocheting through his entire body, sparking every nerve.

It goes on for a long time. He begins to get the hang of it, to move his own tongue in and around, exploring her teeth, the undersides of her wet lips. She pulls away once, but only to smile at him, as if taking a breath in order to dive back under the surface. And Evan is drowning; he hopes no one tries to rescue him. He wills the movie to go on and on, the lights down, the velvet curtains pulled shut. *Please,* he hears himself begging in his head as his hand travels down the slope of her long neck, slowly over the pleasing bump of collarbone, smooth taut back, a dancer's arc, and then around to the front of her dress. Like a man who knows exactly what he is doing. No adolescent grabbing and mashing. He simply cups them, and circles his fingers around, feeling the impossible softness.

"Hey," a voice says just louder than a whisper. A small bright light darts over Evan's shoulder and, as he turns, into his eyes. It is Eddie, standing over them halfway down the row, coming toward them. "Sorry to interrupt," he says, indeed sounding remorseful. "But I can't let kids, you know, fool around in here. You're going to have to leave." As Evan stares up at him, half-blinded and stunned, Eddie adds, "Sorry, man."

Soci stands up, adjusting the hem of her dress, tugging it down, tugging up her tights at her knees, which makes it appear all the worse, as if they'd been doing more than kissing. Evan stands, too, chagrined, angry, slipping a little on the spilled drink and inadvertently kicking the empty cup. He says nothing to Eddie as he brushes past him with Soci behind him, as they walk through the doors and the velvet to the bright afternoon sun flooding the lobby.

"Jerk," Soci murmurs, glaring back toward Eddie, who is not looking at them through the glass, but poring intently over his newspaper as if he'd never left it. "Fucker," she adds under her breath.

Evan doesn't know what to say. "Well," he starts, blinking in the sunlight. "So much for that."

"Forget him. Let's go." Soci says. Evan turns away from the Esquire, hurt and betrayed. He isn't sure if he will ever come back. He wonders, then, if Eddie is jealous. If the reason he seemed to like Evan before was because he seemed to be a lonely kid, not the kind to show up with a girlfriend.

When she says suddenly, "I'm hungry," he wants nothing more than to feed her. He would do anything for her. He has a few hours before he has to show up at soccer practice, something he cannot afford to miss. There is time to eat, to do whatever they want to. Since the Esquire is on the outskirts of a slightly run-down neighborhood, Evan decides to splurge and hail a cab. The town has only a handful of them, but miraculously, one appears. As Evan lifts his arm to flag down the driver, he remembers a line from a poem: "Not waving, but drowning." Suddenly everything is awash in layers of meaning. The car slows to a crawl, and pulls in front of them. Evan opens the door for Soci and slides in after her, settling into the springy backseat as they float away down the street. It is exactly like a scene in a movie.

Suzen arrives home, head down. She is lost in her confusing daydreams, as if she has taken medication with side effects; she cannot shake the feeling that something is wrong with her, her head humming, her skin buzzing. She wishes there were someone she could talk to about it.

"How was your day?" her mother asks when she walks in the back door. Esme is at the sink, hurriedly rinsing dishes left over from breakfast.

"Fine," Suzen says.

"Well, I have to run over to the Phoenix Center to give someone a ride to the doctor's office, okay? I think Ev's still at soccer. So, will you watch Hallie and Aimee?"

"Fine."

"Thanks, honey," Esme says, and she brushes Suzen's hair with a mindless kiss and swishes out the back door in her long skirt with her long hair tossed over her shoulder. *There she goes again,* Suzen thinks. Her mother who used to seem a very part of the house, bearing its scents, its colors and familiar patterns, now is someone who passes through on her way somewhere else. Suzen remembers coming home from school when she was young, always finding Esme waiting there, stirring sauce, or washing out paintbrushes, or brushing Edgar's fur. She would look up and smile when Suzen walked in, as if all day she had been anticipating her return. Now Suzen realizes how egocentric she was, and maybe Esme had, in fact, been living her own life up till that moment, and then was forced to put it all on hold. Perhaps now she's just had it with maternal martyrdom and has transferred her attentions elsewhere. Maybe she figures that the women at the Phoenix Center need her more than her children do—especially with a seventeen-year-old daughter around who can do her job for her.

Suzen sighs, heads upstairs to her room with a bag of potato chips. She eats them on the way, relishing the tang of too much salt. Lately she wants too much of anything, her body demanding sensation, as if silently screaming, *More, more, more.* When she passes her sisters' room she sees Hallie facedown on the floor, eye level with Cupcake, who is sitting perfectly still as if hypnotized. The light glows through the rat's nearly translucent ears, like curled petals. Suzen remembers being small like Hallie, with nothing but time to fill.

"Where's my scrunchie?" a high voice begs behind Suzen. She turns to see Aimee holding her wild hair in a ponytail with one hand.

"Which one? You only have about a million."

"The red one," Aimee is saying.

"Who knows and who cares?" says Hallie from the floor without turning around.

"Have you tried looking?" Suzen asks Aimee calmly.

Aimee says nothing because she has just found the thing she is looking for, an elasticized bunch of cloth she twists around her hair. Or tries to. She can barely reach around behind her own head, she is that uncoordinated. Suzen tucks the bag of chips under one arm and reaches out to help her sister, carefully pulling out the scrunchie and starting over. She knows Aimee is very serious when it comes to her hair paraphernalia. She has fairy-tale hair, long and blond and naturally curly, the kind people always ooh and aah over. Sometimes Suzen wants to cut it off; she fears Aimee already shows signs of irreversible vanity. Yet, it occurs to her that her good looks may be all she has.

"There," she says. "Don't you look beautiful."

"Thanks," Aimee says. "Hey, Hal, want to ride bikes with me?"

"No."

"Why not?"

"Because."

"Because why?"

Hallie rolls over, the rat attached to her chest, its tiny claws stuck in the looped threads of her sweater. She regards Aimee with blank disinterest.

"Come on, Hal, just go with her for five minutes, okay?" Suzen pleads.

"Why should I?"

"Because Mom left me in charge," Suzen says, knowing it is an unfair excuse.

"Besides," Aimee says, "I need help with my bike. It sticks."

"Sticks to what?" Hallie asks, following Suzen and Aimee down the stairs. She carries Cupcake to her glass house in the kitchen and tenderly sets her inside on a nest of cedar chips. She pulls the mesh lid over the top and smiles down on her rat.

"The foot things. You know, the, um—" Aimee is saying.

"The pedals?" Suzen suggests, wondering if her sister is really that stupid. She opens the refrigerator and drinks from the orange juice carton. She wipes her mouth, aware that she is behaving just like Evan, who is often reprimanded for his lack of manners.

"Yes, the pedals. They don't go right. They get stuck and then they get all loose and wobbly."

"Okay, I'll look at it," Suzen says. "In a minute. I have some things to do. Hallie, you go with her and I'll be right out."

Hallie groans, but opens the door. Aimee's bicycle is parked there, blocking the door, and Suzen watches Hallie impatiently shove it open, knocking over the bike and getting the handlebars wedged underneath it. Before Aimee can protest, Hallie picks it up and twists the front end brusquely around.

"Watch out for the flowers," Suzen says sternly, as Hallie drags the bike tire dangerously close to the sedum. Its tiny pink buds are just opening, and butterflies skim over them. Suzen thinks that she needs to weed a little, later, and water the garden, too, since no one else ever remembers to do it.

"Get on," Hallie is ordering. Aimee obeys. "Now, go down the driveway so I can see what's wrong with the bike."

Suzen turns back inside the house but watches from the kitchen window. Since it is ajar, she can still hear the ongoing argument. She finds it entertaining to observe the predictable dissension between her two sisters; they are like an irritable married couple, sharing the same room, griping over each other's bad habits. She can see Hallie, hands on hips, watching Aimee beginning to pedal away, her face twisted in concentration as if she is shooting out of the starter's box at a race. About ten yards down, she yelps and tilts the bike on the rutted brick sidewalk, just catching herself before she falls. She yells to Hallie, "See?"

"Just don't go so fast," Hallie yells back like a coach.

"How am I supposed to stop?" Aimee calls, pushing her golden hair out of her eyes. The scrunchie has slipped halfway out of her ponytail and she looks like a sloppy model, blue-eyed and pouty.

"I don't know. When you hit a tree, I guess!"

"You're *mean*," Aimee says.

"That's my name, don't wear it out."

Suzen turns from the window, laughing. She almost doesn't register the screeching sound she hears next, followed by a harsh crash and a thick surreal silence, as if the world has been turned to slow motion. She knows, but doesn't want to believe what she knows. For a long time it seems she has stopped breathing.

Panting at the sidelines of the soccer field, Evan rubs his knee where Brett Miller has purposely kicked him. "Bonehead," Evan mutters, never daring to insult him out loud. Evan possesses superior intellect, and consoles himself with that secret knowledge as he watches Miller plow downfield toward another victim. Maybe God will intervene, poke out a divine leg and trip him.

Evan turns toward the stands when he hears footsteps thundering over the metal seats. It's his friend, Max, who got cut from the soccer team for smoking in the locker room. Evan believes he did it on purpose, seeking an excuse of defiance instead of admitting that he is terrified of getting on a field again with the likes of Miller, and most of the opposing teams' players. Like Evan, Max is on the slight side, wiry and quick but easily trampled. Evan has managed to overcome his own fears through constant self-aggrandizing pep talks.

"What's up, man?" Evan asks.

"Your sist—" Max starts, breathless.

"You better give up the fags," Evan says, whacking Max on the back. "You sound like a geezer." It occurs to him that he doesn't mind Soci's smoking, that it has given her a kind of worldly allure; with anyone else, including Max, it seems idiotic, childish even.

"Your sis—ter," Max says again, his voice rasping from exertion and edged with anxiety. He stands straighter, his face going pale as if just now realizing the gravity of his news.

"What? Which sister? What *happened?*"

"Aimee was hit by a car, on her bike—you gotta get home," Max blurts. "I'll tell the coach. *Go!*"

Evan runs, fast and hard, in spite of or because of his growing dread. Imagining the worst, he sees his sister flattened, crushed underneath enormous wheels. He wants to murder the driver, the bike manufacturer, everyone responsible. He wants to cry. He wants to run home to his mother's arms, or to run fast in the other direction and never find out what happened. He feels like his life is crumbling, the ground beneath him is filled with unseen fissures, where before he was on solid ground, playing ball, and before that, strutting around with his new girl.

Only two hours ago he was sitting across from Soci in a restaurant booth, watching her dip French fries into catsup, smiling while she ate, tucking a short strand of hair behind her ear, glancing shyly away, then back at him. He couldn't believe his good fortune, just as now he can't believe this turning. He is filled with fear and guilt, as if somehow his happiness caused disaster, as if he didn't deserve it, and now he has to pay.

Okay, okay, he tells himself, taking deep breaths as he races across the field. *Okay, okay. It's okay. Everything is A-OK.* Crazily, he remembers once sitting in the dentist's waiting room, leafing through *Cosmopolitan,* pausing at the photos of large breasts pressed into shiny lingerie. A small man came in briskly and began pacing back and forth. "Okay, okay, okay, okay," he said to himself, loudly, without ceasing. Evan had whipped his head around the waiting room, finding no other

witness, no one with whom to exchange amused looks. Even the receptionist was absent from her desk at the window. "Okayokayokayokay"
went on and on, a paper chain of syllables. Finally, the receptionist
appeared at the window and called out breezily, "Oh, Mr. Windom! I
see you made it. And right on time! Why don't you take a seat now and
we'll be right with you." Amazingly, Mr. Windom stopped pacing and
jabbering, and sat down as if a spell had been broken. Then he looked
straight at Evan and said, "Nice titties, eh," pointing to the magazine
cover.

Running down the middle of the street now, Evan wants to laugh at
the memory—funny what thoughts erupt in the midst of fear—but his
teeth are chattering.

Evan is the one who taught Aimee to ride her bike, unscrewed the
training wheels and let them clatter to the driveway while she watched,
nervous but smiling. If he had just left the damn wheels on—but all her
friends were zipping around the block on two wheels already and
Aimee had come to Evan, petulant, saying, "I'm not a *baby*." When
asked if she had consulted their parents, Aimee shrugged. "Mom's on
the phone, and Dad said maybe but he can't do it right now." Evan, the
doting big brother, picked up his father's slack and the monkey wrench
and did it for her. He might as well have tossed her into the street himself, into the path of an oncoming car.

She has to be all right. He will do anything. Quit school and give
up girls—even Soci Andersson—and become a Jehovah's Witness, if
that's what God wants from him. He'll go door to door in a tight
black suit trying to save souls. Anything. *Please*, he pleads silently.
Please.

By the time he gets home, Evan feels like someone who has
boarded up all the windows, stockpiled supplies and readied himself
for the hurricane gales, only to find out the storm has passed by, the
clouds parting to reveal clear blue skies.

Mrs. Sedgewick, their neighbor, is at the kitchen table, sorting mail as if it were perfectly normal for her to be in their house after school, looking at their catalogues. She smiles at Evan, dog-ears a page. "She's fine," she says. "Your baby sister is fine. Your dad just called from the hospital. She'll have to stay overnight for observation but things look positive, thank God." She pushes a plate across to him. There is only one cookie on it, nestled in crumbs. "Have a snickerdoodle."

Evan sinks into a chair, sweaty, trembling a little. His prayer, such as it was, answered. He thinks of the Jehovah's Witness promise and hopes God has a sense of humor.

Aimee is laughing. Suzen sits on a turquoise chair in the hallway, watching through the door as the doctor tickles the soles of Aimee's feet with his capped pen. He scribbles something on a clipboard, flipping page after page of documents describing Aimee's condition—which, as far as Suzen can tell, is miraculously unscathed.

Moments after the crash, Suzen had run outside to find Hallie standing at the curb, still as stone, and Aimee lying in a lumpen heap in the middle of the street and a strange woman moaning, "Oh my God, oh my God." Apparently Aimee had ridden directly into the path of the woman's minivan, and flown over it like a missile, landing with a sickening thud on the pavement. Though she lay motionless, Aimee didn't appear to be wounded—there was no blood, not even any bruises. Suzen tried to stay levelheaded, though her heart thumped against her ribs like a loose tennis ball; she ran inside and dialed 911, ran back out to wait. Hallie still stood to the side, in shock, with the distraught driver and a neighbor, Mrs. Sedgewick, who slung an arm protectively around Hallie. Suzen crouched beside Aimee then, stroking her hair; she seemed only to have been knocked into a deep sleep. She was breathing and her skin was warm. It wasn't until the paramedics arrived that Suzen began to panic. The two muscled men, one red-haired and whiskered, the other blond and chewing gum so hard the veins in his jaw pulsed, looked alarmed.

"She's not breathing," the redhead said. They worked on her like an inflatable toy with a tiny leak, bending over to listen for air coming from her mouth and nose.

"Come on, baby, don't leave us now," the other man muttered urgently.

On the way to the hospital, in the back of the ambulance, with Aimee attached to an oxygen tank, stabilized, the paramedics looked at Suzen and smiled, wiping the sweat from their brows.

"That was a close one," the blond man said, gum tucked between his teeth. The redhead scratched his forearm and looked away, apparently more shaken than he wanted to let on. She had been that close, Suzen thought then, tipping over the edge—*Don't leave us*—ready to fly away, out of their life forever. Flying toward the light.

Beside her bed in intensive care, Malcolm called softly, "Aimee? Honey? Aimee?" over and over, at first a kind of soothing pattern, until Suzen began to worry that her father had snapped. The only other sound in the room was a faint swooshing, dripping, buzzing, from various machines and fluorescent bulbs.

Then, "She moved!" The doctor darted to the bedside just as Aimee's bright eyes rolled open like a doll's. She blinked. Suzen half expected her to say *Ma-ma*.

"Aimee?" Malcolm said again, his voice muffled with emotion.

"Can you talk?" Esme asked softly, near tears.

Aimee nodded, whispered, "Yes," while smiling, as if basking in the sudden attention. "Mom!" she said, excited, a little breathless. "You should've *seen* it. The rabbits were as big as a car! And there were lots of pretty lights and fountains, and gondolas—" She paused, apparently to relish the memory.

"Gondolas?" Esme said.

"What is she talking about?" Malcolm asked, alarmed.

"It was the trauma," the doctor explained. "It isn't unusual for patients to have hallucinations or dreams, if you will . . . the blow to the head . . . the chemical reaction . . ."

"It wasn't a dream, Dad," Aimee protested. "I was *there*. Don't you know? I went to heaven!" She was beaming, proud. Suzen thought she looked like Dorothy just returned from Oz, lying on her black-and-white bed, surrounded by loved ones, telling them the wonders she had seen—and watching them smile and scratch their heads. "It's true!" Aimee said, angry tears spilling from her eyes. Nurses swirled in and out of the room, checking signs, bearing trays of food—jello dotted with fruit.

"It's okay, honey," Esme said.

Suzen couldn't stand it anymore, the tension, the dread, even the sudden relief. She ran down the hallway and threw up in the rest room, long blond hair falling into the path of vomit.

She has calmed down and sits to wait. Her parents are in charge now; her role is over. Yet, she can't shake the fact that it was partially her fault. If she hadn't sent her sister out alone, supervised only by Hallie, if she had been there, fixed the bicycle herself—but she knows she cannot be there all the time, watching, hovering, protecting. And besides, isn't that her mother's job? And her father's? It turned out that Esme had been just a block away, at a doctor's office with a woman from the shelter; Malcolm, rushing from campus when he got the phone call, beat Esme to the emergency room by ten minutes, since no one knew where she was.

She's never around when we need her, Suzen thinks scornfully.

"What if there's brain damage?" Esme is whispering to Malcolm nearby.

"There's not," Malcolm says. "They already said everything checked out fine." He doesn't sound so sure.

"What if they're wrong?"

"She's fine," Malcolm repeats. "She's just got a head full of imagination."

"It's just—weird," Esme says. She glances into the room where Aimee is playing with the TV remote and swivel tray attached to her bed. She seems blithely unconcerned, unharmed. Yet, Suzen has to admit, there is also something eerily different about her sister.

"She told me she could fly," Esme is saying. "And there were people guiding her."

"I guess anything's possible," Malcolm says, pauses. "Except for the part about the giant rabbits." He smiles, and Suzen laughs. It is a relief to laugh, to believe that everything is normal, even if she fears it is not. And just when she was beginning to think of herself as a woman, she finds herself feeling utterly childlike, helpless.

The television flickers, faces frozen on-screen, a young woman in the midst of turning around to look at someone, her mouth open wide in terror. Like Lot's wife, turned to salt. Evan holds the remote, keeps the tape on pause. He looks over at his sister, who is as motionless as the actress, except that her mouth is clamped tight. Hallie is pale and dazed looking; Evan worries that she has been traumatized.

"Hal. Hey, Hal," he says softly. She doesn't respond. Evan aims the remote at her face and pretends to click it. "Come on, damn it! Why isn't this working?" Finally she smiles, at his attempt to humor her, at his use of profanity. Of course, no adults are around to reprimand. It is just Hallie and Evan, sitting in front of the television watching forbidden movies, R-rated horror films in which hapless teenagers face death and dismemberment. Evan sneaks these home from his friend Max's house, and has tutored Hallie in the predictability of the plotlines, the overtly simulated carnage. "Look at that arm hanging there," he once pointed out cheerfully, when Hallie seemed alarmed. "It's obviously rubber. I mean, the prop guy must've been hung over that day: 'Hey, looky, I'll just use my trusty rubber arm, works every time!'" Hallie laughed and settled back down, arms folded over her flat chest, her gaze critical and appreciative. Though Evan knows his parents, Esme especially, would be aghast, swiftly putting an end to such activity, Evan believes he is doing his sister a favor, inuring her to the lesser fears in life. He plans to teach her self-defense, too, so she can fend off potential attackers. He's read survival guides and likes to share tips with Hallie—on how to avoid bears (talk or sing loudly if walking through the woods; play dead if you have an encounter); how to jump from a moving car (tuck and roll); and to stay away from downed power lines, ticking packages, angry bulls. And when all else fails, scream your head off. Evan has stopped shy of teaching Hallie how to perform an emergency tracheotomy because even he is too squeamish to think about that. Still, he prides himself on filling in the parental gaps. As far as he can tell, Esme and Malcolm have only skimmed the surface by telling their children not to talk to strangers, play with fire, or jam forks into the toaster. They also have warned them not to run or ride bikes into the street, but look where that got them.

Evan thinks of Aimee, how close she came, apparently, to sudden death yesterday. And he knows that Hallie was there, that she feels somehow responsible for it—just as he had, from a distance. When he got home he found Hallie in her room, cleaning like someone possessed. *Out, out, damned spot.* Rag in hand, she was crawling around, dusting baseboards, then Aimee's dresser, arranging the little knick-knacks lovingly. Evan managed to lure Hallie away, downstairs, promising a movie and popcorn while they wait.

"It wasn't your fault," he says now, quietly.

"I know," she says flatly. Her bangs are too long and hang like a window blind just over her eyes. She blows upward, momentarily moving them from her line of vision.

"I mean it, Hal, it was an accident. An accident is something that just happens, it can't be prevented."

"I know."

"So—you okay?" he asks, nudging her.

Hallie shrugs, stares at the television screen. "Just rewind, damn it."

Evan starts to laugh, but he notices there is no mirth in his sister's tone. And he realizes that perhaps she is not referring to the videotape, but to her life—willing it to go backward.

Suzen sits in the backseat with Aimee, whose head lolls sleepily against the car door. Her hair is still tangled and knotted, and she's wrapped in a white quilt from home, her arms like wings in the worn cotton. She looks like a big moth crumpled against the window. Up front, Malcolm and Esme talk quietly about what they need to do when they get home—find something for dinner, call the elementary school, change the filter on the furnace. Suzen marvels that life so readily slides back into the realm of the ordinary. As if nothing much happened. As if a five-year-old catapulting over the roof of a minivan and nearly expiring were nothing more troubling than the dog coughing up a hairball. Clean it up, move on.

Since the doctor signed Aimee's release forms, waving as she was wheeled to the elevator in a wheelchair, Malcolm and Esme have seemed satisfied that everything is fine, after all. Aimee chattered on about her experiences in heaven, and they merely smiled over her head. But Suzen wonders if it is possible. Glancing at Aimee—who is mouthing something silently as her lashes flutter—she thinks maybe she is telling the truth. She knows that people often tell near-death tales of hurtling through a tunnel toward great light, engulfed in warmth and love before being yanked back to this life in the nick of time. Some are disappointed, depressed. They wanted to go on, they say; it was so beautiful and peaceful. *You should have seen it*, they say, enraptured, on television talk shows. It is easy to laugh, Suzen thinks, and to discount them, to believe instead an expert like Aimee's neurologist, who attributes it to brain waves, electromagnetic something or other, synapses of nerves. Suzen would rather believe Aimee. What if it were possible to fly out of this life, even for a split second, into another world?

When they get home, Esme tries to hoist Aimee from the backseat, but can't seem to figure out how to lift her, as she is swaddled like a mummy in her quilt. Malcolm comes around to help her, picking her up as easily as a load of towels, and carries Aimee inside. Esme follows closely behind, stroking her hair, but Aimee's expression is inscrutable. Suzen wonders if she has not fully readjusted to life on earth.

"I think she's tired," Esme says. Malcolm nods and carries Aimee to her room. She does not protest, staring over his shoulder and blinking like a bird from a nest.

Suzen strolls into the family room where Hallie and Evan are watching television. They look startled when she comes in and Evan automatically turns off the volume. The movie continues, however, and Suzen sees that a teenage girl in a cheerleader costume is dangling from a barn rafter.

"You're back!" Evan says. "How's Aimee?"

"She's fine. Just tired." Suzen notices that Hallie has paled, but her ears are bright red. It is obvious she has been distraught and Evan was attempting to distract her. Suzen adds nonchalantly, for Hallie's sake, "Really, they said nothing was wrong with her, just a bump on the head."

"Good, that's good," Evan says. "See, I told you, Hal, there was nothing to worry about. She's a tough little bugger." He nudges her and Hallie smiles a little, sighs.

To change the subject, Suzen says, "What are you watching anyway? It looks lame. And what is a cheerleader doing on a farm?" She does not note that the girl is headless.

"It's a documentary," Evan says, deadpan. Hallie laughs.

"Well, you better lose it before Mom and Dad come down. They're just putting Aimee to bed."

Suzen leaves the room and wanders into the kitchen. The phone machine is loaded with blinking red messages. Twelve in all, as no one has been around to answer calls. Or else hasn't bothered. But *life goes on*, Suzen tells herself, a little breathless with emotion. Until yesterday, she never paid much attention to her siblings' well-being. She did her part, tending to her sisters when asked, but indifferently involved in their small worlds; she paid attention but never worried. Suddenly she seems keenly aware of the tenuous nature of life, how quickly it can change—or end.

To shift her focus, she presses the message button and listens.

"Hello, Esme," says the measured voice of Jennifer Strawbridge, the director of the Phoenix Center. "I have a new client you might be interested in working with," she says. Suzen can hear the tap, tap of a pen in the background. "Call me as soon as you can." She thinks, *That's just what my mother needs, one more person to worry about.* But she writes down the information anyway, and leaves it for her mother to see.

"Hello, Esme? This is Margot, Allison's mother? We were just wondering why Aimee didn't show up at the party. We had her down as a 'yes.' Well, Allison missed her, that's all." *Missed one more present, that's all*, Suzen thinks. *What a snob.* She never liked Margot Munroe, nor her daughter Jenna, Allison's older sister. A family of vain, materialistic princesses. *Good riddance*, she thinks, pressing "erase."

"Es, call me. I'll do anything you need. It's eleven fifteen, but I'll be up till midnight." Esme's friend, Miranda, who would go out on a limb for anyone, though she likes a little credit for it, too. Suzen has always thought it amusing how transparently magnanimous Miranda is. Once, she brought over an entire dinner when half the family had the flu, but then kept bringing it up in every conversation, needing affirmation—

"Did you like the salad? I had never tried that kind of soup before, but I thought it would be good for sore throats. Did everyone survive? I hope I made enough dessert . . ."

Suzen deletes Miranda, too. She can tell her mother later that she phoned.

Five more callers refer to the accident, asking if there is anything they can do—*Tell us what we can do*—which Suzen considers thoughtful, though she knows her mother won't accept.

"Hey, Suzy, it's Mary. I heard about your sister from a customer, and gosh! I just hope everything is okay. Let me know if I can do anything for you. And don't worry about coming in in the morning, you need to be with your family." Suzen pauses, hits "repeat." Mary's voice on the phone is softer than in real life, sweet, almost like a young girl. Suzen listens again. She doesn't know why. She doesn't really want to analyze her feelings, but she can't stop hearing Mary's words in her head, even after she has stopped replaying the message. *Hey, Suzy.*

"Esme?" says a man's voice. There is a hesitation, then, "I thought you were going to call back, when it was convenient to talk, and well, since you haven't yet, I assume either you can't or don't want to talk to me." Another long pause. "But if you do, I just wanted to let you know I am at a different number now—" Suzen stops in her tracks, wondering who he is and why he sounds so serious, faintly desperate. Reflexively she hits the erase button on the machine, holding it too long, thereby obliterating all of the messages, including Mary's and the remaining two she hasn't yet heard. Including the phone number the man just recited.

"Honey?" she hears her father calling from the hallway.

"Right here," her mother answers.

Suzen can hear them talking quietly. When she passes the doorway, she sees her parents at the bottom of the stairs, standing close together in the shadows. Esme's hair is wet from a shower and she is attempting to tuck her shirt into the front of her jeans. Suzen watches as Malcolm takes Esme in his arms, uncharacteristically amorous, untucking the fabric. She realizes that her parents think no one is around, that they aren't being watched. She is close enough to hear the sucking of their saliva as they kiss.

"I love you, Es," Malcolm says huskily. He presses one palm between Esme's legs, slips the fingers of his other hand inside the front of her jeans. She moans quietly with pleasure. Suzen stifles a gasp, steps back against the wall, but not before she glimpses her mother actually unzipping herself and leading Malcolm hurriedly up to their room. When they are gone, Suzen realizes she is shaking a little. It is not so much the horror of her parents' blatant sexuality, but the graphic passion she has never before observed between any man and woman in real life, close up. It is nothing like the movies, slow and backlit, with accompanying violins and piano. And in her imagination, she has always thought of *It* in vague terms, sometimes shot through with a nameless longing.

She knows she could never do what her parents are doing, never. Not like that.

What could be worse, really, than knowing that your parents have sex? Right under the same roof, in their room at the top of the stairs, practically in broad daylight, no less. Evan cannot let himself even think about it. He has heard them laughing, the door slam, the laughter again. Just home from the hospital with Aimee, who was nearly *killed,* and they're off cavorting under the sheets. It's appalling.

Not only that, there's nothing to eat. He rummages through the refrigerator finding only wilting leftovers and snack-sized yogurts. He would give anything for some beef right now, an enormous bloody steak still hissing from the grill, some fries, heaps of them. He is so 1hungry he thinks he might be sick. Unless it is still nausea over what is going on overhead. It is quiet now. He wonders (he can't help it) how long it actually takes. Ten minutes? Two? Thirty? He has an informed sense of what goes where, of course, and how to do It, but he doesn't know enough. For instance, how long does it take to warm up?

He and his friends debate this endlessly, hilariously. Max and Tony think girls need hours of foreplay. Lance says you have to use oils and "all kinds of shit," and give them back rubs. All of them agree that it takes awhile to get near "the scenery," which is their handy euphemism for female genitalia. "Did you happen to notice the scenery?" is the usual line of questioning after one of them has been on a date. Although (according to statistics), at fifteen boys are often well along in their sexual exploration, the truth is, among Evan's closest friends, sex is nearly uncharted territory. None of them has really ever gotten close, save a little groping. They all have opinions, however, based on hours of movie and television research, along with information passed on from older brothers and, rarely, fathers. Evan himself has never had much of a conversation with his own dad about sex, other than Malcolm sitting him down when he was about eleven, and haltingly telling him "the facts." But he isn't helpful at all when it comes to how to get lucky. His advice about girls is for Evan just to be himself. But obviously that would never work. Evan has to be anyone *but* himself; Soci is too sophisticated for an undersized fifteen-year-old who dreams in black-and-white film. Yet, she did go with him willingly, and she was the one to lean over first and kiss him, long and luxuriantly.

Thinking of Soci when he isn't with her, sometimes he cannot remember exactly what she looks like. He still gets her confused with Jean Seberg in his daydreams. When he sees her in person, he is startled to see her darker hair, her arched brows, her obviously teenage features. And she is so layered in black—albeit short, and often tight—clothing that he isn't sure what she would look like underneath. In a way, he doesn't want to find out. Kissing in the Esquire was like walking through a door into a room he didn't know he was allowed to enter; more than that would be terrifying. Still, he can't help wondering—

He cannot let himself start thinking about it. Standing in front of the open fridge, he lets the cold air assault his lower body till the feeling passes.

He is so hungry. *Mom! I'm hungry!* he wants to holler, as he did as a child. He spent his whole childhood yelling from one part of the house or another. Esme used to come running, but nearly always got exasperated when she discovered it was not a bloody nose or severed limb, but a simple desire for cheese crackers or a sandwich. He wasn't really picky. Fed up with the hollered demands, though, she forced him to learn to fix his own snacks when he was six. But he couldn't help it. The word *Mom!* just naturally left his lips when he felt a hunger pang.

"Hey, what are you doing?" Esme asks gently from the doorway.

Evan turns, startled. Looks at his mother but doesn't want to look too closely. He can't really tell by her face if anything has happened. And she is fully dressed, combed, smiling normally. Nothing to betray the fact that she has just seen fireworks or felt the earth move. Or maybe his dad isn't very good at it. Evan feels a little sorry for Malcolm suddenly, thinking he might be a lousy lover. Imagine having to work all the time, raise four kids, and then not even have really great sex? But maybe they do have great sex. Maybe they have it all the time, daily, on his dad's lunch hour. Maybe that's why they couldn't help it; after nearly two days at the hospital, they were starved for it. It is too awful to think about. Yet, it sort of gives him hope: *Sex can last a lifetime!* Evan grins.

"Are you okay?" his mother asks. "You seem sort of dazed."

"I'm fine," he says. "Just starving."

"I know. I'm sorry. It's been so crazy around here. Look, let's call out for pizza."

"Again?" he says, but when he sees his mother's look, he shrugs. "Okay, no problem. What kind?"

"Anything you want on it." She hands him the phone.

"How about sirloin? Can I have that on it?"

She laughs. Malcolm strides into the kitchen then, beaming, practically strutting. "Hey, sport," he says, and Evan wants to crawl under a rock out of mortification.

He turns his concentration to the number for the pizza parlor. As he dials, he remembers something. "Oh, Mom, I forgot to tell you. Some guy called for you last night when you were at the hospital. Kevin something. I wrote it down around here somewhere . . ." He sorts unsuccessfully through the scraps of paper burying the kitchen desk, then turns his attention to the phone. "Oh, hi, yeah, we want to order a couple of pies."

As he lists the items he wants, thoughtfully including the mushrooms he loathes but knows his father and sisters like, Evan notices his mother has found the note in his childish scrawl, which reads, *Call Kevin Wonderhouse? At the Carlton Hotel. Room 448.* The phone number is barely legible (penmanship has never been his forte) as is the last name; *Wonderhouse* is crossed out and *Wonderwoman?* is written above it, along with a cartoonish doodle of a man with breasts and a cape. Some of his finest work, Evan thinks. He thanks the pizza man and hangs up.

Suzen has wandered in. "Did you remember mushrooms?"

Evan shrugs. "No, just those greasy sausage intestines."

"Funny."

"So, who's Kevin Wonderhouse?" Malcolm is asking, looking at the note in Esme's hand.

Esme clears her throat, attempts a laugh. "No one, just some artist I met once, he wants to talk to me about having another show."

"Really? That would be great!"

"Maybe," Esme says. She shrugs and tucks the message into her pocket, turns to busy herself with folding paper napkins.

• • •

My mother is having an affair, Suzen thinks, the idea flickering into her head. It is the only explanation for the man calling, leaving cryptic messages, her mother's distracted reaction, an obvious lie. Suzen remembers the man's voice—the mixture of eagerness and angst—on the answering machine. Her sense of foreboding was valid.

It is like a made-for-TV movie: a normal, happy family, the stranger who enters and tears it all apart. The mother with the secret life. Suzen recently heard on the news a story about a woman who had been on the lam for twenty-five years. She was a fugitive from justice who had been involved in serious, capital crimes and managed to hide out and create a new life for herself. She changed her name, got married, raised children, was active in the community. People loved her. Then the police and FBI came knocking and it turned out she had been living a huge lie. Suzen can imagine being one of the children, just home from school, finding agents in the living room, interrogating the woman she thought was her mother. Well, of course, she *was* her mother, having given birth to her, et cetera, but she was not the woman they all thought she was.

How long has this been going on?

She thinks about Mary having an affair with a woman. How did Philip, her ex-husband, find out anyway? If the woman had phoned their house, surely he would have thought nothing of it. A man's voice might have given rise to suspicion, but not a woman's. Unless there had been signs. Mary flirting with a friend's wife, perhaps. Or losing interest in sex, or watching progressive French films. Suzen wonders if Mary really is a lesbian, or if she is bisexual, or if it is all rumor and innuendo. She thinks about the novels in which missed communications or slanderous talk ruined lives, drove hapless characters to disastrous ends. And often, the punishment was too cruel for the so-called crime. She thinks of Hester Prynne striding through town in her scarlet badge of dishonor, and feels with righteous certainty that human beings cannot help falling in love, nor with whom. It just happens, she is sure, like a weather front that rolls in from nowhere, off the radar, detected by no one until the rain pours in torrents or the snow buries everything in sight.

Unfortunately, in the old novels women were always made to pay for their involuntary passions. Mary has paid enough, Suzen thinks; people should shut up and leave her alone, already. As for her mother, Suzen isn't sure. Besides, she thinks derisively, when would she have the time? At the same time, Suzen knows that her mother is restless, her life and art passing her by, and that she is beautiful, and prone to flirting—with mailmen, male teachers, a plumber who fixed the dishwasher. Suzen watched as Esme leaned over provocatively, her blond hair falling like Rapunzel's toward the man sprawled on the kitchen floor gazing beneath the sink with a flashlight, then flashing a smile up at Esme. Suzen has also seen her mother glide through faculty gatherings, the occasional parties hosted at their house. The way Esme walks, the way she pays more attention to her makeup and hair, the dress she wears—all of it clearly cries for attention: *Look at me! I'm still gorgeous!* And Malcolm seems to think it's all for him. It's mortifying the way he clings to her side at such gatherings, not territorially, but like a boy on his first date, just so pleased that *she* is with *him*. Suzen wants to shake her father and force him to take a good look—at his wife and the way other men look at her, the way she eats it up with a spoon, in slow, sensuous bites.

Suzen feels a sickening dread curling through her, the unexpected, unforeseen calamity rising to the surface. She watches her mother setting the table, clearly distracted, setting forks to the right sides of plates, glasses to the left. Esme gives up folding napkins, as if she cannot remember how, tosses them onto the table. She sighs and strides to the sink. No one else notices that she is standing there, staring at her pale reflection in the kitchen window, that she is running water over her hands but not washing them. Evan and Malcolm are talking, and

Hallie, who has wandered silently into the room, is tending to her rat, and Aimee is still asleep upstairs. Suzen is alone in observing Esme, who seems to have detached herself as effectively as Suzen often does, drifting apart from the noise and activity. After a moment, though, she collects herself, dries her hands on the front of her pants and turns a placid face toward her family. It is as if she has walked out and then back in, all the while not moving from the room.

"Mom?" Suzen says tentatively.

"Yes?"

Suzen cannot think of anything to say or ask, so she simply shrugs. Esme seems not to notice, and in fact, seems to forget that Suzen has said anything. She slips past her daughter and out of the room, and no one pays any attention at all. For the first time in her life, it occurs to Suzen that her mother is a separate individual with a head full of her own thoughts and ideas and secrets. She is not simply tethered to her family, Suzen thinks, swallowing hard, and it is entirely possible she could unmoor herself if she chose to, and sail away.

Evan drifts down the hall to his father's study and stands in the doorway, watching the familiar hunched posture, Malcolm engrossed in his work. Usually he is grading student essays or planning a lesson for the next day, reviewing notes and revising his themes so he doesn't repeat himself too often. He has said that he worries about losing students to television and movies and popular culture, worries that soon none of them will have heard of Henry James or Hemingway. So, the onus is on him to reinvent classic literature for a modern, sometimes indifferent audience. How he does this is a mystery to Evan; he scarcely can imagine his father entertaining a class full of sleepy-eyed college students, telling jokes or relating his own life experiences to theirs.

Still, he admires Malcolm. He knows he is smart and excessively well-read, that he follows politics and current events and can surprise people with his esoteric knowledge of topics like horology and kinesics and word origins. The latter is his special hobby and sometimes the bane of family gatherings. Over dinner Malcolm likes to quiz his children on vocabulary and sometimes the words' Greek or Latin roots. Evan, who has inherited his father's DNA for this talent, usually fares pretty well. It is one of the few situations in which he dominates his female siblings, or lassos his father's attention, and there is no small pleasure in that.

Evan clears his throat so that Malcolm turns around, smiles. "Hi there," he says. "Do you need something?"

"No, not really," Evan says. "I was just wondering . . ."

"What?"

"Never mind." He cannot bring himself to ask his father about women. What would he tell him but to trust his instincts, treat them with respect, keep his hands to himself? What he really wants to know is what Malcolm was like before he met Esme, if he dated at all, and if he knew what he was doing. Evan is pretty sure of the answer.

"Do you really think Aimee is all right?" he asks, ashamed at himself for using concern over his sister as a diversion. He hadn't really been thinking about her at all.

"Oh, sure," Malcolm says breezily. "They kept her under observation for twenty-four hours, which is usual, you know. But the doctor thinks she's perfectly fine, just bruised and shaken." He laughs a little. "And a little delirious, I suppose. But she'll be back to her old self soon, so don't worry."

"Okay. That's good."

Malcolm turns to his papers, then turns back. "Was there something else?"

Evan scratches his head, smiles, then says, "Not really. I mean . . ."

"Go ahead, Ev, I'm all ears," Malcolm says, cupping his hands around his head for emphasis. Then, surprisingly perceptive: "You've got something on your mind besides your sister, right?" He motions Evan into the room.

Evan comes and sits down, loose-limbed, on the stuffed chair opposite the desk. He decides to plow right in. "Did you date before Mom?" he asks.

Malcolm laughs, then rocks a little in his chair. "That's top secret," he says, smiling wryly.

Evan rolls his eyes. "Seriously, Dad."

"You're wondering if I had any experience back in the Paleolithic Age?"

"Ha, ha."

"Well, I always liked girls when I was your age, though I was admittedly a little on the gawky side. I didn't really date much till my senior year, but then—" Malcolm stops, seems to consider whether or not to go on. He scratches his head.

"Then what?"

"Nothing. I mean, I had a few girlfriends here and there but none mattered until I met your mother."

It is so pat and clichéd that Evan sighs, disappointed. Of course, there would be no story.

"Why do you ask, by the way? Do you have a girlfriend?" Malcolm asks, grinning a little too broadly.

"No," Evan says automatically.

"Well, when you do, just remember, be yourself, that's the most important thing. And be a gentleman, and keep your hands to yourself."

"Right, Dad," Evan says. His father has no idea, he thinks. Apparently, when he was young, a girl's hands never came into the equation. *What if she starts it?* he wonders. *What if she is the one to reach for you, to kiss you, and then what if it goes further and further? What then?* He leaves his father to his stories of nineteenth-century romance, maids-in-waiting, gloved hands folded demurely in laps.

She is standing near his locker, radiating a vigor none of the other students passing by seem to possess. She smiles and waits for Evan to come near, as if he is the thing that causes her to glow; the idea causes him to blush.

"Hi," Soci says softly. "You okay?"

"Yeah, why?" he asks, leaning against the cool metal for support. He wonders if he looks that flushed, or otherwise unhealthy.

"I heard your sister got hit by a car."

"Oh. That. Yeah. It was pretty scary, but she's fine." He pauses, remembering his terror at the time. Then he elaborates, realizing as he tells it, what a good story it makes. "She actually flew right over the top of the van," he says. "And the most amazing thing is she thinks she went to heaven—and then came back."

Soci's eyes widen. "No kidding? A near-death experience? That is so cool."

Evan looks at her and laughs. Soci stares back, earnest. "I mean it. I've always wanted to have that happen to me. Actually, I did have an O.B.E. once."

"A what?"

"Out-of-body experience." She smiles secretively, pushing her tiny bangs off her forehead. Her skin is so smooth it appears translucent at the temples. Evan can see the blue thread of vein pulsing. He wants to press a finger against it, gently, but he holds his hands to his sides.

"How did that happen?"

She shrugs. "I'll tell you about it outside." She begins strolling casually toward the exit. Even hesitates—he knows he cannot continue this deviant behavior. He worries about getting caught, about getting suspended, about experiencing his parents' furor and the subsequent fallout. But then he pushes it all away, like a pile of books for a test he surely will fail. *What's the point? Who cares?* Hypnotized, he follows Soci, who is already outside, then across the parking lot. When he catches up with her, she turns and smiles, then continues on, her fingers skimming the tops of shrubs like water.

At the municipal park a few blocks away, she heads for the swing set and runs to one of the black rubber swings, headlong, like a leggy child. Today she wears blue jeans, but with black boots and a black sweater. Her eyes are rimmed in black kohl, and she licks her lips, which are chapped. It is cold outside, and Evan wishes he had thought to take his jacket from his locker. He wears a short-sleeved T-shirt, because the high school is overheated, and he hadn't planned on leaving so suddenly. He wonders what it is about Soci that so tempts him to disregard convention. Her kiss? Her uncanny resemblance to a former movie star? Before he discovered Soci, Evan was a decent student, a follower of rules. He liked to wisecrack now and then, in front of friends, or showcase his cleverness, but he never cared what a girl thought or suggested; he never forfeited his own will like this, without knowing whether the profit would outweigh the cost. He thinks that Soci is like the game show hostess standing before one of three doors, each promising a potentially better prize than the last. He just doesn't know yet what it is she is offering—nor if he is ready to accept.

She pumps her legs to propel herself off the dusty ground, then swings for awhile, happily, head tipped back so that all Evan can see on her downswing is the long white arch of her throat. When she has had enough, she skids to a halt, dragging a boot toe through the dirt.

"What now?" she asks.

Evan shrugs. "I don't know." He almost says, *We could go back*, but refrains. His curiosity is stronger now than his resolve. A police patrol car cruises past the park and Soci automatically dives to the ground, near some shrubs. Not knowing what else to do, Evan joins her, fling-ing himself down low, breathing hard.

"That was close," Soci says merrily. Evan laughs nervously and wraps his arms around himself. "You cold?" Soci asks, as if it has only just occurred to her. "Maybe this was a stupid idea."

"No," he says quickly. "Really, I'm fine. I need to build up my stam-ina anyway."

She smiles at this obviously valiant excuse, and reaches past Evan to yank a stem of clover from the grass. She lies back down and begins plucking the tiny petals, and singing, "He loves me, he loves me not." Now and then, she looks over at Evan, her face so close it nearly grazes his, and he can see that her eyes are the color of root beer, with a fuzzy gold line running around her pupils. He hadn't noticed before, per-haps because the only time he was this close to her, they were in the dark.

"You have amazing eyes," he murmurs.

"—loves me not," she says, dropping the last little petal on the grass and sitting up. "Oh, well. There are plenty of other fish in the sea."

Evan sits up, too, and shoves her playfully, but he doesn't dare con-tradict her. After all, it is only their second afternoon together; too soon to utter the words, "I *do* love you," because she might either laugh or pull out another cigarette and look away. Evan wants the moment to last, just lying on the grass, admiring her smooth legs stretched out before her, ankles crossed. She tugs at the hem of her sweater a little, flicks an ant from her knee. Evan waits for another to crawl from a blade of grass onto her skin so that he can reach over and brush it off for her; he is prickly with desire, but he waits.

"What did you mean before about having an out-of-body experi-ence?" he asks.

Soci lies back down, and sighs. She cups her hands behind her head, as if thinking how to answer. Evan notices that her breasts melt into small mounds when she lies flat, while her hipbones become erect knobs through the denim. His fingers twitch, imagining the hardness of her bones, the softness of her flesh.

Staring into the sky, Soci says, "It happened just like this. Staring into the clouds for a long, long time. I was around eight or nine years old, riding in the backseat of the car, you know, just daydreaming, while my parents talked. I discovered that the longer I looked without blinking at the clouds, the less I felt like I was myself. You know? I mean, I just kind of floated out of my body and it took awhile before I became *attached* again. It was weird. Kind of scary. Sometimes when we were in the car after that I would dare myself to do it again, but I couldn't. I'd panic and make myself read the label on a box of animal crackers or something close up."

Evan lies back down and looks up at the clouds. "Can you do it now?" he asks, turning to watch her profile. She is squinting skyward, then turns to look at him. She shakes her head back and forth on the grass.

"No. I can't. What if I didn't come back?"

Evan laughs, but Soci doesn't. She just pulls her chin closer to his, kisses him, then slides her whole body, tilted on her side, against his, head to toe. He is the warm flat stone, she is pressed against him, as if she needs him more than anything, more than air. And he is floating, floating away.

A imee floats in the bathtub, eyes closed, blond hair fanning in the water like transparent kelp. Suzen sits on the toilet lid beside the tub, reading a magazine and keeping an eye on her sister. Esme has gone to a sculpting class (she said) and Malcolm is working late on campus. Suzen has begun to feel like a surrogate parent, expected to rear her siblings as if they are orphans. She drove Hallie home from a friend's house, and helped Aimee with her homework—five spelling words—and even walked the dog. For dinner she gave everybody canned pasta, stringy noodles in an orange paste that Aimee devoured and Hallie turned up her nose over. Evan opted for cereal, eating at the sink, then rinsing the bowl and moving on to a sleeve of fig cookies. Suzen worries that Esme's absence has become normal, and that even Malcolm doesn't suspect anything.

Last night, the phone rang and Suzen answered.

"Esme?" the voice said. The mysterious Kevin, calling again.

"No, this is her daughter," Suzen said, bristling.

"Oh, can you get her for me?"

Suzen took the phone into another room and said that her mother was occupied, and couldn't come to the phone.

"May I take a message?" Suzen asked politely, pen poised over paper. He spelled his last name for her, carefully, as if it mattered that she have the correct information. As if there might be another "Wunderhaus" phoning and asking for Esme.

"Tell her it's urgent," he said. "Maybe she didn't get my number the last time I called." He slowly told Suzen the new number and repeated it twice, as if she might be daft. He also told her the name of the hotel where he was staying now, the Imperial Motor Lodge.

"I think I've got it. Anything else?"

"Tell her I *really* need to speak to her. Soon," he said with such desperation Suzen was startled. When she set the phone down, she stood for a moment, wondering what to do next. If she repeated the message to Esme, she knew her mother would make up some story on the spot. If she said nothing, chances were Malcolm would answer the phone sometime, and then what? Suzen wanted to protect him from the shock and heartache. She has told no one about her suspicions. She has kept the phone number to herself.

Now, she looks over at Aimee, the mermaid, and wonders suddenly if she possibly is not the offspring of their father, but of Kevin. She doesn't really look like any of them, except for the light hair like Suzen's and Esme's, though neither of them has curls. But then, she does have the telltale VanderZee chin, squared and a tiny bit protrusive. As if aware of eyes on her, Aimee opens her own and turns her head in the water to look at Suzen.

"Where's Mom?" she asks suddenly.

"An art class."

"Oh." She sways in the water, loose-limbed and weightless. Then she sits up against the back of the tub and reaches one hand between her legs, fingers sliding along the padded slit.

"Don't do that," Suzen snaps without thinking.

"Why not?"

"I don't know. It's inappropriate," she adds, unable to think of a good reason.

"Mom says I can, if I do it in private," Aimee says, not taking her hand away. Her face is relaxed as she moves her fingers back and forth. Suzen is shocked to think of her mother having such a conversation with Aimee; there seems to be so much she doesn't know about her.

"Well," Suzen says, clearing her throat and continuing to flip magazine pages, "this isn't exactly private, since you aren't alone."

"Oh," Aimee says thoughtfully, pausing and then taking her hand away. She splashes a little, watching the water wash over her skin in mild waves. "Can you leave, then?"

Suzen laughs, taken aback. "Mom wanted me to keep an eye on you."

"I won't drown," Aimee says simply. "Don't worry."

Suzen hesitates, then takes a towel from a shelf over the tub and says, "Look, why don't you just get out now, you're turning pruney."

Aimee sighs and stands up obediently. "I wish I was still in heaven," she says dreamily. "It was really beautiful."

Suzen does not know whether to gape or laugh at her. She has been watching Aimee in the days since her accident, noting subtle changes, a sublime aura of calm about her, as if she is in a trance. She no longer argues with or pesters Hallie, and she is uncharacteristically obedient and compliant. Sometimes she seems to be talking to herself—or praying. Suzen wonders what, really, her sister's head is filled with, wonders how much of it is real, how much imagined. In just two days, Aimee seems to have been transformed into another kind of person altogether.

Now she stands waiting patiently, smiling beatifically, water streaming from her pink skin, prickled with goose bumps. Suzen reaches around and begins to dry her sister carefully, as if she is fragile, rubbing the damp blond curls until they gleam again with light.

The bluey light from the television flickers and Evan walks toward the family room, wondering who else is awake. His parents both arrived home after nine, when his younger sisters were already in bed, tucked in by Suzen, who then disappeared into her own room. Esme kissed Evan and asked him how things were, did Aimee seem okay, was Hallie eating normally, did anyone phone? Evan nodded and shrugged. He hadn't noticed anything unusual, and the only person who called had dialed a wrong number, a man who seemed startled by Evan's voice and muttered something before hanging up. He didn't think there was any reason to mention it.

Esme said, "Well, I think I'm going to head up. I'm beat. Evan, you should go to bed soon, too. You've been staying up too late lately."

Evan nodded, surprised she had noticed. Yet, Esme had a knack for knowing where everyone was at any given time, even if she seemed distracted. Unlike Malcolm, who was just plain distracted.

At the doorway of the family room, Evan sees that it is his father who is slouched before the TV, the volume turned to low. He has a large red print quilt draped over his lap like an invalid, and his hair is standing straight up on one side. Evan has a sudden, shocking image of his father as an old man, in a nursing home, blank-faced in some generic sunroom. When Evan takes a step, he slips a little on a pile of magazines on the floor, and Malcolm turns around. He is wearing his old glasses, with the outdated aviator frames, which he wears when he is tired and has removed his contact lenses—Evan thinks he now resembles a nerdy agent on a police show.

"What are you doing up?" Malcolm asks, slight accusation in his tone.

"I couldn't sleep. What're you watching?"

"The Travel Channel," Malcolm says. He sounds a little defensive and Evan wonders if he and Esme have argued again about the proposed sabbatical. Evan has thought about it more lately himself, in spite of (or because of?) his infatuation with Soci. Some days he cannot wait just to see her again, other days the suspense is too much and he wishes he didn't have to deal with such complicated feelings.

He sits down beside his father, crosses his feet on the coffee table. He notices how unlike they are in build, Evan stocky but smallish, Malcolm tall and lean, nearly bony. When Evan was a child, people sometimes jokingly referred to the two of them as the Jolly Green Giant and Little Sprout. He was relieved when they stopped.

"So, where is this?" Evan asks. The scenery on screen could be anywhere remote in South America or Indonesia, or parts of eastern Africa, verdant and mountainous. Waterfalls gush like special effects; it is hard to believe such beauty truly exists.

"Brazil," Malcolm says.

"Have you ever been there?"

Malcolm looks over at his son. "No. Have you?"

Evan laughs, unsure how to take his father's mood. "Well, I mean, I know you traveled around Europe—"

"That's it," Malcolm says, "that's as far as I got. There are many more places I *haven't* visited."

Evan pushes his luck. "So, why don't you?"

Malcolm laughs a little, then sighs. "Because you can't always get what you want, son. Like the song says."

"What song?"

" 'You Can't Always Get What You Want.' "

"Oh, *that* song," Evan laughs. Malcolm laughs, too. Evan is glad his father has relaxed. "What about Italy?"

"What about it." He gives a warning look, as if Evan has brought up a taboo subject.

"You know—your sabbatical." Evan shifts on the sofa, feeling the lumps of the old cushions beneath him. "I heard you and Mom talking about it once."

Malcolm shakes his head and says, "We have talked about it, but there are other things more pressing in our life right now." Evan knows he is referring to Aimee's accident; the horror of *What if?* continually hangs over the household, everyone (except perhaps Aimee) aware of how much worse it could have been. And he suspects that both his parents are suffering no small measure of guilt, as parents always think they should be able to protect their children, no matter what. Evan wants to remind his father that the worst *didn't* happen, so they should just be grateful, and go on with the rest of their lives.

But Malcolm has turned back to the television, silent, his jaw clenched. Eventually he begins flipping the channel away from rushing water and spongy green plateaus until he lands on the weather station, where a stout man in a gray suit and yellow tie is predicting "unseasonably chilly temperatures for the foreseeable future."

"Try saying that ten times fast," Evan says, attempting levity. Then he sobers. "Look, Dad, I just thought—if you really want to take a sabbatical, you should do it."

"Well, I appreciate your support, Ev, but nothing is that simple.

And one doesn't just pick up and move to Italy just because one wants to."

Evan looks at his father in the semi-darkness, his profile illuminated by the television, the map of the United States and its weather fronts drifting willy-nilly across the lenses of his glasses. He is baffled and disappointed by Malcolm's resignation, as if everything—even his own dreams and desires—is beyond his control. He wishes Malcolm were more capricious, a word Evan likes, even if it comes from a root meaning, literally, "hedgehog head." Why shouldn't one pursue one's wishes if doing so will bring one happiness?

After a few minutes, he becomes aware of a different silence in the room, and notices that his father has fallen asleep. The remote control has slipped from his fingers and Evan picks it up, turns the volume off. Then he notices that on the sofa beside Malcolm there is a small, worn notebook, the old ring binder kind with pockets for loose papers. It looks like a journal of some kind and Evan stares at it, instantly curious. He sees the date jotted in a corner and does the math, determining that it was the year his father was eighteen, when he traveled through Europe. Surely his writing would reveal a great deal about what he was like then, a young man on his own, on foreign soil.

When he is certain that Malcolm is deeply asleep, Evan tugs the notebook across the sofa cushion toward himself. Carefully, gingerly, like a pickpocket trying not to be detected, he opens the cover. Before he can read one line of the dense prose, single-spaced, filling the first page top to bottom, Evan spies a photograph. It is small, the old style Kodak, three by three inches, and tucked into the inner flap of the cover. When Evan lifts it out, he sees that it is a picture of a beautiful woman, dark-haired, doe-eyed, in a low-cut flowered blouse. Her head is tilted coyly but she gazes directly at the camera. She has what Evan knows from movies and secondhand information to be bedroom eyes. He looks at the image for a long time, then over at his sleeping father, and finds he cannot put the two together. But then, the girl was very young, probably seventeen or eighteen, and so was Malcolm, back then. Evan turns the photo over and sees that a message is inscribed, in faint gray pencil: *To Malcolmi, mi Americano.* Underneath are *Xs* and *Os,* and an illegible name. Perhaps Mona, or Nona. Or Mara.

Evan glances at the first journal entry, but all he finds are routine descriptions of tourist travel and late-adolescent grappling with Life: ". . . biked through Amsterdam . . . not much sleep . . . lost our way near Prague . . . ate bread and jam (again) . . . spent half a day looking for an American Express office . . . When I stand in the elegant train stations, staring at the destination boards, I feel like a runaway, fleeing everything familiar. It is exhilarating and terrifying. Who knows what is at the other end? . . . I feel like I am more myself here, or, at least, a different version of the person I was—or am I someone else altogether?"

Someone else, Evan thinks. Is his father really someone other than the man he thought he was? Or is everyone simply different versions of the same self?

His father stirs on the sofa, so he quickly puts the picture back where he found it, careful to leave as much of its edge exposed as when he found it, in case Malcolm is more observant than Evan gives him credit for. He certainly is more enigmatic than Evan gave him credit for, perhaps even *capricious.* Once upon a time, an Italian girl smiled for him, and wrote a love note. He wonders what the story holds, and if Malcolm would ever tell it. Perhaps it is his great secret, his first real love, before Esme. Perhaps that was what Malcolm was going to tell Evan the other night before he changed his mind and said nothing. And then it occurs to Evan that perhaps the picture of the lovely girl somehow is tied to Malcolm's longing to return to Italy. If so, that would explain Esme's resistance. But then, Evan reasons, how would she know about it? Lots of couples have past lovers that they don't speak of, for good reason. *That was then, this is now.* And yet, if that is the case, why would his father still hold onto his youthful journal, and the picture of a girl from long ago? While Evan is desperate to know, he is uneasy. He remembers hearing his parents laughing in their bedroom and wonders if their marriage is as stable as it seems, or if, like so many others, like half his friends' parents', it is really built on toothpicks, and it would take only a small breeze to knock it over.

The wind has picked up and Suzen wanders the grounds of the nursery, helping right tipped plants and displays. She has arrived early this afternoon, having finagled permission from the school office to miss her last homeroom class once a week; she has made a case for her work-study apprenticeship, promising to write an extra science paper based on her observations. She feels she has won a small, private battle, especially since she has not informed her parents of her decision, partly out of stubborn self-will, and partly out of a growing grudge against her mother for her supposed infidelity.

She has to admit, however, that she could be wrong. Though she has been watching Esme closely lately, and listening in on her phone conversations, there has been no further sign of the man named Kevin Wunderhaus. She wonders if she has unjustly suspected her mother and if she should give her the phone number she has withheld; at least then she could read the reaction on Esme's face. But days have passed and she figures if it really were important, he would have called back. Maybe he has, when Suzen wasn't home. It is not her problem, after all. Is it? Suzen decides not to think about it until she has more—or rather, any—proof.

She strolls through the nursery paths, her shoes crunching cheerfully on the gravel. The sky is blue gray and skidded with clouds, threatening rain. Yet, when Suzen looks around her, all she sees is vibrant color, explosions of life: a woman in a red scarf passes by lugging a flatbed wagon full of orange mums; wooden display tables tower with leggy purple pincushions (*scabiosa columbaria*), and silver reflecting balls like giant Christmas ornaments; fuchsia roses press their faces against the glass of the greenhouse; mounds of white impatiens pillow the trunks of trees; the ubiquitous ivy crawls darkly green around the grounds. Suzen loves the seasons, the way even in autumn there is life, changing, remaking the scenery. She even happily anticipates winter, when everything blooming and tropical will be nestled within warm glass and outside the dormant plants will rest underneath a hard cover of frost. She imagines sitting in the small office with Mary, surrounded by the pungent smell of coffee and damp earth, droplets of mist in their hair.

She is startled by Mary rushing up behind her, a little breathless. "Come here," she is saying, "I need your help." She tugs Suzen with her toward the main building, informing her along the way that she is terribly shorthanded and needs Suzen to run the cash register for half an hour. Before Suzen can object on the grounds that she has never done it before, that her math skills are abysmal, Mary seems to read her mind.

"Don't worry, the machine does all the adding and multiplying for you, including tax." She hands Suzen the silver key, demonstrates how it opens the cash drawer, and gives a cursory lesson on the various features of the machine, then leaves her alone.

Very quickly, to Suzen's dismay, a line forms. A short woman with beauty parlor hair sidles up with a wagon of mulch, fifteen five-pound bags. Suzen smiles at her and starts tallying. She turns to the customer and says brightly, "That will be $381.16, please."

"Excuse me?" the woman says, raising her brows. "Try again, dear. I think you added an extra zero in there because unless I am sorely misinformed, fifteen times two dollars and forty cents is not three hundred and eighty-one dollars. Even with tax."

Suzen blushes, apologizes, hits the return key on the cash register. It does not open the machine as she hoped, nor clear the mistake.

"What's the problem?" a burly man in line asks impatiently.

"She added wrong."

"That's the problem with these computerized cash registers, you know," the man says. "Kids don't have to know a darn thing any more. They think the machine will do it all, the all-powerful machine will do their thinking for them. Now look what happens, when the machine fails!"

"Actually, I don't think it's the machine's fault," the mulch woman says matter-of-factly. "She just added wrong. She hit the extra zero."

"So, can't you just delete that?" the burly man asks Suzen, leaning over the counter so she can see the crust in the corners of his bleary eyes. Behind him, the line continues to grow, like a mutant vine, winding around the front of the store. Suddenly it seems everyone in town is purchasing begonias and English ivy, potting soil and tulip bulbs. Can't they just *wait?* Suzen wants to turn around and abandon her post. She nearly wants to cry.

"Come *on*," someone farther down the line calls out. Suzen perseveres, keeps trying different buttons on the register, turns the silver drawer key Mary gave her, back and forth, but to no avail. Suddenly, there is a hand on her arm. Her skin tingles. It is Mary, come to her rescue.

"It's okay, Suz," she says. "This happens all the time. I appreciate your trying to help out here." She turns and waves to the line of customers, assuring them that everything is under control. "Patience is like sunshine," she singsongs and everyone seems to relax. The mulch lady even gives Suzen a sympathetic little smile.

"I think she just hit the extra zero is all," she says to Mary.

Fifteen minutes later, the rush has died down and only two customers are milling about, taking their time as if on a museum tour. Mary puts an arm around Suzen's shoulder and squeezes. "You did fine! Don't let it get to you."

Suzen tries to smile, but she is still embarrassed by her lack of

skills, and grace. It amazes her how Mary so effortlessly meets everything head-on. Mary hands Suzen a cup of hot tea and pours one for
herself.

"Listen," she says. "I have this new project coming up, and I think
it would be great if you could help me with it."

"Sure," Suzen says, eager to appear competent, capable. She sips
her tea, burning her lip.

"Believe it or not, it's a hedge maze," Mary says, dropping her voice
to a whisper, conspiratorially. "This man called me up out of the
blue—he just bought Conrads', the auto parts plants—you know the
one that makes headlight dimmers? Anyway, obviously he's loaded,
and he and his family spent some time in England, and he has this
infatuation with the mazes over there—"

"Like Hampton Court?" Suzen interjects.

Mary smiles, quizzically. "Chatsworth, actually. But how did you
know?"

"I went there when I was little," Suzen says. "My family lived in
Wales for about six months and we traveled around England."

"Really? That must have been wonderful."

Suzen shrugs. "I really don't remember much, but I remember the
castles, and the maze." She remembers everything, but doesn't want to
seem self-important.

"I've seen photos of it in a book. It is impressive," Mary says. "Mr.
Andersson—that's this man's name—wants a design like the
Chatsworth maze, or the one at Leed's Castle, though on a much
smaller scale, of course. I've never done anything like this, but I love
the idea. Apparently, he tried to hire some maze expert, but none were
available to come to Michigan for another year or more, and he's impatient. We talked a few times and I guess he figured I could do it as well
as anyone, given the right plans."

"I'd love to help," Suzen says boldly. Automatically she envisions running through high green tunnels of clipped hedges, her feet silent on the path, chasing after—whom? It doesn't matter. Her blood pulses with the romance of it all.

"It will take awhile to lay out the plans on their property," Mary is saying, "but he has given me a rough blueprint, and carte blanche to figure out how to implement it, revise it as needed. And if it goes well, we can start planting before the first freeze." She glances at a calendar on her desk, as if it reveals exactly when that might be. She sighs. "There isn't much time. We should go over there and at least walk it out."

"When?"

"How about Friday afternoon?"

"Okay."

"Mr. Andersson said his daughter would be there after school to show us around if he's running late."

D id soccer run late?" Esme asks when Evan walks into the kitchen. He glances at the clock, considers a line of defense. He can lie, or he can tell the truth, that soccer practice was canceled and he spent the hour and a half with Soci at a coffee shop, handing her quarters so she could monopolize the jukebox and make him guess her selections while he sipped his mocha and watched her walk back and forth in her tight black skirt.

"I was with some of my people," he says, which is more or less the truth, as there were, indeed, others in the shop.

"Your people?" Esme smiles.

Evan shrugs. "Language is always evolving, Mom."

"I see. How's your education evolving?"

Evan pauses before answering, suspecting a trick question. His mother isn't usually glib unless she knows more than she lets on. Sometimes she asks questions to which she already knows the answers, just to check her children's veracity. For instance, she might very well have been informed about the schedule change for practice, so Evan is relieved he didn't lie. Furthermore, even if he had lied, she would know it. She always knows, claims she can read minds, and Evan believes her. Still believes he can see the extra eyes in the back of her head blinking through her hair if he squints.

"I just have to review for a biology test on Monday," he says earnestly, thinking it will suffice. It is true, it is valid, and if she will just let him go, he will commence studying immediately.

Esme stares at him and then she sits down at the table, hands smoothing the surface in small circles. It is a habit she has, a kind of displaced painting. When Esme quit working on her art, or "put it on hold" as she explained it, she threw herself into other things. She is frequently away, attending to the affairs of Troubled Women (Evan has heard this euphemism so often he thinks of it in capitals). Evan wonders if she does so to get away from her own domestic duties, from her children and marriage. Yet, she seems perfectly serene most of the time, so his doubts could be wholly unfounded. And Esme has begun attending a sculpting class one evening a week, returning to the artist self that she has long neglected.

"So, how's your class going?" Evan asks, partly out of sincere interest, mostly to divert attention from himself.

Esme laughs. "Fine. Thanks for asking. I'm not sure it's my style, or if I could make it my style, but it's fun to try something new."

"That's good."

"But enough about me," she says wryly. "We were talking about you. So, do you have a girlfriend?"

Evan is startled by the question, but he shrugs. "I guess. I mean, it's not official or anything." He isn't sure what would make it so, unless it would involve jewelry or a declaration of some sort—or going further than kissing.

"Because I don't know if your father has talked to you about—"

"*Please*," he interrupts. "You don't have to worry." He is deeply embarrassed.

"Okay. Fair enough. So, what's her name? What's she like?"

Evan thinks it over, a loaded question. "Her name is Soci Andersson, and she's—nice."

Esme smiles. "Nice. Well, that's good." She pauses in her invisible painting on the table and says, "She isn't prone to skipping class or anything like that, is she?"

Evan swallows, tries to meet her eyes but can't. There isn't a good excuse, he knows, and he can't blame it on Soci's bad influence, nor would he want to, and besides, he knows that one is responsible for one's own actions, as his father would put it. Yet, when his mother is looking at him like that, steady and patient, waiting for the confession, words fly out of his mind, small and illegible, then out of sight. He can only stammer and fidget.

"Um, well, we—it only happened a couple of times," he says.

"I thought so," she says. "The assistant principal said Soci Andersson was absent the same two afternoons you were. Funny coincidence." Her tone is no longer patient, but cool. Her arms are folded across her chest. She almost looks like a jealous girlfriend demanding to know if he's been unfaithful. She waits for him to explain.

"It's nothing, really," he manages to say. "We just cut class once or twice—and there wasn't much going on those days, I swear. I didn't miss much. And we don't do anything but talk, you know, hang out together and talk. That's all." He doesn't mention the movie or the kissing, or that he knows what her tongue tastes like, that he wants nothing more than to feel the skin underneath her clothing.

Esme sighs. "Okay, I believe you, Ev. But I thought we had already talked about this, getting distracted, skipping classes. You have got to stop it or you will be in serious trouble. Understand? You can 'just talk' on your free time."

Evan, earnest, nods. But even as he agrees, promises to change, he knows that there is something about Soci that latches itself to a strange new part of him, a part that cannot or will not obey rules, that blithely disregards his own conscience. *I am . . . a different version of the person I was.* The ironic thing is that just the other day, on their second flight from school, Soci informed Evan that he was lucky to be a Libra, which meant he was "balanced."

"You represent harmony," she'd said.

"What about you?" he asked. "What's your sign?"

Soci grinned. "Trouble."

He is starting to see that she wasn't kidding. And that if he continues to follow her around—which is how it is, she leading, he following—Evan knows without his mother telling him that it *will* be trouble, a disaster. And aptly enough, he's learned that "disaster" comes from the Italian word *disastrato*, which means "ill-starred." Perhaps, Evan thinks, he was born under the wrong sign.

Suzen has spent so much time watching Aimee for signs (of what, she isn't sure—latent brain damage?) that she has virtually ignored Hallie. Since the accident, however, Suzen has noticed that Hallie has grown even more introverted. And she avoids Aimee, stepping gingerly around her as if she might be a ghost, or made of glass.

Coming home from the nursery, Suzen finds her sister sitting crouched on the back porch steps, hair drooping over her hanging head. When she looks up, her peaked face is so sorrowful, Suzen impulsively sits down and puts an arm around her. It is unusually cool, and Suzen wraps her cardigan tighter around herself with one hand, still holding Hallie with her other. She can almost feel the hum of anxiety emanating from her sister's small body.

"Hey, there," Suzen says softly. She racks her brain for something more to say, some wise form of comfort, though, in her experience doling out advice, it seems usually no one listens. In the past, she has tried to teach her sisters how to shoot basketballs through the hoop *not* like a girl, and to complete difficult tasks before the easy ones—but both of them still throw balls with flippy arm movements, missing their targets, and Hallie always rushes through her homework, leaving the hardest for last, usually around bedtime when she is in tears and Esme is scolding her.

Through the kitchen window just behind them, Suzen can see their mother moving about now, preparing dinner. Aimee is sitting cross-legged on the countertop, dipping her fingers into a bowl. For a moment Suzen takes in the simplicity of the scene, the silence of it as she cannot hear what her mother is saying to Aimee, just sees her smile, turn back to stir something. It occurs to her that Esme is behaving like a normal, doting mother, and that Aimee seems, from all appearances, like a healthy child.

"You know, you can stop worrying about Aimee now," Suzen says. "She's perfectly fine."

"I know," Hallie says, a little impatiently. "I wasn't even thinking about her."

"So, what's bothering you?"

"It's Lily. She has a new best friend." Hallie looks away, as if this information pains her to share. Suzen knows that Lily, their next-door neighbor, an adopted Korean girl with black-ink eyes and razor-edged bangs, has been Hallie's constant companion since they were six. One third of their lifetime.

"Really? Are you sure?"

"Yes, she even *told* me."

Little bitch, Suzen thinks. She wants to march over and demand that Lily explain herself. "Who is it?" she asks.

"Some girl called AnnaLisa, she's new. She has really long hair, the longest in the class, she can even sit on it." Hallie tucks her own short, stringy hair behind one ear. Her hair is brown and fine, cut to a chin-length bob, with bangs that always seem too long. Sometimes Suzen offers to trim them for her, but Hallie just pushes them or blows them habitually out of her eyes. Though she is always clean and usually combed, by the end of the school day she tends to look scruffy, unkempt, like a forgotten child left to her own devices. Suzen vows, looking at her, to pay more attention. In spite of her tendencies to shut herself off from her family, she finds that lately, she really does care.

As she listens to Hallie trying to hold in her tears, sniffling softly and wiping her nose with her sleeve, suddenly she has an inspiration. "Hal, you know, once when I was about your age, this one girl, Alexis, the most popular one, had a pool party and invited every girl in the class, except me. And a counselor at school, Ms. Hernandez, found out about it. She asked how I felt and I said that I didn't care, I didn't even want to go, because I hated Alexis.

"Ms. Hernandez let me just say all the horrible things I wanted to without judging. Then she told me that instead of carrying all my bad feelings around inside me, I should drop them in a mailbox on my way home." Suzen glances at Hallie, who regards her skeptically. She goes on, "I don't mean literally, because that's impossible, of course. But I would just open up the lid and pretend to drop it all in there—my angry and hurt feelings, my loneliness. All of that. And you'd be amazed what a relief it was."

Suzen sits quietly for a moment, recalling. She had bent over and squinted to see inside the dark mail slot on the wall of their house, where there was a flier for a Chinese restaurant and some rust stuck to the sides. Then she imagined herself a giant, dropping in not her feelings but cruel Alexis Macmillan with her perfect teeth and her miniature tribe of followers. It seemed she could almost hear the girls from school dropping down down down, their screams small and shrill, until they were swallowed up in metallic darkness. *There.*

She is pleased with herself for coming up with a solution for Hallie, being able to relate to her elementary school angst, and she waits for her sister to respond. If she wants to, Suzen will stand with Hallie while she tosses Lily and AnnaLisa into the dark abyss.

"I don't think that would work. It sounds kind of childish," Hallie says finally. "No offense." She has composed herself and straightened up. Suzen lets her arm fall away from Hallie's shoulders; she tries not to take personally her rejection.

"I wish I was Aimee," Hallie blurts then.

"Why?"

"I don't know. She just seems so—peaceful. And she prays all the time, like she has this magic connection to God or something."

"Well, anyone can pray."

"Not like that."

Suzen remembers when Aimee's prayers were limited to "God is good, God is great, let us thank him for our food." She always got the rhyme wrong, and once, Evan suggested she just end with "let us thank him for our *plate*," but Aimee didn't get the joke. Now, Suzen knows, Hallie is right. Aimee is like a small nun, lost in her heavenly thoughts. She has heard her whispering in her bed at night, her voice a quiet lilt, the words unintelligible. Suzen has entertained the disconcerting idea that since the accident, Aimee has lost part of her mind, that, although she seems *better* in some ways—sweeter, more thoughtful—she has developed a crooked view of reality.

"Hallie," Suzen says. "I think you should just talk to Lily. I'm sure she still puts you first, and this new girl is just—new. A novelty. She'll get over it."

Hallie shrugs and stands up. "Thanks," she says, though Suzen knows she is not satisfied. Suzen watches her sister go into the house, past the mail slot, still carrying her small woes. Suzen imagines dropping Hallie's nemesis in herself, the girl's excessively long hair flying behind her as she screams.

• • •

At dusk, there are screams, first one, then another, in a duet of panic. Evan runs outside, after his parents, to find Hallie and Suzen pointing—at the roof, where Aimee is perched on the edge, one foot toeing the flimsy gutter, clotted with leaves. Aimee is waving at her family on the ground. Her arms flap slowly. She hooks both feet underneath the gutter and leans forward, knees locked, so that she resembles a figurehead on the prow of a ship.

"Aimee!" Malcolm yells. His voice is hoarse, but booming enough that she stops waving and looks down at him. "Stop right now. Stand still and we'll come and get you." He seems afraid to move. Esme beside him is shaking.

"Watch me fly, Dad," Aimee says merrily, her voice small and far away.

"Not right now, okay, honey?" Malcolm pleads. "Just sit down. Please."

Aimee hesitates, considering. Evan thinks she seems torn between wanting to show off and obey. She sits. He can hear his mother sigh, almost a moan, then she murmurs, "We should call 9-1-1." Still, no one moves, as if sudden motions might startle Aimee.

Evan is fast sifting through his memorized survival techniques. The roof isn't that high, a gradual slope, forty-five degrees, he calculates—even if Aimee did fall (or jump) she might just break a leg. He wonders if he should advise her to jump, allowing the shrubs below to soften the fall. She might miss them completely, though, unless she drops straight down rather than succumbing to the urge to wing herself away from the edge, as experts say is a common inclination of leapers. While Aimee sits there, a doll against the darkening sky with her family frozen below, Evan quietly goes back into the house.

A few moments later, he is shoving himself through the attic window, which is small, opening inward on a chain. Bats enter the attic each fall through the window, which hasn't been closed in years. It is amazing that even Aimee could fit through it. But Evan forces it wider, and manages to shimmy his weight through. For once, he is grateful to be on the slight side. He sidles, barefoot, along the rough shingles and down the slope toward his little sister. He sits and slings one arm firmly around her waist.

Evan whispers, "Hey, knucklehead, what do you think you're doing up here?"

"I like it up here, it's so high," she says dreamily.

"No kidding. You could have gotten yourself killed, you know."

"No, I couldn't. I wasn't going to fall."

"But you said you were going to fly," Evan reminds her, gently accusing. He can see his family below, still staring up, but a little more relaxed now. Suzen is shaking her head in disbelief.

Aimee scissors her legs on the shingles, as if making a snow angel. Then she says quietly, "I flew before, you know."

"When? Over the van, you mean? When you had the accident?"

Aimee nods. "I flew over it, way over it, and over the trees and everything. I could see everything really small below, even myself in the street. It was me but it wasn't me."

Evan looks at her, his arm still tight around her waist. "What else?" he asks then, suddenly interested. He can't help wondering if in the few moments the paramedics said she was without a pulse, Aimee's short life ran through her head like a movie—a short-short, he thinks. He suddenly is aware of the absurdity of the situation, perched on the rooftop, acting as his sister's therapist. *Tell me about it. What happened? How did you feel?*

"I can't remember everything now," she says, her tone petulant. "There was a bright light, but it didn't hurt my eyes like staring at the sun. And there were nice people everywhere, *really* nice. They held my hands and pulled me."

Evan listens patiently, He tries to piece together her vague descriptions. "What did they look like?"

Aimee sighs, as if she has been through this a hundred times, the witness queried again and again. "They had robes. White, or gold. There was a river. A gondola. A big brown rabbit." She says this a bit woodenly, as if perhaps she doesn't even believe it herself anymore. Evan pictures each one as if peering into a Viewmaster. *Click, click.* He thinks, but doesn't say, that Aimee's experience might have been a combination of a true near-death experience (consistent with other stories of bright lights and loving guides) and childish imagination, too many cartoons. Even so, her tenacious grip on her vision startles him. Who knows? Maybe she really did "cross over" for a few seconds.

"How about if we go back inside?" Evan says, remembering his mission.

"Okay," Aimee says. She seems tired, even a little bored. Evan pulls her slowly, carefully back to her feet and leads her toward the window. When she is safely through, he turns and yells down to his family on the ground, "It's okay. You can go home now. There's nothing to see here, folks." He can hear them laughing, relieved, but Evan himself is trembling uncontrollably.

M ary shakes a drooping pine tree, a baby really, to check the status of its growth, to make sure needles are not falling off. Suzen watches, waiting for instructions. Finally Mary just shrugs. "I guess it's all right," she says. "It just doesn't look right to me."

"Because it's so droopy?"

Mary laughs. "No, it's supposed to do that—it's a Weeping Eastern White Pine. It just looks lethargic to me."

"How can you tell?"

"Instinct."

Suzen nods, wondering if she will ever possess the ability to assess plant life so confidently. She thinks she can read people far more easily. Then again, she is beginning to doubt that, too. Her own family baffles her—her brother, her suddenly enigmatic mother, her distracted

father, her sisters pensive and pious. And Mary, well, there is so much
yet to discover.

"We should get going," Mary is saying. "I told Mr. Andersson we
would be there by three. Are you ready?"

Suzen nods, follows Mary to her truck. When she climbs into the
passenger seat, she winds her long hair into a bun and pokes a bobby
pin in to hold it. As they begin moving, wind blowing through the windows, she notices that Mary's pixie hair flutters atop her head like little
feathers. Soft and golden. Her skin is flawless, flushed from sun, faintly
freckled across her nose. She dangles her left hand out of the window
and drives with the other, sunlight glinting off a trio of silver bracelets.
She seems to sense Suzen's eyes on her, because she glances over and
smiles. Suzen feels herself blush, caught so blatantly staring, but Mary
says nothing. It occurs to Suzen that one of the things separating Mary
from every other adult she knows, is the way she can sit in amiable
silence, apparently lacking the need to fill up the space with chatter,
asking the usual, pointless questions (*How's school? What's new? Got
a boyfriend? Play any sports?*). When she drives, she seems to lose herself temporarily in wandering thoughts; Suzen is careful not to inter-
fere. Only when they approach the Anderssons' house—a mansion,
really, of sand-colored limestone and leaded-glass windows, at the end
of a long, curved drive, with a veritable wall of stately pines and maples
obscuring the house from the street—does Suzen speak.

"This is it?" she says. "I've never seen this house before, I had no
idea it was back here." Her eyes scan across a sweeping lawn lined with
perfectly spaced and manicured shrubs. The driveway is pea gravel, so
level it looks like someone has spread it by hand, smoothed it over with
flat palms.

"I know," says Mary. "It's like a secret, this place."

"It looks like an English country manor."

Mary laughs. "I think that was intentional."

They park near the four-stall garage and get out to stroll around toward the backyard, where Mary has said they are to meet their client. Suzen noted that Mary referred to him as "our illustrious benefactor," because he was paying so much for Mary's expertise and labor—but what Suzen caught was the fact that she'd said *our*, as if they were a team, in this together. She stands up straight and tall, trying to look professional, and older.

The backyard, if something so vast can be called such, wraps around an enormous flagstone verandah with a low wall and stone benches. The yard has subtly elegant landscaping, with curved garden paths, thickly blooming hostas, perfect, velvety grass. The trees are spaced in seemingly random but well-placed intervals, and many are old growth, hundreds of years old. Everywhere Suzen looks around her, the view is stunning. There is a large tiled fish pool, deep blue, etched with the darting orange fins of koi. Above it, a small waterfall trickles through the mouth of a marble trout, the body of which is embedded into a blue and white tiled wall, which, in turn, is draped in ivy. All of it looks pristine, yet as if it has always been there. Suzen catches her breath. What kind of people are lucky enough to live in such a place? she wonders. And yet, she feels fortunate just standing in the middle of the lush and lovely lawn, awaiting direction, ready to help transform an already paradisiacal setting.

For ten minutes they walk around the grounds, Mary guessing the proposed location of the maze to be to the right of the middle of the backyard, where the lawn is level, and only two trees would need to be removed to accommodate the plan. "This is great," she says more than once. "I can already visualize it." She waves her arms around as if conjuring the image for Suzen, who squints a little in the sunshine and tries to see it.

"Hello there!" a voice booms out, and Suzen turns to see a tall man, fortyish—or fifty, it's hard to tell—striding toward them in a suit and tie. He is tan, like an actor on location, and just graying at the temples. His face is vaguely lined, not with telltale signs of stress, but of hard work and hard thinking, and everything from his clothing to his posture to his broad-smiling demeanor seems confident and rich.

"Hello, Mr. Andersson," Mary says, walking to meet him, holding out her hand.

"Call me Ted," he says, his eyes sparkling. He turns his gaze toward Suzen and smiles. "And who's this?"

"Suzen," says Mary, before Suzen can speak. "My assistant."

"You look about my daughter's age," Mr. Andersson says. "She's fifteen."

"I'm seventeen," Suzen says quickly. Both Mr. Andersson and Mary laugh, which makes Suzen blush.

"I remember being that young," Mr. Andersson says, addressing Mary. "When you *wanted* to be older." Still smiling, he says to Suzen, "So, are you in school? Is this a part-time job, an apprenticeship?"

Suzen nods. "Yes. I get some work-study credits."

"And a measly paycheck," Mary adds, laughing. "But she works harder than any other intern I've ever had."

"Maybe you'd be a good influence on my daughter," Mr. Andersson says ruefully.

Suzen doesn't know what to say, but thankfully, Mary does. She deftly turns the subject back to the project as if she didn't hear his comment. "We've been talking about the best spot for your plans." She waves an arm. "Right about here?"

"Yes, that's exactly what I was thinking," Mr. Andersson says. Mary nods, jotting something down in a thick notebook. "Have you had any time to work on my blueprints?"

Mary flips some pages and turns the notebook around to show him. Suzen, standing nearby, leans forward to look, too. It is the first time she has seen the plan. With a sharp charcoal pencil, Mary has drawn boxy outer walls with curved concentric rings and half-rings inside, diminishing toward the center, all of the twists and dead ends plotted carefully. She has noted, in the white margins, ideas for plantings: yew, boxwood, and hornbeam, with a question mark.

"I used your drawings, of course," Mary is saying. "And incorporated some of the designs from the English mazes, but made it smaller. When it's finished, though, I think it will be just as beautiful."

Mr. Andersson smiles, gazing at the plan. "How long will that be, do you expect?"

"Well, we—my staff—can begin marking off the borders as early as next week, and then try to plant as much as possible before a freeze sets in, by Thanksgiving. After that, of course, we would have to wait until spring. The ground gets too cold and hard and nothing would thrive. The ones we manage to get in before then will simply lie dormant until spring."

"Oh," he says, sounding faintly disappointed.

"And you have to remember that the mazes you visited, the ones you showed me in books, have been there for thirty or forty years, some even hundreds. It takes a long time for hedges to fill in and look like a wall." She shrugs a little, as if to indicate that she is sorry for bearing such discouraging news.

"Surely you aren't suggesting this won't look like anything for forty years?" he says petulantly, like a child misled.

"No, no, of course not," says Mary. "But it will take a few years to grow to the height I imagine you are hoping for—perhaps ten years."

"Oh, well, I'm not going anywhere," Mr. Andersson says, more cheerfully. "Maybe my grandchildren will be able to enjoy it." He laughs, as if the idea is absurd. "I still want to do it, though, so go ahead, as soon as you can. And I will be willing to pay extra for the largest hedges you can plant, to get as far a head start as possible."

When they finish the preliminary discussion, Mr. Andersson turns to lead them back toward the driveway. Suzen lags behind a few feet, taking her time, reluctant to leave. She glances up at the huge house, its windows clear as water, reflecting a stark blue sky. In one of the upper windows, Suzen sees a figure suddenly appear. It is a girl, with dark hair short as a boy's, staring back at Suzen, who feels compelled to look away. But when she glances back, the girl is waving, unsmiling, like a princess trapped in her turret. Suzen waves back, then hurries to catch up with Mary.

A train rushes past, churning litter in its path, thundering the ground beneath Evan's feet. Beside him on the wood-slatted bench outside the train station, where they are sitting, killing time, Soci glances up to watch the cars rattling by, one after the other, her head turning with each one as if she is silently counting. Then she turns back to her work, digging open an orange with her thumbnail. She peels loose one segment, plucks out a seed, and hands it to Evan. He takes it, smiling, and eats it in one bite. He watches her lick the juice from her fingers.

Soci leans on Evan's shoulder and says dreamily, "I can hear the trains in the middle of the night when I have the windows open. I always wish I were on one." She turns to look at Evan. "Chicago is only two and a half hours away by train, you know."

"Yeah," Evan says. "I haven't been there in awhile." He doesn't know what else to say. The orange lingers on his tongue, tangy, causing his glands to water painfully.

"It's only fifty bucks, round trip," Soci says, smiling. "How about it?"

"Now?"

She laughs. "You're not enough of a yob, are you."

"A what?"

"A *yob*. It's British for a delinquent—you know, 'boy' spelled backwards?" When she sees his expression, she softens. "I was kidding. Anyway, I didn't mean right now. Amtrak only goes once a day, around nine." She pauses. "How about next Friday?"

Evan's mind races. Friday afternoon is a biology midterm test, in a class he is hardly acing, barely passing. But what if he says no? While he is considering, Soci leans over on the bench and kisses him, nudging her tongue between his lips. Evan tastes the fruit on her mouth, mixed with cherry lip gloss. He feels himself going, going, gone.

When Soci finally pulls away, her cheeks are flushed, her lips swollen. She looks pleased. "Let's meet here Friday, eight thirty a.m.," she says simply.

"Okay," he says without thinking, his mind a whirl of colorful confusion. In three days he may be going to Chicago on a train, with a girl, his girl. Sure, he'll also fail all of his classes and get grounded for the rest of his life—but he's in love. He wipes his lips with the back of his hand. "Do your parents mind?" he asks nonchalantly. "I mean, don't you have to get permission?"

Soci shrugs. "Yes, and no. Why bother asking when you already know the answer? What they don't know can't hurt 'em, I say."

Evan says nothing for a moment. Then, "What does your father do? For a living, I mean."

"Works at Conrads'," Soci says, without looking at him.

"Oh," says Evan. "Doing what?"

Soci laughs. "Making headlights, what else?" Then she pauses, and sighs. "Why does everyone care so much what a person does for a living? How much they make and all that?" She scrapes more flesh from the orange and tosses the pieces like scabs onto the ground.

Evan flushes, realizing his mistake. "I didn't mean—"

"Oh, I know," she says, shoving him gently with her shoulder. "I know you didn't mean anything by it, just conversation, right? So, what does *your* dad do?"

Evan hesitates, wondering how to phrase it. He doesn't want to imply that because his father works in academia and has three degrees to his name, he feels superior to her, daughter of a factory worker. He doesn't feel that, anyway, but he sees how sensitive she is about it. "He's a boring teacher," he says finally.

"What about your mother?" she asks, her eyes suddenly eager.

"The usual. A mom," he says, then adds, "She used to be an artist, but put it off because of us."

"Us?"

"My sisters and me. I have three."

"Oh. Funny, you never told me that."

"You never asked. Do you have any annoying siblings?"

"Nope, just me. I just have me to annoy myself."

"There's nothing annoying about you," Evan says softly, taking her hand in his in a gesture that feels at once right and corny. "What about your mom? What's she like?"

"Hah," Soci says harshly. "Hard to say. In fact, let's not. I don't want to talk about our boring parents, okay? If we go to Chicago, we can forget all about them and everyone else for a day. Pretend we're running away together."

Evan thinks of his father's European journal, descriptions of him standing in train stations and choosing where to go, feeling like a runaway. *Exhilarating and terrifying.* Exactly. He laces his fingers through Soci's tightly, as if making a pact. Silently, he promises himself he will just go forward, make the leap, like Aimee standing on their roof, fully confident not only that she wouldn't fall, but that she could fly.

When Eduardo landed in America, he is telling Suzen, "everything change, just like that." He snaps his fingers and smiles. "It is better than I expect."

"That's good," Suzen says, smiling back, but unsure how to respond to the sudden attention being lavished on her. Until today,

Eduardo, senior exchange student and widely idolized dreamboat, has been occupied by a growing posse of teenage girls. They follow him everywhere, and Eduardo often can be seen gesticulating wildly, laughing and entertaining his audience, who laugh and nudge each other, jockeying for closer proximity to the handsome foreigner. Suzen, too, has admired Eduardo, dreamed about him from afar, too proud to latch on so obviously like the others. Lately, however, she has forgotten all about him, and now here he is, solo, unencumbered, choosing to sit beside Suzen in the back of the school auditorium. Suzen has arrived early for a science film to be shown, of a real open-heart surgery. Eduardo, who isn't even in the same class, has simply appeared.

He keeps staring and grinning. Or is he leering? Suzen looks down at her sweater to make sure none of the buttons are undone, checks the zipper of her jeans. Everything seems okay; she looks back at Eduardo with a question in her eyes. *What? What is it? Why are you staring at me like that?*

As if reading her mind, Eduardo answers in his honey-thick accent, "You look 'specially beautiful today, Susannah."

"It's Suzen, actually, but thank you," she says. A month ago she would have savored his words, drinking in the compliment over and over. But now she is confused, flattered by his attention, yet strangely unmoved. Also, she wonders where all the other girls have gone; did they finally grow bored, the novelty of Eduardo worn off after the first six weeks of school? And why has he chosen her, now?

"You have very nice tooths," he says suddenly, pointing to his own, as if unsure he has used the correct word. He pauses, thinking. "*Teeth,* I mean." He laughs, embarrassed. Suzen laughs, too, and blushes. It is (almost) the same compliment Mary gave her. She cannot help but grow conscious of her mouth, feels her teeth sparkle and gleam as she smiles at Eduardo. A movie star acknowledging a fan.

"What are you doing here?" she finally asks.

"Look for you," he says, shrugging, smiling. "And now I find you."

"What about all the other girls you hang around with all the time?"

Eduardo laughs, a deep-throated laugh like a grown man. That, Suzen realizes, is a large part of his appeal, aside from his foreignness; he looks so much older than the rest of her peers. At her age, girls tend to look upward, drawn to older men, the allure of the adult world just ahead. Suzen thinks about how she prefers Mary's company now to that of her old friends, Lisa and Rebecca. And the less time she spends with them, the more they join together, as if closing the gap she left behind. When she sees them in class they seem to have turned into Siamese twins, heads pressed together, long hair—light amber and chestnut brown—entwined as they whisper whisper whisper. Sometimes she feels a pang of dismay, left out, bereft, a self-anointed loner, but most of the time she doesn't even care, just counts down the minutes until she can resume her other life in the sunlit nursery.

Eduardo touches Suzen's arm and whispers, "I ditch them."

Suzen laughs. "Really?"

"Yes, I cannot go anyplace by myself. They always so near to me. And the other guys do not like. They think I show off, they think I—steal?—their women. But I not trying to do anything like that. It just happen to me." He sounds so sincere and guileless, Suzen smiles and shakes her head. Eduardo stretches up in his seat to dig something out of the pocket of his blue jeans. Though the light in the auditorium is dim, Suzen can see that the thing he is holding in his palm is a perfectly round blue stone, with a single white stripe running all the way around it, as if drawn there.

"Here, take it," Eduardo says. "For good luck."

"Where did you find this?" Suzen asks, picking up the stone and inspecting it more closely. The stripe, she sees now, is not simply white, but nearly transparent, like a strip of ice. It is exquisite.

"On beach, one time. I keep it always."

"Then why are you giving it to me?" Suzen tries to hand it back, but Eduardo shakes his head.

"Because you are very beautiful. Especial. Like this," he says, folding her fingers closed over the stone.

Suzen stares in wonderment, speechless over such bald sentiment. *You don't even know me*, she wants to say. His words seem somehow farcical, as if Eduardo has watched too many soap operas. At the same time, she senses he is sincere, that he is not just uttering a line, but that he has been plotting and waiting for the right moment to offer his lucky stone along with his strangely intense admiration. Suzen fears that he will—he must—expect something in return, but she has nothing to give.

She can feel his presence close upon her, though he has not moved in his seat. It is the thick hum of sexual attraction, the eagerness of a man for a woman; Suzen feels it in her gut, and it terrifies her. She holds the blue stone in her hand, turning it over and over with her fingers, not daring to look at Eduardo.

Just then, students begin arriving from the back of the auditorium, brushing down the aisle past Suzen, who is in an end seat. She seizes the opportunity, and says, "You have to go."

"Why, Susannah?" he whispers.

"This isn't your class," she says, looking away from him.

"Oh. Yes, I know." He smiles—she can hear it in his voice—and says, "I see you later, right?"

Suzen nods, finally meeting his gaze. He is looking at her and smiling so winningly, she melts a little, smiles back. When he is gone, Suzen slides down in her seat and tries to concentrate. Even when the lights go down and the movie begins, however, she cannot focus. She watches the bloody and beating heart, exposed in an open chest cavity, as around her classmates groan and murmur, but after awhile, she does not even know what she is watching. All she can think about is the way Eduardo looked at her, his musky aftershave lingering like a cloud, and how it was nothing like she expected. In all of her dreams of the beautiful Peruvian boy, she couldn't wait for him to touch her; in real life, she felt herself curling up, pulling back. *Don't,* she'd thought, and it wasn't from fear of getting caught.

When Evan thinks of Soci Andersson, he feels like a fugitive. More and more, that is how their relationship appears to be evolving. He finds himself checking over his shoulder for authorities—parents, teachers, police, even—anyone who might stop them. Skipping last hour has become routine, hiding in restrooms, sneaking out between class changes, watching for patrol cars. Now Soci wants to run away, to Chicago, just for the day, as if that lessens the nature of the crime. Evan knows that, if he asked, his parents would let him take a train to the city accompanied by a friend—and the friend's parent. So, of course, he cannot ask.

That was part of the agreement, anyway, that they would tell no one. All he had to do was round up enough spending money for food and incidentals. And forge a parent's signature on a note to allow him to miss an entire day of school.

"Just say it's for a funeral," Soci suggested.

"Yeah, mine," Evan said morosely.

"C'mon, it's no big deal. Life is to be lived," she said. She wore her shortest dress.

Riding home from soccer practice on his bike, Evan takes a detour. It is a long one, seven miles out of the way, but he is in good shape, his heart and lungs and legs pummeled daily by the coach, so it is effortless, and he allows himself to ride and not think. It reminds him of being a kid, nine or ten, when his mother finally began to let him ride alone, home from friends' or on short errands. He loved the sense that he was out there on his own, no one watching, no one warning. At ten he was well old enough to cross the roads, wait for lights, avoid the tracks, and he had a feeling that this was what it would be like to be a man, going where he wanted to go, thinking his private thoughts. Now he rides and thinks that it has been a long time since he simply went where he wanted to go, solo. He is glad to be without Soci for a change, though the relief is interrupted by periodic longing.

He rounds the bend and Lake Michigan emerges in full view, gray blue and seemingly endless. It strikes Evan that no matter how many times he comes here, or at what time of the year, he is impressed by the sight. The horizon is sharp as if pencil-drawn, and tiny waves whip the shoreline. The sky is darkening, with bruised clouds, and Evan knows that the sand is already hard packed and cold, the water icy. By January there may even be small mountains of icebergs floating out toward Chicago or Milwaukee. Evan thinks of Chicago lying across the lake, its narrow streets and crowded cafes, the Magnificent Mile of store upon store, the gum-colored Wrigley building, the emerald river running through the middle of the city. He can picture it all perfectly—he's been there dozens of times—yet somehow cannot see himself wandering around it with Soci leading the way. It sounds exhausting. It seems that she wants him to prove himself to her, to show that he is as daring and cavalier as she, willing to take chances and flee adult authority. Her kisses are beginning to seem like a form of bribery. She knows he wants more and she will give it to him a little at a time, like Gretel dropping her bread crumbs through the woods, until he is thoroughly lost.

Evan rides slowly home, cool and windblown and pensive. The sky is nearly dark now, and the windows of his house are squares of light. He waits in the driveway for a few moments, leaning on his bicycle, just watching from outside the home he knows so intimately. There is his mother in the kitchen, standing at the window beside the sink, her unseen hands involved in some task, cleaning potatoes, perhaps. It seems to Evan that Esme is the perfect mother, always present, always where he expects her to be; she is like a page in a book you always turn to, knowing what will happen, comforted that the plot never changes. When he walks in, she will turn and smile, glad to see him—while also reprimanding him for tardiness. He knows she watches over them all, counting in her head, content only when all are accounted for. Evan glances at his watch. He is forty minutes late because of his detour. He also knows, however, that when he explains, she will accept it, forgive, move on. Esme does not bear grudges; she sees the best in everyone. As he watches her from the driveway, she turns her head, says something to someone in the room he cannot see. It is like watching an art film, the camera angled so that the viewer is left wondering what is happening offscreen.

In an upstairs window, he sees Suzen strolling back and forth, head down, hands on hips, as though she is arguing with someone, though clearly she is not. She is always alone. Evan has begun to wonder if his sister even has any friends. Rebecca and Lisa, who used to come around regularly, are nowhere to be found. Evan used to enjoy their visits, the raucous laughter from the kitchen or den, their hushed voices if he ventured in. Rebecca, with her long copper hair, was his favorite. He liked to watch her swish it over her back, or pull it over one shoulder and grasp it in one hand, stroking it like a cat. Evan had always been drawn to girls with long hair, until he met Soci.

Suzen's long golden hair is habitually tied up now, like a spinster in an old Cary Grant film, the secretary always just to the side, at a metal desk. He worries sometimes that she is going through an emotional turmoil and no one is bothering to check on her. Esme is always there, true, but occupied, and she and Suzen never see eye to eye; and Malcolm, well, when it comes to the girls, he is somewhat useless. He seems even more baffled than Evan in their midst, a part yet not a part of the scene. Like the father in *Little Women* (Evan has seen the movie version, starring Katharine Hepburn) wandering in from the war, gathered happily into the family bosom but clearly not one of them. Evan wonders if he should try to talk to Suzen himself; perhaps they could help each other. While she could break the code of women, he could tell her not to worry, that guys are more transparent than you'd think, that they are more approachable and less reprehensible than they let on. That deep down, they all want to do the right thing. Whatever that is.

As Evan starts to park his bike in the garage, he sees another light click on, in his father's study. Malcolm walks across the small room, obscured for a moment by crooked blinds no one ever adjusts. He reaches across his desk toward a shelf, glancing behind him quickly as if afraid he will be caught. Evan is intrigued. The lamp on his desk casts a circle of soft light on his father's hands, on whatever it is he holds. A book, it seems, nothing shocking (What did he expect? A gun? Drugs? A thick wad of cash?). It is a notebook, Evan can tell from its standard size—his father's diary. Evan suddenly wants to hold it himself, turn the pages, read more about Malcolm as a young man on his quest for himself, for romance, for the wide world out there. He wonders what he dreams about now, a grown man with a wife and four children—does he regret his choices, his deeply entrenched routines? Evan watches, standing still in the dark yard, as his father turns the pages slowly and seems to lose himself in the adventures of his youth, his distant past.

Evan resolves to grow old with no regrets. He will neither miss out because of his own fears, nor follow blindly in order to impress. If he goes to Chicago, it will be on his own terms. He jerks his bike and shoves it into the cluttered garage. Walks to the back door and enters the movie.

"Oh, good, you're home," Esme says, right on cue.

If Suzen could, she would slip between the pages of a book, Alice in Wonderland falling through the chute, landing on another plane. The sky still would be dark outside her window, but the window would be leaded glass, the yard beyond an endless heath. She would listen for the sound of approaching hooves, a rider she cannot see, half hidden by a heavy cloak. In her room, she dims the light, ignites a candle on her sill, opens *Tess of the d'Urbervilles,* and reads:

> ... *the sun blazes down upon fields so large as to give an unenclosed character to the landscape, the lanes are white, the hedges low and plashed, the atmosphere colourless. Here, in the valley, the world seems to be constructed upon a smaller and more delicate scale; the fields are mere paddocks, so reduced that from this height their hedgerows appear a network of dark green threads overspreading the paler green of the grass. The atmosphere beneath is langorous, and is so tinged with azure that what artists call the middle distance partakes also of that hue, while the horizon beyond is of the deepest ultramarine.*

When Suzen absorbs the scenery, she is transported, nearly physically. She wonders at times if she possesses a gift for illusion—if, like Aimee, she can propel herself into another realm, a parallel universe, a sliver in the wall of time and place. She so vividly smells the damp earth, the soft fragrance of lavender and thyme, the thickly pungent manure spread on fields, and sees that deep azure sky, that it seems she really is *there,* not here, at least for a few moments. And it seems entirely plausible to her that if such an ability is inherent, a kind of sixth or seventh sense, then maybe Aimee has inherited it, too. Perhaps when she hit her head on the solid pavement, her brain was jarred, and a section opened in which she found she could slide into the other, better world, her own imaginary version of reality. What she describes as "heaven" was simply her own personal paradise, just as nineteenth-century England is Suzen's. She knows, of course, that anyone else would call it simply daydreaming, but it seems more real than that to her.

Lately, for instance, she's had strange recurring dreams about the Brontës in which they visit her. They always come together, Charlotte just ahead of Emily, and Anne lurking in the doorway, remote and sullen. Sometimes she wanders away, leaving the other two alone with

Suzen. They don't speak, but perch on either side of her bed, Charlotte sitting a bit more fully on the mattress as though she feels somehow more entitled. Emily seems not to mind being relegated to the few inches on the edge of the bed, near Suzen's right thigh, and she fans her wide taffeta skirts around her. They are deep purple, the color of eggplant, and the fabric whispers when she adjusts herself on the bed. Then both women simply sit there and look at Suzen, or a little off to the sides of her, their faces milky white, their features slightly fuzzy as if Suzen were viewing them through frosted glass. Suzen waits, holding her breath, holding her limbs tense beneath the blankets. But she always wakes up before anything happens. But what would happen? The long-dead Brontës just sit there in their bustles, tightly collared bodices, their hair arranged in fussy braids or buns atop their regally held heads; there is nothing remotely threatening about them. Even so, Suzen always awakes a little scared, searching her room in the dark for evidence that anyone was there.

It seems she is always looking for something, half-holding her breath. Even with Mary, whom she regards now as a friend, she sometimes feels nervous, afraid of saying the wrong thing. There are so many things she would like to ask her—for instance, if the rumors are true—yet worries about crossing an invisible line. She is aware that on the other side is the adult world, and that, though she has one foot squarely there, she is not ready to step all the way in, much as she wants to.

She wishes there were a manual of instructions, a guideline for girls like her, teetering on the edge of eighteen. Hardy and the Brontës are no help, of course, and even modern literature seems to offer no advice, not for her, not for this—Mary, the maze, her dreams, or Eduardo in the auditorium. *This is my life,* she sometimes thinks, happy that no one else is living it exactly as she is, feels exactly the way she does, but it would be nice to find some clues, somewhere, to help her find her way.

• • •

I t is easy to find the secret hiding place, as it is in full view, on a bottom shelf. Evan knows his father has a faculty dinner tonight, which Esme is also attending, swishing out of the door in her best clothes and lipstick, as if she were heading to the opera and not some dour professor's house, where undoubtedly the fare will be trays of limp hors d'oeuvres, pink wine in a box. The same parties have been held at their own house and Evan has observed, bemused at the predictability, the lack of imagination, considering the caliber of the crowd. He expects better of people who supposedly read and travel and spend their waking hours exploring the depth and breadth of life with rooms full of students. But when it comes to socializing, they are sadly inept. Or so it seems to Evan. Perhaps there is more going on than he can see.

Which is why he has been drawn to his father's study and his private diary. Because of the little he has already read, and the clandestine way his father pulled it out the night Evan watched through the window, he is sure there is a story there, something no one else knows about, perhaps not even Esme.

Of course, he feels some shame in sneaking around, prying into pages not meant for his eyes (and perhaps not even Esme's), but he cannot help it. He has become inured lately, to the stress of misconduct. *What's next?* he wonders. *Shoplifting?* Even so, he tells himself that reading something his father wrote as a young man is not much different from reading a novel; surely he embellished, fictionalized anyway. What harm could there be in just looking?

He opens the notebook to the first pages, skims through the early days of backpacking and hostels, the overawed ramblings of a boy in the world for the first time. Though he has hardly traveled himself yet, Evan feels strangely superior to this young version of his father. In the same situation, Evan never would be so ardent, or so fatuous. Some of the passages cause him to cringe.

"When Jim and I reached Paris, finally, we were besotted with happiness. It was just as I hoped it would be. We spent whole afternoons at the cafés, watching people, sipping au laits, drinking it all in. It was like dying and going to literary heaven—Hemingway was here, and Balzac, of course, and Henry Miller . . . I knew then I wanted to be a writer of great importance, changing the face of the world through words, mere words."

Two pages later, Evan reads about how Malcolm and his friend, Jim, "lined up with the rest of the tourists to enter the sacred Louvre, since it is something you're supposed to do—who can go to Paris and not tour the greatest museum in the world? But once inside, I admit I was enthralled. The *Mona Lisa* is amazing, you can't help but think she is nearly alive, ready to break into a real grin any minute. And then room after room of extraordinary paintings, Greek sculpture thousands of years old. Jim was a little less impressed. We hadn't eaten breakfast, and when his blood sugar gets low, bad moods roll in. I should have known better than to insist we go so early. Or maybe I should have known better than to go with someone like Jim, who appreciates food far more than art, and always will."

Evan laughs at this, both the sudden change in tone and the fact that at eighteen, Malcolm likely was years ahead of most of his peers. He may have been full of grandiosity, but he was also intelligent, and surprisingly gifted at putting his experiences into words. Evan wonders if he still writes anything other than academic papers and occasional commencement speeches.

"What're you doing?"

Evan jumps, startled from his reverie on the floor of the study, by Aimee, who has appeared out of thin air and is standing directly behind him.

"Jeez, you scared me," he says, abruptly shutting the notebook, though it is unlikely Aimee would suspect anything. It is the gut reaction of a guilty person, he knows, and in a moment, collects himself enough to lie, "I was just doing my homework, Aimee, what does it look like I'm doing?"

She shrugs, flops down on the rug beside him. "You never do homework in here. I thought you were doing something else."

"Well, I'm not. Why don't you go do something else?" Evan says, impatient. "Where's Suzen?"

"She's upstairs, and she said I should go find something to do, but I'm bored, and Hallie won't play with me."

"Why not?"

"She's drawing."

"So, go draw with her," Evan says, trying to sound encouraging, rather than annoyed, knowing that the former is more likely to get the desired results.

"She says I can't, it's a project. I don't see what's so important, it's just paint."

Even registers this, but barely. He wants Aimee to leave him alone, but he is aware, like everyone else in the family, that leaving Aimee to her own devices can be dangerous. He's irritated that Suzen is ignoring her duties, though, on the other hand, he can't blame her. Being the eldest must get tiresome, always expected to take care of the younger siblings when their parents are out, the unpaid, unappreciated live-in help. He decides that if he can find something to occupy his little sister, it's the least he can do. And then he can resume his reading in peace.

"Here," he says, inspired. "Why don't you hook these together." He hands her a box of paper clips from Malcolm's desk.

"Why?"

"Dad likes them that way."

As Aimee busies herself with her task, cross-legged beside him, Evan opens the notebook, forgetting where he left off. When he scans a new page, he is astounded. He has happened upon a gold mine—his father's blossoming sex life, written like a romance novel.

I will never forget the train ride through undulating fields, broom-swept villages built around stone fountains, or the stately cypress trees, the blue depth of Mediterranean sky, the crusty warmth of just-baked pan, and a brown-eyed girl in a pale blue sweater. The buttons were small as peas and I tried to twist them loose carefully, my mind racing for the right words in Italian.

How can I begin to describe this amazing encounter? Jim left me for two hours, in search of a bakery because he had to have bread or die, and I relished the time alone, wandering the shoreline of the village. After Rome, a tiny town with five restaurants and two hotels is a welcome change. And everything is so cheap, we could stay here for weeks and not run out of cash. And now, I could stay here a lifetime, and not run out of desire . . . she was walking there, just ahead of me, picking up stones like a scientist. I watched her and she turned around, her smile shy but welcoming. She came over and asked if I was an American. We started talking and her English was impressive, even though she had to stop and think of words now and then. Her name was Mara Torelli.

Before I knew it, we had a date. I wondered what to tell Jim, but decided I would make up an excuse—tell him I had a headache, so he should go and find dinner without me. I didn't want him to know—Mara was like a gift from the gods, and I didn't want to share anything, not even her name. She would be my secret.

To make a long story short (though why would I want to? I want to tell it all, relive it over and over again), we met at her house. Her family was out, she still lives at home, though she is eighteen and works full-time at a florist's shop. It was as if we had known each other our whole lives. And when she asked me to come inside—into her room, into her bed—what could I say? The word "no" no longer existed. Everything was yes, yes, yes. Or si, si, si . . . I wondered if I dreamed it. But I could not have made up those breasts, her belly flat but soft, her legs opening like a flower, or what it was like to be inside her.

Evan pauses, suddenly aware that he is perspiring a little, shocked and not a little aroused, picturing himself and Soci. Just as suddenly, though, he is also mortified, to read in his father's own handwriting so graphic and lurid a description of his experience with a woman, a woman not his wife, Evan's mother, though that, of course, would have been far worse. In fact, the more he thinks about it—Mara, his dad—he feels queasy and disgusted.

"Evan, look at this," Aimee is saying from a corner of the room.

"What," he says flatly, not looking.

"It makes sparks," she says delightedly. Evan turns his head and notices a chain of paper clips running from the top of the desk—cleverly affixed to a stapler—and leading down to the corner, out of his line of vision. The clips turn and glint in the lamplight and Evan laughs, amused that Aimee took the work so seriously. And then she yelps.

Evan jumps to his feet when he sees Aimee hunched on the floor, silver chain in hand, pressed against the outlet. Evan grabs her, pulls her away, panicked.

"What are you *doing*, for God's sake?"

"Making sparks," Aimee repeats. "But the last time I did it, it was really big. It made me feel sort of jumpy."

"Aimee, you can't do that. *Ever!* Do you understand? Don't you know you aren't supposed to put things into outlets? That's electricity, Aim, it can kill you." Only as he says it out loud does Evan realize what has happened, or nearly. And five feet away from him, while he wasn't looking. "Are you sure you're okay?" he croaks, still holding her.

"Yeah, I'm fine," she says, sighing.

"You almost gave me a coronary."

"Sorry."

Evan lets her go only long enough to shove the notebook back in its place on the bottom shelf, under a book about sonnets. He shoves away any thought of Mara Torelli, or Soci Andersson, his heart pounding.

• • •

"There has to be a goal," Mary says, "something in the heart of the maze that the path finally leads to." She points to her drawing, now more precise and polished. In the center she has sketched a fountain, three-tiered, with tiny ripples of water and lines to indicate it flowing down from one level to the next, drawn slightly crudely, like ropes.

"I've been reading all about them," Mary says. "There are two main kinds of mazes—unicursal, with one path that leads to the center; or multicursal, which has dead ends and twists and turns so you have to backtrack and get lost before you figure it out. Most people like that kind best, probably because it's more of a challenge."

Suzen nods, walking along behind Mary as they check the posts and lines erected by some of her staff over the past several mornings, before Suzen arrived. Mary had given specific measurements and entrusted them to Sal, her assistant with a master's degree in horticulture and ecology, and like Mary, an artist's eye for design. Suzen has only met Sal twice, as he is usually out on job sites. Now, Sal and several other men from the nursery are walking the outer lines of the maze-to-be and jabbing flat-edged shovels to begin the trough into which yew shrubs will be planted.

"They liked them for hiding, too," Suzen notes, as she has done her own kind of research.

"Who?" Mary asks, bending to adjust a listing stake.

"Couples, you know, in the old days, when they couldn't go anywhere without escorts or chaperones. They used the mazes as an excuse to get away from everyone so they could be alone."

Mary laughs. "How romantic," she says. "Sometimes I think it would be nice if there were still a bit more discretion in societal etiquette." She pauses. "On the other hand—"

"What?"

"Never mind. I just meant—" Mary actually blushes, Suzen notices with surprise. "If things hadn't changed, some of us would really be out of luck. You know?"

Suzen nods, but Mary is already walking ahead, as if not expecting an answer. Clearly, she doesn't want to pursue the subject, whatever it was she was beginning to reveal. Suzen busies herself with straightening the string that drapes from post to post, not knowing what else to do. The yews have not arrived yet and planting won't begin for another week or two; she is merely along to observe. For the first time, she is somewhat bored. Mary is talking to her crew now, and Suzen holds back, moving away from the maze, wishing she had a task.

"Hey, there," a voice calls out and Suzen turns to see the girl from the window, loping toward her. She is smaller than Suzen expected, but with sharp, knowing eyes, like someone who has seen much more than most her age. She looks young, and yet somehow old. Her hair is pixie-short, shorter than Mary's, which enhances her delicate features, her beautiful smile. She is smiling broadly at Suzen now, shielding her eyes from the sun with one hand.

"Hi," Suzen says.

"I'm Soci," the girl says, holding out her hand like an adult. Suzen takes it and shakes it, but lets go quickly.

"Suzen. Nice to meet you," she says, tucking her hands into her pockets, suddenly shy without knowing why. "I'm working with Mary," she says, nodding her head in the general direction of the maze.

"I know. I've seen you here before. So, are you full-time, or what?"

"No. I'm still in school," Suzen says, smiling, flattered to be mistaken for older.

"Oh, yeah? Where?"

"Lincoln High. I'm a senior."

"Lucky. I go there, too," Soci says, "but I'm a lowly sophomore. I just moved here this fall."

"Really? From where?"

"New York. Gosh, I miss it."

"I'm sure. A lot more exciting than here, huh."

Soci shrugs. "Yeah. But it's nice to have a little more space, I guess. And the lake is great." She laughs. "I guess that's why they call them the Great Lakes." She sits down on the sloped berm. "This is some project my dad has going," she says, and Suzen cannot tell from her tone if she is approving or derisive.

On impulse, she sits down beside her, suddenly curious about the girl from the mansion. Does she have any siblings? Is her life as grand as it appears? She dresses like anyone else, Suzen notices, in torn jeans and black boots. Only her modish hair sets her apart from most of their peers with their long locks. Suzen is embarrassed by her own, tied into a nondescript ponytail. It feels childish to her for the first time, and passé, as if she has unwittingly followed the example of all the other girls in her middle-class, midwestern town. She is tempted to lop it off with one clip of garden shears. Out of the corner of her eye, she studies Soci.

"So, what does your mother think?" Suzen asks.

"About what?" Soci says sharply, looking intently at Suzen.

"The maze," Suzen says, a little taken aback by the reaction.

"Oh." Soci looks down, plucks a handful of grass a little violently, like pulling hair by the roots. "She has no idea about the maze—or anything else." She hesitates, as if wondering how much to tell. "She hasn't been in the picture for a long time," she says simply, dropping the grass from her fist.

"Oh, sorry," Suzen says, chagrined for bringing up an obviously taboo topic.

"No, don't be. I just never talk about it. I mean, I don't have that many friends here yet, and you know—you never know who to trust."

Suzen looks at her. "I won't tell anyone, I promise. I really hate gossip."

"Me, too." Soci smiles, apparently relieved. "Anyway, the thing is, in a nutshell, my mother ran off to 'find herself' when I was nine, and then she met some guy and—that was that."

"Gosh," says Suzen quietly. "That's terrible. I have a sister who's nine. It's so young." She thinks fleetingly of her own mother, wondering.

"Yeah. Well, anyway, it's just me and my dad, though he has a date now and then for official things—fund-raisers, holiday parties, whatever. He should have found someone else by now, but I guess it's kind of a relief he hasn't. You know, the wicked stepmother and all that."

Suzen nods, silent. She glances up and sees Mary waving at her, indicating that she wants to show her something. Suzen stands. "I guess I better get to work. Nice meeting you," she says again, this time meaning it.

"You, too. Maybe we can talk again," Soci says, a hint of eagerness in her voice. Suzen can tell she is used to guarding herself, possibly afraid to let people get too close. As she watches Soci walk back toward her enormous house, for the first time she pities rather than envies her. And she silently vows to be her friend, even if she is a "lowly sophomore," same as her brother.

In history class, Max slides into the seat beside Evan and says, "I need your notes."

"What for?"

"Friday's test, moron. You said we could study together. I don't know a damn thing about the Civil War."

"Don't you ever watch PBS? They did a whole, like, ten-week series," Evan says. "If you only watched more TV, you would be so much better off."

Max slugs him. "Come on. Just let me copy your notes—you're so organized. I'll give 'em back tomorrow and we can study. I'll bring pizza."

Evan slouches into his seat. "I don't know."

"What do you mean? You aren't going to let me use them?"

Evan turns to him and whispers urgently, "I mean, I don't know if I'm going to be here Friday."

Evan doesn't know how much he can tell Max, though he is his best friend. If he lets him in on the secret of Soci, he fears it may all evaporate, like a dream. On the other hand, he isn't sure he wants to go to Chicago with her Friday—or ever—and it might be good to bounce it off an objective party. As objective as Max can be.

Max's thick eyebrows have lifted in anticipation, but before Evan can begin to explain, the teacher, Mr. Selner, has entered the room, so he straightens up, alert. Mr. Selner has a reputation for no-nonsense order. No talking. No whispering. No sailing paper notes between desks. No sleeping. No slouching. All eyes facing the front of the room. Like the military—or kindergarten. Evan opens his notebook but the words blur on the page.

When he met Soci earlier, between classes, she cornered him at his locker. While he feigned nonchalance, reminding himself not to be pressured by her but to do things on his own terms, his heart was pounding. She was standing so close, he could smell shampoo residue and nicotine. She was wearing the short red dress she'd worn to the Esquire.

Soci smiled. "So, are you ready for our outing?"

"Yeah," he said, shrugging, unable to argue. Unintentionally, though, he leaned farther away from her into the cool metal of his locker door. The cigarette odor was a little too strong so early in the morning and he wondered if offering her gum would be too obvious. She grinned at him, her paper-white teeth gleaming. Her lips were so shiny with gloss, he could nearly see his own reflection.

"Okay, then," she said, touching his chest lightly. "Let's meet at the train station at eight. We can pay for tickets once we're on board." She looked at him slyly. "Or not."

"Or not?"

"Yeah, there are ways, you know. Little rest rooms, big enough for two . . ." She turned and drifted away from him then, and Evan stood there as if pasted, unable to pull himself free.

Staring now at his history book, chapter five, he sees himself crammed for two hours into an Amtrak water closet, pressed against Soci's smoky breasts. In his vision he cannot smell her, though, but can almost feel her breasts under his hands, underneath her dress, *her legs opening like a flower.* He is kissing her and he is no longer Evan the sophomore with stocky legs and hairless chest, but a grown-man version of himself, muscular, stubble on his chin brushing against Soci's bare neck, her shoulders slipping free of fabric—

"Mr. VanderZee, are you with us?" Mr. Selner is calling in a half-mocking tone, "Or agin' us?" Evan starts. The class is staring at him. "Gettysburg," Mr. Selner prompts. "Did you read the assignment?"

Evan clears his throat and words come out of his mouth as though a tape were inserted. "Um. Yeah, I read it. The British invaded America because—"

Max is motioning to him. He whispers, "Wrong war, man." His expression indicates that even he knew that much. Everyone is laughing, though not the teacher.

"Right," says Evan, with a self-deprecating smile. "The war between the *states.*" Mr. Selner is boring a stern gaze into Evan's forehead. He feels branded, a giant letter *A* for *ass* for all to see.

He slides farther into his chair. There is no way he can go; he has to study and take the test, there is too much at stake. Even though a girl is practically offering herself to him on a platter, he can't go through with it. He imagines standing on the platform, Soci watching him from the train window, her pale face pulled into a scowl. Instead of getting off, she sits down, and the train leaves without him.

• • •

Suzen's mother is waiting for her in the front seat of her car. It is the first time Esme has come to Strohman's and it feels like a kind of invasion. So far, Suzen has managed to keep her work life separate from her home life, as if the former represents the adult side of her, and home, the child. She does not want the two to cross paths. She scowls as she strides to the car and gets in.

"I told you I would walk home. I always do," she says, petulant as a ten-year-old. She can't help it; her mother seems to bring out the worst in her. She wraps her corduroy coat around herself and looks ahead through the windshield.

"I know, but I figured maybe you could run an errand with me and we could talk," Esme says, her tone light, though clearly she is just as tense as her daughter is; her gloved hands grip the steering wheel so tightly Suzen can see the knobs of each knuckle through the leather.

"Where are we going," Suzen says flatly, barely a question.

"I thought we could get you a new coat," Esme says cheerfully, placating. "That one isn't going to make it through another winter, and anyway, it isn't really warm enough. And since you've always hated the down one you said makes you look like a marshmallow, I thought we could find something in wool, if you want. Maybe something a little more sophisticated. Something you could take to college next year."

Suzen thinks all of this over, the notion of buying something "sophisticated," her mother's unexpected attention—and college. *I'm not going*, she thinks, but isn't prepared to say.

"How about Jacobs'?" Esme is saying brightly, pulling out of the parking lot. "They always have nice coats, and it's early enough in the season, they probably have lots to choose from."

"What about Hal and Aimee?" Suzen asks.

"They're both at friends' houses. I pawned them off so we could have some time together," Esme says. She looks pointedly over at

Suzen and smiles. "I feel like I never see you. And at home there's so much going on all the time, we don't get to talk."

Suzen shrugs, neither agreeing nor disputing this fact. She cannot remember the last time she and her mother really talked. She thought she didn't care; she had grown used to the way things were. Now, faced with an opportunity, she doesn't know what to say or how to behave. The circumstances seem contrived, suspicious. She cannot believe her mother really just wants to buy her something and talk. It occurs to her then that Esme is laying a soft nest before shoving Suzen down with bad news. She thinks of Soci, her mother running away to find herself, a new lover, never coming back, and she looks at Esme, suddenly anxious, filled with dread. Or what if it is something else, something worse? Like cancer? Esme's mother had it, breast cancer that later spread through her bones until they looked, in X rays, like moth-eaten lace. She died at sixty-eight. Suzen remembers the doctor saying she might have been carrying the disease for years, in her forties, though it went undetected.

"Mom, are you all right?" Suzen asks.

Esme laughs. "What do you mean?"

"I mean—never mind."

"What? You obviously have something you want to say." When Suzen says nothing, Esme continues driving for a few minutes. Jacobs' department store, an old but popular family business, is on the outskirts of town, surrounded by a newer development of shops and restaurants. When they are stalled by a line of traffic at a red light, Esme turns to Suzen and says, "I know you think I don't pay enough attention to you, that I'm always preoccupied or something, and it's partly true. And I'm sorry. That's why I wanted to pick you up today. I called your boss—Mary, is it?—to find out what time you would finish. She seems very nice, articulate, gracious. Anyway, I hardly know what you are up to these days. Your work, for instance. How's it going?"

The light changes and Esme slowly moves forward, waiting for

Suzen's response. Suzen is thinking, however, that if it were cancer, Esme would have said so—she wouldn't have blithely changed the subject if she truly wanted Suzen to know. Now it seems that her mother's motive is entirely selfish. She is trying to pry into Suzen's life, as if she didn't have enough to worry about on her own. She thinks of her mother talking to Mary and wonders what they said, if Mary offered an opinion about her, if her mother seemed overly solicitous. More and more she resents the intrusion. Strohman's has felt like her secret garden, a place only she knew about, a place where Mary was always waiting on the other side of the wall.

"It's just work," she says finally. "I help plant and move things and sell things sometimes. Nothing exciting."

"It doesn't have to be exciting, sweetie," Esme says, "for me to be interested."

"You don't need to be," Suzen says dully.

"What do you mean? Why are you being so difficult?"

"Just forget it," Suzen says, gritting her teeth.

"Forget *what?* You haven't told me anything," Esme protests.

"The coat, everything. I don't need one. I'm fine."

"Suzen—"

"Can we just go home, please?"

They ride home in silence, though there is a moment—during an abrupt U-turn, tires squealing—when Suzen is as aware of her mother's anger as if she were shouting. She can't look at Esme, wishing for an awful moment that she had confessed something terrible, anything, so Suzen could have ranted at her, justifiably. As it is, she knows she is now in the wrong—the resistant, belligerent teenager, making her mother's life hell.

When did things change? When did Suzen stop wanting to be near her mother? It was before the phone calls from Kevin What's-his-name; that merely pushed Suzen into a quiet rage, whereas before she simply felt inexplicably irritated by Esme. She hated the way she sipped her coffee, blowing and pursing her lips at the rim; her hair, girlishly long; and the way she strode into a room like a long-limbed model, though lines were creasing the corners of her eyes, the edges of her mouth. She was pretty, there was no denying that, but Suzen had begun to suspect a barely concealed vanity was always threatening to peek out from behind her earth-mother veneer, like a lace bra underneath a flannel shirt. In fact, she looked better than ever lately, as if she were readying herself for something. And she was always in constant motion, stirring dinner with one hand while answering the phone with the other, or skimming her children's homework and school notes while scribbling a signature on the bottom; distracted, with one foot out the door. And now Suzen thinks her mother may really be heading that way, burrowing deeper into a secret life, a separate life that doesn't include any of them.

She looks at her mother beside her, for just a moment, and sees her jaw clenched, her eyes cold and resigned; there is no way to know what she is thinking or feeling. And Suzen is aware all at once that it was her own doing that has just shut the door solidly between them.

Evan opens the door to find the Redhead, with a man on her arm. He looks about twenty-five, roughly ten years younger than his date, with a goatee and hints of acne. The Redhead has a name, which Evan cannot recall, but it doesn't matter; everyone thinks of her by various code names—she also is known among the English faculty as the Poetess, the Flower Child, and (secretly) the Harlot, a typically old-fashioned term because no one would stoop to using modern slang. Once, when Evan heard his father refer to something as "radical," he cringed, and rushed to set him straight ("Dad, don't, under any circumstances, ever use that word around anyone under the age of forty, unless, of course, you're referring to a protester from the sixties.").

The Redhead smiles at Evan and waltzes past, with her latest catch

clinging closely. "Where should we put our coats?" she sings. She is
already slithering out of hers, which is fake fur, lined in green satin,
revealing a blue body-skimming dress made of something synthetic. It
might be plastic, Evan thinks. He tries very hard not to focus attention
on her cleavage, partly because he knows it would be rude, and partly
just on principle—he knows she expects it. According to Frederick
Watley, Malcolm's friend from the sociology department, the Redhead
thrives on male attention. He once told Evan, "She's like those plants
that curl up at night but as soon as the first rays of sun touch their
leaves, they pop right up. That's what happens to her breasts when a
man glances at her; just watch sometime. It's highly entertaining."
Evan wishes Watley were going to be here tonight, so they could hide
in the kitchen together and mock the other guests, but unfortunately, it
is an all-English-department party.

It was Esme's idea. When Malcolm told her that one of the creative
writing professors, Bryan Dylan (whose name alone, Evan thinks, pre-
determined his fate), had just published his first novel, she seemed to
jump at the chance to host the impromptu celebration. Esme loves a
party. She loves the frantic preparation, digging out extra glasses and
plates, dimming lights, dressing up. When Evan was little and his parents prepared for the rare party at their house, he marveled at the
transformation of his mother from laid-back nurturer in faded jeans, to
red-lipped siren in a black dress. She seemed to delight in the change
herself; he noticed she even walked differently. And Evan liked the way
the air in the house seemed to crackle with excitement, the sudden
wealth of wine bottles and unfamiliar scent of hors d'oeuvres, candles
brought out of hiding. He liked the crowds of grown-ups, talking and
laughing too loudly, and jazz throbbing, as if teenagers with good taste
had taken over the house.

Now the house has been cleaned, top to bottom—all the family
enlisted, grumbling, to scour and dust—and wineglasses line the dining table, gleaming in the lamplight. Malcolm expects around twenty

guests, but Evan has observed that when free food and booze are offered, the English department seems to double in size. Suddenly part-time staff and adjunct professors and even lowly teaching assistants appear at the door, wearing their most stylish clothes and an expression of expectation—that this will be a party worth writing about. This is something else Evan knows, based on his own nonscientific research: every English professor at Field secretly thinks he or she understands human nature better than everyone else, and furthermore, is more equipped to shine a fictional or poetic light upon it. Evan loves watching the watchers, their blatant attempts to hold breezy conversations while simultaneously taking mental notes on the other speaker's posture, body odor, self-importance.

Evan leads the Redhead and Goatee to the kitchen, where Esme is frantically throwing (literally) tiny *spanikopita* onto tarnished silver trays. One slides off and the crisp phyllo pastry scatters across the floor like dry leaves.

"Mom? People are here," Evan announces.

Esme whips her head around, and smiles automatically, her game face in place. "Oh, hi! Serena, I'm so glad you came. Malcolm thought you were still in Vermont. Did you have a good trip?"

Serena, thinks Evan. He never would have guessed that; he prefers "Redhead," anyway. And as introductions are made, he learns that Goatee is named Paul, though Redhead refers to him as "Paulie," which makes him blush and Evan think of a hitman, for some reason. Esme leads them to the living room, where a fire is blazing in the hearth and the coffee table cleared of books and half-finished card games. Aimee threw a fit earlier because she was ahead in Crazy Eights when Esme swept the cards into a drawer. Now Aimee and Hallie are tucked upstairs with a movie on a television hauled into their room for just that indulgent purpose. Esme knows how easily children are placated by unexpected perks; in addition to the TV, there is a treasure trove of candy on the bedside table between them. Earlier, when Evan, on his mother's orders, checked on his sisters, they didn't even glance up at him, licorice sticks dangling like limp cigars from their lips.

Suzen also has remained out of sight, which is unusual, because she usually accepts waitressing duty at parties, being graceful and adept at carrying trays among throngs of tipsy guests. Evan senses new trouble brewing between her and Esme, though he doesn't know its exact nature. All he knows is that Esme hasn't once yelled Suzen's name during the party preparations; she seems resigned to her daughter's self-imposed exile. It seems, then, that Evan is going to be the evening's maitre d'. His parents are too preoccupied—Esme in the kitchen and Malcolm in the basement searching for a case of wine he is sure he bought—to greet anyone at the door.

The doorbell chimes again, and Evan lets in a familiar cast of characters. There is Stu Farnberg, the ancient Shakespeare authority who threatens to retire every year, then opts for a "stay of execution" claiming that if he stopped teaching the Bard, he might as well be dead; Florence Fast, who belies her name by speaking in painfully drawn out sentences, so that unwary victims who find themselves in conversation with her often begin to fidget and look around for an exit; Margo Streep, who fancies herself a distant relative of the actress and tends toward drama herself—Evan has heard that she sometimes teaches class wearing masks, unaware that no one can understand a word she says from behind papier-mâché; her husband, Jimmy, a contractor, who always looks uncomfortable around the academics, unless they are in the midst of a remodeling job and thus pepper him with questions to which he knows the answer; and a pair of recently hired creative writing professors, David VonDamm, who looks like a soap opera actor, and Lucy Sjelraj, who seems to pride herself on her unpronounceable name. Both are single, and bear the intense look of young professionals eager to make their marks and be noticed.

Once all have shed their coats and scarves and voluminous handbags, they make their way to the living room, milling about, oohing and ahhing over the decor (standard hostess stroking), then on to the dining room for drinks. Evan smiles and endures the usual questions and pointless banter as they pass by—*So, how's school? Got a girl-friend? Are your parents paying you enough tonight? I hope you're smart enough to avoid this crowd. You look like you could use a drink.* Then he watches them from the semi-darkness of the front hallway, as they make themselves comfortable; as more arrive, including the guest of honor, Bryan Dylan; as Esme glides among them in a red dress. It is knee-length, but slit in the back, and, Evan thinks, dangerously low-cut in the front.

Squinting, he looks at Esme and realizes that from a distance she looks much younger, like a movie star, her eyes bright, her makeup enhanced. And all the men glance her way, there is no mistaking it. They even ignore the Redhead, curled seductively in one corner of the sofa. VonDamm, who looks barely twenty, a child, can't keep his eyes off Esme, and in fact, has positioned himself close to her, engaging her in conversation. Dylan, too, the novelist, seems to bask in her attention when she turns to greet and congratulate him. He leans in for an air kiss, then impulsively embraces her.

"Thank you so much for having this party, Esme," he says. "I really appreciate it."

"Oh, it was my pleasure!" Esme says, releasing him, but squeezing his forearm as she does.

Evan wonders if his mother has always been such a flirt, and that he just hasn't noticed because he rarely sees her in social settings. His friends have always told Evan that they think his mother is pretty, but fortunately they go no further in their observations, because they know that if they did, he would be forced to hurt them. Evan knows his mother is an attractive woman, for a mother, but standing at the stove or unloading groceries, or hauling laundry baskets up and down the stairs, she offers no indication of this other side. Perhaps it is just that tonight she has decided to shine, to pour on her charm for the sake of the guests, to show that she's a good sport, that she knows how to entertain, and it means nothing else. Just a good show. Still, there's something unsettling about watching another man watch your mother—stare, in fact, at her cleavage while pretending to hang on her every word. Evan considers intervening, brusquely nudging aside Von-Dammit and pretending he urgently needs to speak to Esme. But then Malcolm appears, hoisting a box of wine onto one shoulder, while his colleagues yell out their approval. Esme turns then, too, quickly rushing to help him with the load, busying herself with the corkscrew she flicks open like a knife. Her cheeks are pink, and Evan wonders if she is just flushed from activity—or shame.

"It's such an incestuous crowd," Fred Watley once said of the English department. "Someone should write a book about it." He laughed and added, "Probably fifteen people already are." Evan hasn't read Bryan Dylan's novel, but he suddenly remembers hearing that it involves a love triangle set on a small midwestern college campus. No, his mother isn't like that, he tells himself. As if to confirm it, Malcolm pauses in serving wine to run a hand down Esme's back, leaning in to kiss her forehead, and she smiles into his eyes, like a girl madly in love.

Suzen feels like a little girl again, peering between rungs of the banister from upstairs to watch the party-goers. Most of them she knows, though there are some new faces, fresh faculty members trying to fit in, and the rarely seen spouses or dates of regular staff. Right off she sees the Redhead, who stands out like a beacon of color in the sea of muted-toned sweaters. Her shiny blue dress, midthigh length and clearly made of rubber, is so tight Suzen can see the faint outlines of lingerie from upstairs. She can't help but admire the woman, and wonders what it would be like to be so blatant in one's sexuality, to just flaunt it in the most staid circumstances. Amazingly, no one ever comments or jokes (aloud) about her scant attire, though, of course, she has a reputation. At the same time, Suzen has heard, the Redhead has a Ph.D. in English literature, which she couldn't have attained without at least some intellectual prowess.

It is late and the party is winding down. Before Suzen ventured out of her bedroom, she heard guests passing her closed door in search of their coats, which were flung across her parents' bed like pelts. When she was little, she would sneak in to try on some of the coats—always one or two furs, back then, before it became a social taboo—and she wonders why Hallie and Aimee haven't thought to do the same. Perhaps they are too much the product of their later generation, reared on videos and content to watch fantasy on-screen rather than invent their own. She sighs, watching the guests depart below her perch on the stairs, the door slamming, the cheerful and drunken farewells, the music still playing, CDs set on "repeat" for the evening; Dean Martin is singing, "You're Nobody 'Til Somebody Loves You," for probably the twentieth time.

And then she sees her mother, dancing with Bryan Dylan, who is singing along drunkenly. Esme is laughing, swinging around the front hallway in his arms, in her red dress, her hair combed to gleaming gold, her cheeks blazing. Dylan holds one of Esme's hands, wraps his other arm around her waist; they look like a couple in a nightclub, oblivious to the audience. Though, as far as Suzen can tell, no one is around to see them. How could her mother be so blatant? And how many men *are* there, exactly? Where is her father, she wonders, though he might not even notice.

He notices now, however, sidling up to his wife and making a show of cutting in, though good-naturedly. Dylan, the guest of honor, demurs, looking a shade flustered, it seems to Suzen.

"Hey, I just can't resist a woman in a red dress," Dylan says, laughing, slurring slightly. "It's a character flaw, like a weakness for Belgian chocolates."

"Well, get your own," Malcolm says, pulling Esme close. They both laugh then, Esme curling into her husband's arms as if to say it was all a joke, it meant nothing. She and Malcolm dance for a moment, badly, and look at each other as if they can't wait to be alone.

In spite of his inebriated state, Dylan takes the hint and clears his throat. "Well, thank you both again for a great party and—um, everything. I guess I should go find my coat."

"I think it's up on our bed," Esme says, smiling brightly, but making no move to get it for him.

Dylan heads up the stairs, slowly, as if unsure what his feet are doing. Malcolm, watching him go, mutters, "I suppose someone should drive him home, but everyone's left already."

"Yeah, he's in no condition to drive."

"Maybe he could walk," Malcolm says.

"He lives near the lake," Esme says.

"Exactly."

Esme laughs. "You're cruel."

"Yeah, well, you're a flirt."

"You knew that when we met," Esme says, a hint of challenge in her voice.

Suzen has pulled away from the banister, so that no one can see her, not even Bryan Dylan when he finally, painstakingly makes his way to the landing and the last four steps. He walks right past Suzen, crouched in the shadows, and stumbles down the hallway. He opens a door—Evan's—then abruptly closes it. Evan, the last Suzen heard of him, has retired to the den and is probably asleep on the sofa with the television on. Dylan is about to open the door to Hallie and Aimee's room, so Suzen leaps up to stop him before he wakes them.

"The next one down, on your right," she says.

He jumps. "Shit! You nearly scared me to death," he says. "I mean that lit-er-all-ee." He laughs. "Who might you be?"

"Suzen. We've met before," she says. She is used to being over-looked by adults, lost in their own lofty thoughts.

"We have? Sorry, but I think I'd remember someone like you." He grins. Leers. Suzen backs away.

"Your coat is in there, the next door," she says.

"Coat-shmoat," Dylan says. He sighs. "Yes, I suppose I should get my coat and take my leave. Don't want to wear out my welcome. *Welcome* is a funny word, isn't it?" he says. He turns toward the bedroom, murmuring the word over and over like a madman. When he finally comes out—it seems to take an inordinate amount of time and Suzen wonders if he has been snooping, or just trying to figure out how his sleeves work—he walks past Suzen once again, as if she is invisible, as if he has no memory of their conversation a moment earlier.

Suzen slides back down to the polished wooden floor, scoots across to her post and peers down. Dylan and Malcolm are gone. She can hear her father's car in the driveway. Esme is alone now, with Dean Martin still crooning. She has her high heels off and bends to yank down her pantyhose, tossing them aside, too. Then she waltzes around the living room, gathering paper plates and tossing them into the dying fire. She stands there, watching the tiny bursts of flame. " 'You're nobody, till somebody loves you,' " she sings softly to herself. And Suzen, watching, listening, her heart in her throat, wonders what her mother is thinking.

Trees cling to the sides of a cliff like moss, and a waterfall and deep turquoise pools ring the walls of softly jagged granite. Evan finds himself staring, squinting, to make it come to life. The colors aren't very realistic, he thinks. His gaze shifts to the Eiffel Tower pasted against a backdrop of crazily pink and orange skies, swirled like melted sherbet. Posters line the wall of the travel agency and Evan picks up a brochure on tours of Italy, tucks it into his back pocket. Waiting for someone to assist him, he sits down, idly looking around. Phones are ringing and a few people stand at the counters, handing over credit cards. All of them going somewhere, or planning to, with a sense of urgency as if travel were the most important thing to do in life, and to do now, before it's too late.

Travel, Evan recalls from one of the family word games, derives from the same Latin source as *travail.* In fact, both words come, originally, from *trepalium,* an instrument of torture made of three sharp stakes. This evolved into an old French word, *travailler,* meaning trouble, pain, hard work. (Malcolm seemed delighted to point that out. "Nothing worth doing is easy," he'd intoned, adding that "every trip I've ever taken was effort, but worth it.") Eventually *travailler* was borrowed by the English as *travail,* or "wearisome journey," and then shortened simply to *travel* itself, which meant "to go from one place to another," or—in Evan's favorite definition—"to be transmitted, as light." He loves the notion of words emerging from words, the layered meanings coated over from one culture and age to another, like paint, as if each time a slightly more pleasing shade is discovered.

While he waits, Evan thumbs through a worn copy of a Berlitz guide to Italian. He found it in the family room at home, near the television, and surmised that Malcolm had been up late again, planning the trip they never will take. He glances up again at the fake orange sky of Paris, the twinkling lights. Then he studies the waterfall, the mountains, and the verdant valley that surely lies beyond, dotted with gnarled olive trees, their fruit dangling like ornaments. There probably aren't waterfalls in Tuscany, he thinks, but he likes to imagine it nonetheless.

"May I help you?" a manly woman barks at him over the counter. When Evan jumps up and walks over to her, he can see her mustache beneath a layer of makeup.

"I was wondering about flights to Italy?" he says.

"Where."

"Uh, Italy," he says again, more loudly.

"I'm not deaf, hon. I meant, where in Italy—Rome, Florence, Milan? You need to pick a point of entry."

Evan laughs, embarrassed. "Oh. Rome, I guess. Is it near Tuscany?" *Ignorant*, he chides himself. He memorized the map; he should know. But under scrutinization, he can't remember anything. He realizes he would fail under interrogation. He'd be tortured to death before remembering his own name, probably. Of course, the travel agent isn't interested in torture. She just wants him to get a move on. While Evan stands there dumbly, she excuses herself, answers three phone calls, puts two on hold and clicks rapidly on her keyboard. Then she looks up at him over black rimmed glasses.

"Florence is closer, by the way, though it's more complicated—most people fly into Rome, and you could always take a train from there. How long are you planning to go for? What's your departure date?"

Evan stammers. "Um, I'm not sure."

The woman looks at him again, lips terse. "Are you booking a flight right now, or just inquiring?" In other words, *I don't have all day, hon.* It occurs to Evan that he should have looked it up on the computer at home, but he thought he needed an expert's advice. Some expert, he thinks, watching her turn to pick at a dried-up jelly danish.

"Never mind," he says sheepishly. "I guess I should get some more information first." And he heads quickly through the door. He thinks of Soci, trying to coax him to take a simple trip with her less than three hours from home, and how he has resisted—yet here he is trying to find a way to flee not only his home, but his country, the entire continent. It is as if the harder Soci tries to pull him along, the more he thinks of plotting his own escape. Maybe it is genetic; he is just like Malcolm, dreaming of flight. But unlike his father, Evan intends to make it happen, one way or another.

Meanwhile, he reasons, there has to be a way to prove to Soci that he is willing to take risks—just not necessarily the ones she wants from him. While she relishes the regular escapes from school, smoking a pack of cigarettes a day, and, he recently learned, "borrowing" money from her unwitting father, Evan is finding that he doesn't really want to be a *yob*, disregarding parental and other authority. He wants to be with Soci, but not at the cost of getting in trouble. Trouble, he is finding, is not as appealing in real life as it is on film. In movies, the danger is always accompanied by effective music and suspense—and the certain knowledge that the hero will always come out ahead in the end. For instance, James Bond may be hanging upside-down from the skiff of a helicopter, choked by the giant hand of a silver-mouthed ogre, but he'll find a way out. With Soci leading the way, hinting, tempting, and prodding him, Evan doesn't feel confident that he will come through so cavalierly.

He has had one lucky break, however. A reprieve. The night before their scheduled rendezvous at the train station, Evan was pretending to study his notes with Max when Soci called. Suzen appeared at the door with the cordless phone and said, "A girl. For you." Evan went cold and sweaty.

"Hello?" he said, turning his back on Max, as if then he wouldn't overhear.

"I can't go," Soci was saying, her voice petulant. "Something has come up at home, and I can't get out of here. Dammit." Evan, flushed with relief, put on his best disappointed tone. "Soon, though, okay?" she said, sounding hopeful and eager. Because her eagerness had to do with *him*, Evan found himself agreeing again.

When he hung up, Max was swiveling around and around in Evan's desk chair, smirking. "So, what's up?" he asked. And Evan told him everything then, watching his friend turn green with envy, twirling.

"You know anything about her?" Max asked.

"What do you mean—I just told you everything about her."

"I don't mean that you made out in the theater or cut class. I mean, she just showed up out of nowhere, you know. She could be a psychopath." Max was grinning. He loved to torment.

"She moved here from New York, or Connecticut, the suburbs. Not that different from here, probably. She doesn't talk about it and I don't care about her past," Evan said, whacking his friend as he rolled past him in the desk chair. But later, it got him thinking. He really didn't know anything about Soci, what her life was like before, or even where she lived now. She never suggested meeting at either of their houses, as if they really were adrift, loners without home or family; she seemed to like it that way. And Evan used to think that was what he wanted, no complications, just the two of them, alone. Now he knows that he is scared—of Soci, of getting too involved, of going too far and not being able to come back to the way he was.

As he walks home from the travel agency, hands deep in his pockets, Evan thinks that if his father really did plan a sabbatical, he would go in a minute, without looking back. Maybe all he has to do is convince Malcolm that they need to go, and help him figure out how.

M alcolm points through the windshield at the sign on the corner, which reads: *We won't be undersold! Biggest sale in the "history" of retail! So get you're tail in to see us now!* He shakes his head in disgust. "Can you believe that? Someone actually *paid* to have that billboard painted! I mean, why is 'history' in quotation marks? Is it an inside joke? And then, 'you're tail'? *You are* tail? What does it mean?"

Suzen laughs. "It means they're morons, Dad, that's all." She is used to her father's ranting about the apparent lack of appreciation for the English language that he fears is growing epidemic. Malcolm brings home horror stories of nineteen-year-olds who don't know the difference between a noun and a verb, let alone participles and gerunds. Their spelling often is atrocious. Malcolm likes to laugh (then moan) over his students' personal essays, about how one wrote a paper detailing the number and variety of "girl *fiends*" he claimed to have, and another described her plan to start a "physical *fat*ness club" after she "*gradiated.*"

Suzen tilts her head back and stares through the sunroof. Clouds drift overhead, softly collide. She feels sleepy and warm in the car with her father, though they are only driving across town to the hardware store. It reminds Suzen of when she was small, curled into the front seat watching the scenery blur past, glad to be included in a simple errand with her father. He knows she loves hardware stores, so it has become a tradition for them to go together. It is so much easier to be with her father than her mother; he doesn't expect anything from her, except proper grammar.

"It's just so *depressing*," Malcolm is saying, still fixated on the bill-board. He sighs. Someone behind him honks loudly and he moves the car forward without acknowledging the other driver's impatience.

"What a jerk," Suzen says.

"Oh, well," Malcolm says, suddenly magnanimous—he is more bothered by words than behavior, Suzen has noticed—"You can never know what's going on in someone else's life, so you have to give him or her the benefit of the doubt." Suzen wonders if he exercises this prin-ciple with his wife, and if he has any idea that Esme is having an affair (allegedly) with someone called Kevin Wunderhaus. She wonders, too, if Esme has told him about their Cold War, if he has noticed that they aren't speaking.

"So, how are you doing?" Malcolm asks suddenly, cheerily.

Suzen sits up, adjusts her seat belt. "Fine. You know, nothing new." Apparently, he is that oblivious.

"Are you giving any thought to college?" he asks, and she knows his nonchalance is only thinly shading his anxiety—she has not requested an application from Field's admission office, nor any other school's, though most of her peers sent forms in last year already.

Suzen is in the first semester of her senior year and has yet to make a decision regarding her future. What she cannot explain to her father, however, is that her future only just began opening up when she walked into Strohman's Nursery and met Mary.

"I think I might just work awhile, Dad, you know, take some time before college."

"This *is* before college," he notes. "Now is the time you should be thinking about what you want to do, and college helps prepare you for that. And you don't even have to have a solid idea about it when you enter; you figure it out as you go along."

"That's what I am doing," Suzen says, defensively. "I'm figuring it out as I go." She flips the door-lock button up and down. Malcolm keeps his eyes on the road, takes deep sighing breaths, slowly letting them out as if he is practicing Lamaze. It seems they have reached an impasse and neither knows what more to say. She wonders if she is doomed to spend tortured time in the car with each of her parents.

"Your mother is worried that—" he starts.

Suzen glares straight ahead. "She doesn't understand a thing about me."

"That isn't true, Suz. Your mother loves you." He pauses, she says nothing. Then he asks, tentatively, "It isn't a boy, is it?" he asks.

Suzen gapes at her father. "What do you mean? What are you talking about?"

"I mean, sometimes kids form their plans around someone else. I know lots of students at Field who have transferred in or out to be near their sweethearts. I'm not saying it's a bad thing, necessarily, but I just wouldn't want you planning your life around a guy when you have your whole life ahead of you."

"I'm not, don't worry. Jeez."

"Okay, okay, you don't have to get upset. I mean, I can't help thinking about your mother and how she put her own plans on hold because—"

"Because of me," Suzen says flatly. "Because she was pregnant with me." Maybe that's why they don't get along, Suzen thinks. She is the reason her mother's life turned at an early age and she never got it back the way it was. Suzen changed everything.

"Well," Malcolm stammers. "That is true. But, well, I guess that was because of *me*." He is blushing, and it occurs to Suzen that though she has known for years now, it is the first time her father has ever mentioned it. They have arrived at the hardware store, and Malcolm parks near the door, backing in as if they will be loading up lumber, though all they have come for is a bathtub snake and some lightbulbs.

"Well, okay, here we are," Malcolm says. It is clear he doesn't know how to drop or change the subject gracefully.

Suzen decides to help him out. "I can promise you, Dad, that whatever I decide to do will have nothing to do with a man in my life." Malcolm smiles, evidently relieved.

In the hardware store, Suzen wanders up and down the aisles as usual, fingering the silvery bolts and inhaling the sweet odor of sawdust. Her father has tracked down a salesman and is holding up various snakes, comparing lengths, asking advice. She watches other men confidently gathering sockets and screws, a thin man scrutinizing a welding torch; she can tell by his half-smile as he holds and aims the tip into the air that he is just like a small boy, imagining the fire gushing forth, annihilating an imaginary foe. They are all like this to her, transparent, simple, soporific. Except of course, her father, and maybe Eduardo.

She has hardly thought about her encounter with him in the auditorium, though she has kept his blue stone in her pocket, liking the small hard rub of it against her upper thigh when she walks. She wonders if maybe it really is good luck. After all, Eduardo comes from a culture open to superstition, magic, mysticism. She wants to believe in his luck, and the notion that there is much beyond that we don't know or can't see. It makes the mundane bearable. In fact, daydreaming has become her way of life, a way out of life.

Wandering the hardware store, turning randomly down one row to the next, she imagines the floor she trods is really soft moss, and the walls are hedges high overhead. And just around the next bend there will be a gurgling fountain, or a velvet bench. And someone, the right someone, waiting for her.

"Ready to go?" Malcolm asks.

"Sure, Dad," Suzen says, following him out.

D ad?" Evan says as his father passes his doorway. "Can I show you something?"

Malcolm walks in, stands over Evan's desk. "So, what's all this?" he asks, though he doesn't seem unusually surprised to see that Evan has possession of the family passports, stacked neatly on his desk beside his alligator stapler and baseball cards. Before Evan can explain, Malcolm sits down across from him, sinking deep into a red beanbag chair.

"I know what you're up to, Ev," Malcolm says, looking long at his son, as if he has caught him rolling a joint. "I've been talking to Fred."

Frederick Watley, he means, of course, who has been fielding Evan's questions for the past two weeks.

"Well, if it isn't my favorite faculty brat!" he said when Evan first showed up. When he discovered that Evan wanted information about sabbatical protocol, Watley chortled over his meddling. "Are you secretly going to fill out the applications, renew passports, book tickets—and then spring it on your parents?"

"I just want to find out what's involved. You know, so I can present a logical case."

Watley got up and strode across his office, and returned with the faculty handbook. He flipped some pages, folded the book open, and handed it to Evan. "Section c12, part II," he said. Evan took it and read aloud, "The sabbatical leave program at Field College is designed to encourage the professional development of faculty members. This, in turn, will advance the educational objectives of the institution.' " He looked up. "What does *that* mean?"

Watley winked. "Good question. No one really knows. It is one of the great mysteries of Field College."

"No, really," Evan said. "What does my dad have to do, to get it?"

"Grovel and beg, basically." He laughs. "But, then, that isn't easy to do if he doesn't even know he is applying. Are you planning to include him in the process?"

"I asked him about it, but he's kind of busy," Evan said, shrugging. "I thought I could save him some time if I did the legwork myself. I've already looked into airfare."

"And you thought I could aid and abet, right?"

Apparently, while Watley delighted in humoring Evan, he also found it amusing to divulge his plans to Malcolm. Evan wonders if they had a hearty laugh over it.

Malcolm leans up and plucks one of the passports from the desk, flipping it open.

"You know, Ev," he says, "I'm not as naïve as I may seem. I know what you're doing. I knew even without Fred telling me. The fact is, even he's been hinting to me I need a break for years. He just thought I should know my own family members felt the same way."

"Mom doesn't," Evan blurts.

"How do you know that?" Malcolm asks, his tone firmer.

Evan shrugs, says, "I mean, she's so busy and involved here. It would be hard to get her to leave."

Malcolm studies his son. "Just why are *you* so hell-bent on leaving, anyway? Are you in trouble of some kind?"

"No! I just want—I don't know. I just want some adventure."

Malcolm laughs. "You know," he says, "life is supposed to be an adventure in itself." His tone is lightly facetious. "Well, let's see what we have here."

He stands up and lines up the passports, opens them one by one, Evan standing over his shoulder. They are all out of date. Aimee doesn't even have one, as she hadn't been conceived when they took the last sabbatical. The other children's passports were only good for five years and have expired. Evan looks at the black-and-white photograph of himself, his face at six still babyish, a gap in his front teeth as he grinned for the camera. Hallie was just a baby, unsmiling, her eyes as serious at three months as they are now at nine years. Making a mental list, Evan figures the most pressing issue is money. He has yet to estimate the cost of living off savings for a year. He has tried to find out just how much money—if any—his parents have stocked away, but it is no simple feat. He knows his father's general salary, but isn't clear about what other assets he might have. He knows that a year-long sabbatical would mean a half-paid leave.

He paces his room, waiting for his father to decide. It seems Malcolm is standing on the brink, that if Evan can nudge him, it will all work out. They will go. He has earmarked advertisements in the back pages of the magazines, for Italian villas to rent. Probably there is a friend of a friend of a colleague of his father's who knows someone who has lived in Tuscany, or has relatives in Florence. Venice is out of the question—too congested, too watery; Evan has done research. He wants to be in the hillsides, waves of golden semolina rolling in the afternoon sunlight. He sees himself driving a used Fiat into town— who would care whether or not he had a valid license? Watley told him that Italians are notorious for their lax driving laws, and remarked that in Italy, stoplights "are merely ornamental."

He thinks about his father's journey there, the descriptions in his diary, and the girl with whom he fell in love (or lust). There was no mention of how it ended, though obviously it did end. Evan wonders if there is a way he can ask Malcolm about her, without revealing that he has snooped; he just wants to know how serious it was, or if it was just a sudden, one-time event that happened, like a car accident, and the two of them went their separate ways afterward without reporting it to anyone. There was no indication in the writing one way or another, but Evan assumed Mara was his father's first lover. And thus, he can't help wondering if Malcolm's continuing attraction to Tuscany has anything to do with her, with his coming of age there, and if that is why he wants to return for a sabbatical.

"It's not as simple as you think," Malcolm says finally, leaning against the cluttered desk. "There are a million things to consider. I appreciate your interest in all this, Evan, but it isn't going to happen right now. There's just too much going on." And he sets the passports back down, walks out of Evan's room and closes the door behind him.

What *is* going on? Evan wonders.

H ey. What's new?" Soci asks. Suzen looks up, smiles. She is bent over a yew, trying to shovel soil over the ball of roots she has just dropped into a hole. The maze in Soci's backyard is now fully a third planted and Suzen comes daily to check the progress, to work—and to avoid going home for as long as possible. Mary has arranged for some of her staff to work evenings, after Strohman's closes, paying them overtime as she is being compensated generously herself by Mr. Andersson. He wants the work finished before the weather turns cold, if possible, so it won't have to wait till spring.

"Hi, Soci," Suzen says. "What do you think?" She motions toward the maze, its low walls curving into shape.

Soci says, "It's okay, I guess," not looking, and Suzen wonders why she is so disinterested in the maze, which Suzen thinks is wonderful. Perhaps it is simply because Soci and her father don't get along—it's his project, after all—just as Suzen wants nothing to do with her mother's life. Suddenly, she feels guilty, like an accomplice for the enemy. She stands up, wipes her hands on her jeans.

"I was just going to take a break," she says. "I have some hot chocolate in a Thermos—want some?"

"Sure," Soci says, smiling. They sit together on a wool stadium blanket Suzen has taken from home; the days are getting colder now, as it is nearly October.

"So, do you like working on this?" Soci asks, sipping from the plastic cup Suzen handed her.

"Yeah, I guess. I mean, I love anything that has to do with plants."

"You're lucky."

"Why?"

"I mean, to have a definite interest," Soci says. "A *raison d'être.*"

"Oh," Suzen says. "Do you speak French?"

"Some. We used to travel when I was little. We lived in England for a year when I was five."

"Really? I lived there when I was seven!" Suzen says. She considers this, then adds, her face lighting up, "We might have been there at the same time, since you're two years younger than I am. That's amazing."

"It is," Soci agrees, eyes twinkling. "Small world."

"Didn't you love it there?" Suzen asks. She wants to talk about her longings, her dreams of the English countryside, everything.

"I suppose. But I loved New York more. My dad went and got the harebrained idea to buy the headlight company. 'A great investment and all that,' but really, it's because he can do whatever the hell he wants to, money is no object. And he grew up around here, you know, and thought it would be a good place for me. Safe." She laughs, bitterly. "So I would stay out of trouble, live the nice midwestern life, and find some wholesome friends. God, he's so fucking stupid."

Suzen sits still, staring into her hot chocolate, her delight over their English connection evaporating. She feels deeply sorry for Soci, a girl with everything but, apparently, happiness. "Don't you have any friends?" she asks, looking at Soci.

"You," Soci says, and smiles. "And a sort-of boyfriend, but with the emphasis on *boy*. I'm not sure it's going to go anywhere." She nudges Suzen with her elbow. "What about you? Got a boyfriend?"

Suzen considers lying, pretending that there is something between her and Eduardo—it would sound exciting, exotic, but she knows it isn't true. She isn't even sure anymore that she wants it to be. She shakes her head "no."

"Well, who needs them, right?" Soci says. Suzen laughs.

"I'd better go," Soci says. "I'm supposed to go meet the new cleaning lady." She rolls her eyes. "The last one quit because of arthritis and the one before that said the house was too big. I don't blame them." She looks up at her house. "It is too fucking big. If I could, I'd live in a trailer." She smiles and walks away across the lawn. *"Au revoir."*

"So, that's the notorious daughter," Mary says, coming up behind Suzen. She pulls off her soil-stained gloves. "She's cute." Mary laughs then, looking at Suzen. "Oh, I didn't mean it like *that*, I hope it didn't sound like that."

Suzen looks at her quizzically, laughs nervously. Then, since they are alone for the first time in awhile, Suzen asks what she has long wondered. "Does it bother you?"

"What?" Mary asks.

"You know," Suzen says, shrugging. "The rumors, the things people say about you."

Mary eyes her quizzically. "What do they say?" She laughs at Suzen's red face. "I'm kidding. You mean, that I'm a dyke?" She pauses thoughtfully. "It's just too bad there isn't a nicer name. I mean, gay men get to be called 'fairies'! Why not us? *I* would like to be a fairy."

Suzen doesn't know what to say. Her feelings are muddled. She starts to clear her throat; it feels as if she has swallowed a small bird. "Oh," is all she can manage to croak.

"I hope it doesn't change your opinion of me," Mary says. She looks into Suzen's eyes as if she really means it, needs to know.

"No! Of course not!" Suzen says, too emphatically. There is more she wants to say but the words catch in her throat, wings folded flat.

"The thing is," Mary says, reaching down to level a yew, though it is already straight, perfect, "I've always believed that it shouldn't matter who you love, anyway. Your heart often goes places you least expect, and all you can do is follow. Long as you aren't hurting anyone, right?"

Suzen nods. Mary hands her back her shovel and smiles. "It's getting dark earlier now—we better finish up and get out of here." As she winds her way through the rows, Suzen watches her, and thinks about what she said, and wonders whom she loves. She pictures a faceless woman, Mary's size, holding her in her arms. It is strange at first, the slender arms wrapped around slender ribs, but then it isn't. She sees them tilt their heads, lean in to kiss. Their hair touches, their fingers grasp each other's faces lightly, gently. It is not so odd a vision, and Suzen feels she is looking through a window or a keyhole at Mary's secret life.

Evan decides that he is going to find out more about Soci—or at least, where she lives. He looked for her name in the phone book; there was only one Andersson with the same spelling, but its number was unlisted and Evan was unfamiliar with the street name. Evan just wants to be able to picture her in a particular kitchen, neighborhood, bedroom. He wonders if her room is like his sisters', decorated with art posters and throw pillows, soft carpeting, and a girlish mess of things he finds foreign. In Aimee and Hallie's room there is always a heap of clothes and smaller piles of doll shoes and hair paraphernalia, while in

Suzen's, which is more Spartan, grown-up, there are only books and small potted plants on the window sills, and some makeup. Once, Evan nosed around, opening tubes of lipstick and sniffing them, out of curiosity. They all had names like Sugared Maple and Raspberry Glacé, or Envy and Divine. Some smelled like bubble gum or wax, but others, obviously more expensive in silver tubes like bullets, were sublime and alluring. He opened one all the way, a deep blood red called Vixen, and licked it, then quickly rolled it down and put it back. He wondered why Suzen owned so much lipstick, when all she ever wore was clear balm for chapped lips. Maybe she was just waiting for the right occasion, a big date, though she never dated anyone.

He waits for Soci after school, as usual near the lockers, a wall of ugly beige metal, watching the sea of people pass and part, rushing on and on, until there is a mere trickle, a few stragglers, and finally, Her. He grins, unabashedly happy at the sight of her, and feeling all at once lucky and doomed. He doesn't care about the latter; he knows she may be bad for him but Soci is a drug he must have now or die.

"Hey, sweetie," she says, using a term of endearment for the first time. "Hey," he says, oddly stumped for a counterpart. He figures "honey" sounds old-fashioned, and "baby" like he'd be trying too hard. So he says nothing, deciding to mull it over and surprise her sometime with just the right word.

"Why are you still here?" she asks.

"Waiting for you. I was hoping you hadn't left yet."

"Well, I was supposed to stay and go over my science test—which I bombed, surprise, surprise—with Mr. Watson, but he had to go home. Some emergency with his wife or something. Too bad, huh." She smiles wickedly, taking Evan's hand. "So, where do you want to go?"

"I don't know. How about your house?"

Soci lets go of his hand, busies herself with her book bag. "Naw. That wouldn't be any fun," she says.

"Why not? I want to see where you live. I want to see your room."

Evan slings an arm around her neck and starts to walk her down the hallway, though she has to adjust her backpack, awkwardly holding it over her forearm.

"I live in a trailer," she says flatly. "If you really must know."

"Oh," he says, his voice level.

"Yeah. 'Oh.' That's what I'd expect you to say."

"What do you mean? Why would you say that?" Evan asks, wounded, but still holding his arm around her, trying to maintain his cool.

"I mean, everyone has preconceived ideas about people based on how they look and where they live and what they drive. It's ingrained in us."

"I don't judge you," Evan argues.

"I know you don't—I mean, I know how you feel about me. But you don't know my father or anything, and if you did, you might change your mind."

"I wouldn't."

"Maybe not. Maybe you're above that—I shouldn't have assumed you're like everyone else. Sorry." Soci ducks out from under Evan's arm so she can face him. She smiles. "Anyway, why don't we go to your house?"

Evan shrugs. "Okay, I mean, if you really want to. But it's a zoo there, sisters, pets, parents—though they might be out. If we're lucky, everyone will be out, but that hardly ever happens."

"I don't care. I want to meet your sisters. It'll be fun," Soci says.

"Sure," Evan laughs. "But you have to promise you'll take me to your house sometime. Okay?"

"I promise," Soci says, and laughs as if it is a great joke.

Listening from the kitchen, Suzen can hear the girl's short, musical laugh that is probably infectious. It sounds like the type of girl

Evan would hang around with, though Suzen knows it's not fair to judge a person, unseen, based on her laugh alone. Whoever she is, she's Evan's new girlfriend—his first, as far as Suzen knows. He has dropped a few hints, and living in the same house it's impossible not to pick up information about family members, by osmosis if not direct contact. Suzen also has noticed that her brother has been paying more attention to his usually haphazard appearance, and that he has been in trouble for skipping school, though he seems reformed now, as the topic hasn't surfaced lately at the dinner table.

As far as girls are concerned, Evan is so woefully inexperienced; Suzen eavesdrops and thinks of her brother as an actor with a new, unrehearsed script, fumbling for the right tone and inflection, uttering lines that he never would in his normal life. Now he is explaining the origin of a scar on his collarbone. "Here, see? It looks like lightning, or a sideways Z?" Yet, the girl seems to find him amusing, fascinating. Suzen pictures Evan with her in the hallway, trying out his cocky stance, arms folded over his T-shirted chest so that the biceps inflate, the veins perfect ridges along his smooth hairless skin. Suzen has watched him practice this in his room, the door ajar.

Now she hears him saying, "So, what do you want to do?" followed by the girl's punch line, "I don't know, what do *you* want to do?" as if they are children. Which, Suzen supposes, they are. She rolls her eyes and steps around the corner on her way upstairs; she can't resist getting a look at the person who would be so enthralled by her brother.

"Hey," the girl calls out automatically. Suzen is startled both by her forthrightness and then by the fact that it is Soci Andersson, the girl of the mansion and the maze. She has taken off her shoes, as if she is fully at home, and she is gazing at Suzen with bright, direct eyes. Suzen finds her own voice and mutters hello in response, struck dumb by the situation.

Evan is saying, "Hey Soci, this is Suzy. Suzy, Soci."

"We've met," Suzen says.

"At the library," Soci blurts, glancing at Suzen. "Small world."

Suzen feels herself blushing, confused. Soci manages to divert the conversation easily, turning cheerfully to Evan. "We were just trying to figure out what to do, weren't we?" She nudges him. "How about hide-and-seek? You guys have a big house, it would be a blast."

A big house, Suzen repeats to herself, thinking of Soci's thirty-room home, enough bedrooms that she could sleep in a different one every night of the week. For a moment Suzen and Evan look at each other over Soci's head, as if silently agreeing she is crazy, just humor her. They both shrug.

"What about your other sisters, should we ask them?" Soci says. "The more the merrier, right?"

Before they know it, Soci has commandeered the four VanderZee children into a game of hiding in their own house, something they haven't done in years. She also insists they close shutters and window blinds to make it more frightening. Hallie and Aimee seem delighted to be included in the affairs of the teenagers.

"Only inside, though, okay? No one can go outside to hide," Suzen says, as she has been instructed by her parents to keep a vigilant eye on Aimee. After everyone has darted off in different directions, Suzen grudgingly closes herself into the coat closet, pressed against old wool and vinyl raincoats that feel strangely like skin in the dark.

Since Soci has declared herself It, and is thumping around the house on her search, Suzen resigns herself to waiting, thinking about the awkward exchange with Soci, wondering why she lied about where they met. And she is utterly bewildered by the astounding coincidence that Soci is with Evan, of all people. Suddenly, she remembers Soci's comment about her "sort-of boyfriend, but with the emphasis on *boy.*" It makes sense, then. And it probably won't last, though why Suzen cares, she has no idea.

She is suddenly irritated at having been coerced into their silly game; she has better things to do. Even so, settled in the soft darkness she sighs and succumbs, leaning into the cushioned wall of cloth.

Suzen remembers the last time she played hide-and-seek, at a slumber party when she was thirteen and the host, Rachel, suggested they play the game with her older brother. Rachel knew most of the girls had crushes on Michael, a tall, athletic senior, and she took obvious pride in her connection to him. The nine or ten girls eagerly rifled through their duffel bags and small suitcases, slipping shirts over their heads, or leaving them on to remove bras discreetly. All of them wore baby doll pajamas, popular then, lace insets at the bodice, tiny ruffled cap sleeves, matching panties. They looked to Suzen like a gathering of oversized toddlers. She wore a long soft T-shirt with the Detroit Tigers logo, and snowflake-printed boxer shorts. Someone called her "tomboy," affectionately.

When the game commenced, Suzen had hidden in Rachel's private bathroom, locking the door behind her. She sat on the edge of the porcelain tub, surrounded by pink and white tiles like giant Chiclets. Bored, she studied herself in the mirror, opened the medicine cabinet and sniffed Rachel's collections of perfume, lip gloss, and powder tins with oversized puffs. Outside the door she could hear the far-off squeals of the other girls, feebly attempting to "hide" from Michael, hoping to be caught. After awhile, Suzen heard the bathroom door rattle, a pause, then a deep voice saying, "Hey, come on out of there, cheater." Beyond him, laughter. Someone murmuring, "Maybe she had to *go.*" More laughter. Suzen, blushing with anger, yanked open the door. She saw Michael, surprised, appraising her. It seemed that, surrounded by a bevy of budding breasts in filmy nylon, he only had eyes for Suzen in her sloppy shirt.

"A Tigers fan," he noted. "Cool."

Suzen slipped past him, relieved the game was over, more relieved when Rachel's mother announced it was time to settle down and sleep. Suzen was happy to curl into the zippered flannel comfort of her sleeping bag, watching the other girls sleep. She studied their profiles, their loose lips, fluttering eyelids.

Standing in the closet, the close padded air almost suffocating, Suzen suddenly remembers wanting to lean over and kiss one of the sleeping girls, then feeling shocked at the notion. What harm was there in kissing, though? she wonders now. It is such a natural impulse, the yearning for the sensual. Suzen imagines Soci opening the door slowly now. Instead of calling, "Gotcha!" Soci would step in and close the door. Saying nothing, her arm would brush against Suzen's; it could be a mistake. She might think it was Evan. Stepping closer, reaching blindly, feeling a nose, lips. Leaning forward, tipping into the darkness, lips against lips. She would know, of course, in an instant that it wasn't Evan, but she wouldn't care—Soci would let her tongue linger, press her mouth over Suzen's. Pulling away, she would only say, "Wow," so softly it could just be a breath.

Maybe there is something wrong with me, Suzen thinks. Perhaps she has been spending too much time with Mary, and it's rubbing off on her. But Suzen reminds herself she isn't like *that.* Thinking about kissing Soci was just out of curiosity; it is not the same thing as lusting—after her brother's girlfriend. Disgusted with herself, she shoves open the door, her hair alight with static as the coats release her.

"Hey," Soci says, spying her as she passes through the hallway. "I guess you're found," she laughs.

"I quit," Suzen says, not looking at her.

"Why?"

"I get claustrophobic."

"Your hair is standing straight up," Soci notes. She reaches out a hand and smoothes Suzen's hair over her scalp. Goose bumps erupt along Suzen's skin and she ducks her head. Soci glances around. "Hey, don't tell Evan, okay?"

"What?" Suzen asks, blushing rapidly.

"About—you know, where I live."

"Oh. Why not?"

"He doesn't know. He thinks—never mind. I just don't want him to know about it, okay? Promise?"

Suzen nods. "Don't worry," she says. "I never talk to Evan."

After everyone has been found, and grown bored, Evan and Soci sit in his room, talking. Evan was nervous about letting her in—not just because of what she might think of his decorating style, but about what might happen if they were alone there, with the door closed. He knows it is risky, having a girl over, his sisters within earshot, his parents likely to return home at any moment. So far, though, no one has bothered them, and Soci seems perfectly happy just to tour his room, taking her time lifting and looking at the objects on his shelves and desk. Sometimes she smiles to herself—turning over the alligator stapler, for instance, and finding the framed photograph of Evan with his fifth-grade soccer team—and sometimes she just looks and says nothing. Evan wonders what conclusions she is drawing from his things, wonders if she thinks him juvenile, or interesting, or clever. He hopes she notices the posters for old movies—classy, he thinks, and sophisticated—and not the baseball cards or the *Sports Illustrated* swimsuit calendar partially hidden by a coatrack loaded with clothes. The calendar is several years outdated, but Evan has kept it up nonetheless—along with a poster of a blond swimsuit model over his bed. It has been there so long the colors are faded beige and sherbet, and the woman looks slightly ghostly; in fact, it has been there so long, Evan no longer even sees it. He sees it now, however, and panics. *I don't objectify women,* he wants to say, though there isn't a graceful way to drop the line into conversation.

Soci looks at the poster now, as if reading his mind, as if her gaze is directed there by his guilt. She laughs. "Typical," she says.

"What?" Evan says, deciding to play innocent. "Oh, *that.* I just have that there as a joke. You know, like I'm the stereotypical teenage boy who likes stupid, brainless models."

Soci looks at him, smirking. "So, do you?"

"No."

"Yes, you do. All boys do. I'd worry about you if you didn't."

This is a new one. Evan is surprised by her honesty, then worried that he is so transparent; he'd always fancied himself more intelligent and worldly than his peers, slightly above their blatantly boyish tendencies. He may be fifteen, but he often feels closer to twenty. Evidently, he doesn't give that impression to the outside world, though, including Soci.

Soci sits down on the bed, scoots back so that her back is against the wall, her head obscuring the model's upper thighs. "You know what my dad likes to say?" She pauses, turning to Evan, who has positioned himself beside her, close but not too. "He says he thinks there are two kinds of people—those who fulfill stereotypes and those who defy them."

"Oh," says Evan. He processes this, considers it insightful, especially for a factory worker. Immediately, he is horrified by the very stereotype he has drawn about her father. Obviously, the guy knows what he is talking about, and he embodies the latter group.

"So," Soci says. "Which are you?"

Evan frowns, dejected and disappointed in himself. "Well, you seem to think I'm the kind who fulfills stereotypes." He feels like he has been caught by a security camera, unable to hide his actions from a sharp and infallible eye.

"Actually, I don't. I think you are unlike almost all the boys I know, except for the girls-in-bikinis pictures, and really, that doesn't bother me at all."

"It doesn't?"

"No. It just means you like girls. And that's good, right?" She turns to him, smiling, twinkling. Evan laughs, relieved, happy. He leans over and kisses her lightly, afraid to fool around too much. Soci, however, has other ideas. She shoves him down on the bed and climbs on top of him. She is wearing blue jeans, thankfully, and not a miniskirt. Even so, straddling him, pressed against his groin, it is clear that she is not thinking about the impediment of clothes.

"We can't—" he starts to say.

"Can't what?" She is smiling, folding herself over so that her chest is lying against his, and they are face-to-face. Evan feels himself stiffen—all over, in fear more than lust.

"You know."

"What?" she whispers. "You don't have a condom handy?"

Evan stammers, stunned. "No."

"Sure you do—all boys have them, in their wallets or back pockets, right? I bet a hundred dollars you have one somewhere."

Evan shakes his head back and forth on his pillow. Soci sits up, still on top of him, but leaning back now and planting her hands on either side of his hips. She looks a little like a child riding a mechanical pony, disappointed that she doesn't have a quarter to make it move.

"Okay, then," she says. "I understand. Not now, right? Because someone might walk in?"

"Yeah," Evan says. "See, there's always someone barging in—that's just how it is in a big family. Sorry." He adds the latter, hoping to placate her, and hoping the excuse sounds valid.

"I guess. I've never had to worry about that." Soci slides off Evan's body and stands up beside the bed, leaving him lying there like an invalid. "The funny thing is, most boys would jump at the chance to jump a girl's bones. You really are different, aren't you?"

When she leaves a few minutes later, announcing that she had better go in case her father has started to worry—something she has never cared about before—Evan thinks about what she said. He knows that his being different, this time, wasn't exactly a compliment.

• • •

"Y ou don't know me at all," the girl on the television screen is saying petulantly to her boyfriend. He is trying to push her thick hair out of her face so he can look at her and kiss her but she will have none of it. Hallie sits closer to the screen.

"Stop it, that's bad for your eyes," Suzen says. She doesn't want to admit she also cares about what will happen next on the soap opera.

"I like it like this. All you can see is tiny dots."

Suzen knows what she means. She used to do the same thing, watching the screen vibrate. It was mesmerizing. Lately, it is how she feels about life, as if she wears new glasses that tilt the world, sifting it so that each angle and shadow comes into clear view and the picture isn't what it seems. She wonders if anyone else feels that way.

Still. She shoves Hallie with her foot. "Hey, move it, Hal. Besides, you watch way too much TV lately. You know that? It isn't healthy."

"You're not my mother."

Suzen rolls her eyes. Hallie moves back a few feet, obliging, but continues to fixate on the screen. Their mother walks into the den and says, "Hey, I could use some help around here. Okay? Setting the table, cleaning the animal cages. I guess you know who should do what." Suzen notes that her mother never looks at her directly as she speaks. "Dinner's in the oven and Dad and Evan are on their way home. I'm going up to take a quick shower."

Hallie reluctantly unfolds herself from the floor and heads up to her room. Suzen rises from the sofa, sighing, and wanders into the kitchen to gather silverware. Aimee is at the long table, coloring. Her curls hang over her face as she concentrates, the crayons swishing across the paper. Suzen says nothing, just works around her, setting down plates and forks. The phone rings and Aimee looks up, briefly, then back down as Suzen reaches for it.

"Hello? Esme?" a voice asks. Suzen realizes with annoyance that she answers the phone with the exact inflection as her mother. People often mistake her for Esme. She is about to correct the caller, but it occurs to her that it is *him*, and without thinking she begins playing along.

Taking the phone into the pantry, she takes a deep breath and says, "Kevin?"

"Esme?"

"Yes, it's me."

"Wow," says the man on the other end of the receiver, his sigh so close it seems he is in the same room. "I thought you'd never be there. I keep leaving messages, you know." There is a pause, as if he is trying to remember what was so important to begin with, while Suzen waits, wondering how much she should say—she knows that her voice, though it closely echoes Esme's, still has remnants of a girl's lilt in it, and if she is not careful, she could give herself away.

"So, when can I see you?" he says.

"I don't think that is such a good idea," Suzen says levelly.

"Why not? You didn't used to think that," he says, and laughs. There is something wavering in his tone and Suzen wonders if he is drinking.

As if reading her mind, he says, "I don't drink anymore, you know. I don't do anything. I am a bonafide on-the-wagon recovering *add*-ict. You know, AA meetings, lots of bad coffee, one day at a time, and all that. I thought you would be happy to know."

"That's good. I'm glad for you," Suzen says. She is pleased with how steady she sounds.

"So, you didn't answer my question. When are you going to see me? I think you owe me that much, Esme. After all these years."

Years? Suzen cannot believe her ears. Does he mean it has been happening for years, or happened years ago? Though she has been waiting for a sign that her mother is indeed having an affair with Kevin

Wunderhaus, Suzen has found no tangible evidence. There are no love notes, no new lingerie. She rifled through Esme's drawers when she wasn't home, and found only graying cotton underpants with stretched-out elastic. Not a single pair of racy panties or a lacy bra. Yet, she still cannot help but suspect there is more to know. Whenever the phone rings, Esme seems to startle. And now here he is, the man himself, demanding to see her.

Suzen holds the phone so tightly in her grip, her wrist trembles. She forces herself to relax—and think fast. "The kids," she blurts. "My husband." The words sound so strange on her lips. She almost wants to laugh and admit the charade, but she understands there is too much at stake.

"Right, the *husband*. I almost forgot! What's his name again?"

"Malcolm."

"Right, Malcolm. Malcolm the Lucky Bastard. So when do I get to meet him?"

"Kevin—" Suzen says his name as calmly and flatly as she can.

"Never mind. I'll meet him when I'm good and ready. I just hope you are." And he is gone.

There is a soft knock on the pantry door. Suzen opens it and finds Aimee standing there. "Who are you talking to?" she asks.

"No one," Suzen says sharply. Her hands feel ice cold but her cheeks are burning; she presses both palms to her face to cool them. When Esme walks into the room a few moments later, Suzen cannot stand to look at her. She drops a pile of silverware on the end of the table and walks out of the room.

You're home," Esme says, but there is a little edge to her tone. "I thought you would be here forty minutes ago. I think the pasta is about to become glue. And Deirdre is coming for dinner—I told you that."

"Oh, right. Well, Evan's practice went overtime, and I got talking to the coach," Malcolm says. "Did you know he graduated from Michigan the same year I did?" He comes forward to kiss Esme. She turns her cheek to let him, but continues pressing garlic through a metal sieve as if it is surgery. Evan watches Malcolm help himself to a glass of wine. A big glass. He fills it so full he has to lean over like a kid and lap from the rim before he can carry it safely to the table.

"Who's Deirdre?" Evan asks.

"Someone your mother has helped find a job and an apartment," Malcolm says. "I forgot she was coming. I'm sorry. Chianti?" he offers Esme, who scowls.

"Not now. There isn't time."

"Need help?" he tries again.

"No, thanks," Esme says tersely. "It's too late. I think I might have ruined it."

"I'm sure it will be great," Malcolm says. Esme says nothing. Evan can sense that tension is building between his parents, perhaps has been for days. Their anger is like snow, he thinks, quiet and cold, accumulating in the background until you are surprised by its depth.

He wishes he were allowed to drink Chianti, for more reasons than one. He hasn't seen Soci since the other day in his room, when she left abruptly. He tells himself it's a good thing; they could use some time apart. Even so, he finds himself watching the clock, daring himself to call her, but he lets the hours pass without doing anything, waiting for her to act first. Unfortunately, for once she hasn't.

The dinner guest still hasn't arrived, and everyone lingers around the table, not sure whether or not to sit. Evan notices that his sisters seem quieter than usual—Suzen glum, Hallie lost in her own world, Aimee probably praying to the saints. Malcolm continues to sip his wine. When the doorbell rings a moment later, Suzen says, "I'll get it," as if hoping a car is outside waiting to take her away.

"No, I will," Esme says. "That must be Deirdre." When she returns a moment later, it is with a woman trudging reluctantly behind her. She is short and doughy, with beige skin and a matching sweater, carrying a purse the size of carry-on luggage.

Esme puts an arm around the woman's rounded shoulders. "Everyone, this is Deirdre, she just moved here from Detroit." Deirdre, of course, is one of the Troubled Women. Until now, Evan has never seen any of the clients and he wonders if they all look like this, pale and uneasy, with a heap of psychic baggage. He chides himself for his instant prejudice, thinks again about what Soci said and wonders if she was right.

Evan looks at his mother, standing there smiling benignly like Glinda the Good Witch—eager to make wishes come true, to help lost souls find their home, even if it is *her* home. She is clearly in her element.

When everyone is seated, and grace has been uttered (halfheartedly, Evan notices) by Malcolm, there is no noise for a few minutes except the passing of plates and the tinny clink of silverware. Evan watches with curiosity the drama unfold at his own dinner table. It is like a scene from a movie: "The Client who Came to Dinner." He waits to see who will blunder first. (*Blunder*, which originally meant to "stumble around blindly, bumping into things." It is something he is sure he has done himself, with Soci, so he is sympathetic.)

"Would you like a glass of Chianti?" Malcolm asks the woman.

Esme stares wide-eyed at him across the table, a warning look, and Evan suspects that Deirdre from Detroit is a recovering alcoholic. *Oops,* he thinks, watching his father's smile fade.

"No, thank you," Deirdre says, never once looking at Malcolm. It is as if she resents his attempts at congeniality. A man-hater, Evan thinks. She is a man-hater and a recovering addict. It is getting more interesting by the moment.

Suzen and Hallie smile politely and offer Deirdre bread, salad, more sauce. Evan notices the obvious appetite of their guest and he can't help feeling a tug of pity. She probably has a good reason for her biases. But he wishes she did drink a little; it might put color in her pasty cheeks, make her lighten up a little.

To his dismay, he hears his father saying, "Hey, we haven't played our game lately."

"Come on, Dad," Suzen pleads. The others groan.

"Not tonight, hon," Esme says, with a flicker of warning in her eyes.

Deirdre is looking around the table with brows raised, but she seems too polite to ask. Or else, she is too busy eating; Evan notices she hasn't stopped chewing since they sat down.

Aimee explains for her. "It's a game we play at dinner sometimes."

"What kind of game?"

"A word game," Aimee says. "Daddy tells us a word and the first person to say what it means wins. I don't usually win."

Hallie says nothing but watches the family for signs of discord.

Esme is looking at Malcolm again, her expression loud and clear. It is saying, *Not now. We will look pretentious. Don't do it.*

Evan thinks that Malcolm is likely still miffed over Esme's bad mood before dinner. He also can be intentionally stubborn when it comes to linguistics; he invented the game in the first place, he claimed, so that his children would appreciate their native language and its roots. Why should they be ashamed of being intelligent and inquisitive?

Malcolm looks at his wife and takes a bite of garlic bread. For a moment, Evan can't decide whose side to take. After all, it's not as though Malcolm has proposed reading *The Europeans*.

Malcolm's own childhood was steeped in literature, art, and weekly trips to the symphony. His parents did read Henry James aloud at the dinner table, for instance, and thought it better if he continued his studies in the summers instead of assembling window frames or armoires at the local factories. He never had much chance to connect with normal working-class folk, though he still prides himself on his socialist leanings, developed in college and fortified by constant contact with a liberal arts faculty, many of whom never got over the sixties. Evan thinks his father maintains an elevated view of reality, believing that things could always be better, and that people can rise above their slender means and even bad habits, with enough education and moxie; they should try.

Suddenly Hallie comes to their father's aid. "It is sort of fun," she says. "Sometimes we get it right away and sometimes we are all wrong." Ever the moderator.

"Sounds like fun," Deirdre says flatly.

"Okay," Malcolm says amiably. "Here's how it goes. I call out a word and whoever gets it first, gets—more salad." Everyone laughs, even Esme. She passes the bread to Suzen, who plucks a little piece apart on her plate, not eating. "Hey, Suz," Malcolm says, teasing. "How about 'mortify'?"

She rolls her eyes. "The definition of mortify is 'father,' " she says.

Malcolm laughs. "Atta girl. Okay, let's play for real." He looks around the table, then up at the ceiling for effect, as if deep in thought. "Here's a good one: 'arcane'."

He waits. It is silent except for the clinking of silverware on plates. It often happens this way; depending on the general mood, they are either racking their brains or stubbornly refusing to participate. Evan is tempted to speak up, to show off, as he remembers *arcane* from a vocabulary test last week; when Malcolm quizzed him, Evan had impressed him by knowing the meaning as well as the Latin root. A chip off the old block. He decides to say nothing, to see if anyone else answers first.

It is Deirdre who speaks up. "Arcane, ain't that where they play video games? You know, like at the mall?"

The silence is harsh, like bad lighting, and it falls on Malcolm the hardest. Evan sees that his mother is glowering at his father, and Suzen is twirling pasta around and around on her fork. Finally Malcolm laughs a little, tries for a combination of self-deprecation and gentle candor.

"Close," he says. "You got 'arcade' right. I actually said 'ar*cane*,' but maybe I didn't say it very clearly. It sounds very much the same. It means, uh, mysterious. Hidden, secret."

"Oh. Whatever," Deirdre says. "I wasn't sure."

"That's okay," Malcolm says brightly. "You still get extra salad for trying." He passes the bowl over and she accepts it as if she doesn't know what else to do. Evan watches as his father digs himself a deeper hole and peers in. "Hey, now that I think about it, arcades *are* kind of secret and hidden, aren't they? They're usually dark, and the games are sort of complicated and mysterious, right?"

He looks at Evan, clearly hoping he will help him out. Malcolm took him to an arcade once, for his twelfth birthday, with three of his friends. It was a horrible experience. Even as the one who thought he had wanted the experience, Evan found himself in a panic. Rowdy kids and derelict characters wove in and out, and the lighting was dim, the noise at a decibel level that had to be dangerous. He kept losing track of his father and friends, afraid that he was going to be lured away by drug dealers or some other evil element. He felt like he was in a bad dream and he kept winding around among the pinball and video machines, looking for the bright light of the exit sign. Afterward, Malcolm took the boys to a fast food restaurant and Evan was struck by how suddenly sane and cheerful it seemed, familiar as home.

"Anyone want dessert?" Esme is asking, standing up and starting to collect empty plates. Evan thinks it funny how she does her best to be cheerleader of the pack, deflecting bad moods and ill humor, placating and distracting. Suzen rises to start, removing glasses, and Hallie automatically gathers dirty silverware. Aimee, of course, is oblivious enough not to grasp the tension in the air, though it is thick, snow falling on their heads. She bounces a little on the chair beside Malcolm.

"Hey, Dad, I learned a new word at school today."

"Really? What was it?" he asks eagerly.

"Motherfucker."

*P*riceless, thinks Suzen, standing at the door with a handful of glasses. She notices the way mouths drop open, the uncomfortable laughter. The Parental Unit apparently is trying to decide how to react—Reprimand Aimee? Pretend it didn't happen?—while the word hangs in the air like a smoke bomb. Malcolm and Esme so obviously want to blink it away, but there it is. *Motherfucker.* The vulgar syllables chirped from their child's lips. And Deirdre the dinner guest is guffawing, like it is the best thing she has witnessed in a long while.

They asked for it, Suzen thinks. For the past ten minutes she has sat in abject discomfort, watching her father make a fool of himself, embarrassing them. And her mother, the martyr, falling over herself to keep everyone happy, acting like everything's *fine, fine, fine!* Putting on a show for the guest, as if they are the Perfect Family, welcoming in the lost and needy.

The word is still hanging over the table, but Esme is overreacting, her distraction tactics are at an all-time high: "Aimee, why don't you take Deirdre to the yard for a few minutes, show her your pumpkins. Oops, watch out for Edgar. Suzen, could you take him outside, around the block? He hasn't been walked today, poor old dog. Hallie, start with the dishwasher, and Evan, it's your turn for the trash, okay?"

The others obey slowly, shaking their heads—*What's all the fuss?*—taking charge of their assigned tasks. Aimee actually is holding Deirdre's hand as she leads her to the backyard. They stand outside in a halo of porch light as Aimee waves her arms around, showing off a patch of garden that Suzen helped her plant. Suzen bends to attach the leash to Edgar's collar, though the dog is spread flat as a throw rug on the floor. As she tugs him to his wobbly feet, Suzen sees that her father is busying himself at the table, distractedly folding soiled paper napkins. She feels a little sorry for him.

"Hey, Dad," she says. "Want to walk with us?"

Malcolm turns to look at her and shrugs. Then he sets down the napkins and follows her out the door, hands in his pockets. "Come on, Edgar, you can do it," he says.

When they are a block from home, engulfed in the comforting silence of the evening, all the houses closed against the chilly air, the only sound the rustle of leaves stirred by their feet, Malcolm chuckles a little. "I guess I asked for it, huh?"

"Well, maybe you should be proud," Suzen says, deadpan. "You know—that Aimee has an appreciation for language."

Malcolm laughs, hard. He bends down to pet Edgar's ears, as the dog has sat down to rest.

"Dad—" Suzen begins. Malcolm glances up, waiting. She wants to tell him about the phone call, but she stands planted on the sidewalk, halfway between wanting to punish Esme and not wanting to hurt her father. Telling him what he may not even know would tip open a can of something potentially flammable. And she knows that a little information is a dangerous thing, liable to scorch the innocent. She waits. "Never mind," she says.

"We should get back," Malcolm says, standing and taking the leash out of Suzen's hands. He pulls Edgar out of the nest of leaves he has settled into and the dog reluctantly arches to his feet. "I don't know how long this old boy can hang on," Malcolm says sadly, "before he gets called to the sweet hereafter."

S he's an angel," Aimee whispers.
    "Who is?" Evan asks.

"That girl. Deeder."

"It's *Deirdre*," Evan corrects. "What are you talking about?"

Apparently, at Sunday school, Aimee has been taught that anyone can be an angel in disguise, and that one should be kind to strangers, *just in case*. An interesting philosophy, Evan thinks, though he isn't sure how theologically sound it is. Nor how plausible. He looks at Deirdre—who is on the back porch talking to Esme, smoking a cigarette—and considers the notion of her otherworldliness. He tries to picture wings folded flat against her back, underneath her lumpen sweater the color of Band-Aids. She is trying to blow her smoke away from Esme, but the wind is carrying it in a little cloud directly toward her face. Esme, to her credit, does not move away, but continues to smile.

"I think she's nice," Aimee is saying.

"You've known her for about five minutes."

Aimee shrugs. She is eating a second bowl of ice cream, and no one has stopped her. Evan notices she has poured enough chocolate syrup over it for three servings.

"I don't think she's an angel, Aimee," Evan says quietly. "No offense."

"She might be."

Evan decides to drop the argument; what's the point trying to convince a five-year-old that angels don't drop in for dinner with giant purses full of unfiltered cigarettes? He sees Deirdre now in the driveway, grinding her heel into the grass, looking up at the sky. Esme hugs her good-bye, and then waves as Deirdre ambles to her car and disappears, probably on her way to minister to other lost souls, Evan thinks wryly.

At school, Evan searches for Soci, worried that something is wrong. Since the day she came over, he has seen little of her. She still smiles and touches his arm when they pass in the hall, but she doesn't linger. She no longer suggests breaking out of school together and Evan suspects that she is beginning to tire of him, and he watches for signs that she has found someone else. So far, she seems to wander the halls alone.

In fourth-period homeroom, she still sits in front of him, and turns around to acknowledge him sweetly, then turns back, as if deeply engrossed in the teacher's daily lecture on developing positive study habits. Evan stares at her long smooth neck, the hair just covering the nape like down. He knows how soft it is now, and how it feels to run his fingers along her skin, her jawline, to kiss her lips, to feel her tongue inside his mouth. He remembers the pressure of her body atop his on his bed and wonders if he made a mistake, making an excuse. Maybe he should have just followed through; maybe it was time. He's nearly sixteen, after all. Not just a kid.

Yet, that is exactly what he is. A kid. Lately it feels that instead of growing he is tumbling backward, feeling less and less sure of himself. He wonders how experienced Soci really is, how many guys she has been with. He wanted to ask her that day, "Have you ever—?" but he feared she would laugh, making it clear that she had, and that he was a hopeless novice.

Today, she doesn't show up for fourth period and Evan sits through the class, agonizing over her absence. He skips soccer practice in the afternoon and walks home, slowly, feeling a part of his life is over. He convinces himself that he doesn't really care; it wasn't meant to be; she was too much for him—or worse, he wasn't enough for her. He is desperate to know, to make it up to her, however she wants him to.

When he trudges up the back steps, he finds his mother and Aimee rocking on the porch swing. Esme smiles when she sees him.

"How's school, Ev? You look like you had a bad day."

He shrugs. "Um, it was okay."

"Girl trouble?"

He laughs, nervously. "I guess." He stands on the top step, waiting for his mother to interrogate him.

"Soci, right?"

"Yeah."

Aimee lights up then. "I know her! She's nice. We played hide-and-seek."

"Really?" Esme says. She looks at Evan quizzically. Then she turns to Aimee, "Why don't you run inside and get yourself a little snack, okay?"

"Okay," Aimee says obediently. It occurs to Evan that she never argues anymore. It's almost spooky. When she has gone inside, Esme motions Evan to sit beside her. He knows what's coming.

"Evan, I know you're really smitten with this girl—"

He laughs inadvertently, at her choice of words. *Smitten: to be inflicted by a heavy blow.* "Sorry," he says.

"—but I'm still concerned. I get the impression that she is a bit of an instigator. I mean, I don't think you would have skipped school if she hadn't encouraged you, right?"

Not this again, he thinks. The truth is, he skipped class before on his own, out of sheer boredom, to go to the Esquire. He doesn't feel inclined to share this information, however, so he shrugs. Besides, he thinks, slightly offended, Esme doesn't even know Soci, and she is treating Evan like one of her troubled clients, someone she can help straighten out, set on the right path—though she really has no idea which path he is on, nor even if it's the wrong one.

"I just want you to be careful, so that you don't get hurt."

Too late, Evan thinks, still silent, as he rocks the swing, glowering, and Esme looks off into the distance, seemingly lost in her thoughts. Evan starts to get up, discomfited by the conversation, and eager to escape. But she holds him there with a hand on his arm.

She looks into his eyes and says, with some emotion, "I know how it is to be attracted to someone who is a little wild. And you always think you can have an effect." She pauses, leaving Evan to wonder what—whom—she is talking about so cryptically. Obviously not Malcolm. "Anyway," she continues, "people generally are who they have always been, and you can't change or save them. You have to be true to yourself, first. Do you know what I mean?"

Evan nods, thinking, *No.* "I guess so."

"Well, believe it or not, your father and I weren't born yesterday; in fact, we weren't even just born when we met. We both have lived lives, been in and out of love, so we know what it's like. *I* know. And I know you think you're different, but everyone goes through this for the first time. Just don't let it take over your life."

By "it" he knows she means *her,* and he stands up. "I have homework."

"Just think about what I said," she says, but already Evan has forgotten every word. He heads inside and closes himself in his room. He finds the phone number Soci handed him weeks ago, scribbled on the back of a test she failed. He dials the phone in the upstairs hallway and waits, but not for long, as she answers on the second ring.

"Evan?"

"Yeah, it's me. Are you okay?"

"Of course—why?" Her voice sounds small as if she is holding the phone away.

"I just thought—I didn't see you at school today. And lately, you've been—I mean, I feel like you're mad at me." It feels good to say it out loud, the fear he has held, like dropping an overloaded backpack to the floor.

"No, of course not!" She says. "I just took a mental-health day, you know, to catch up on sleep and soaps." She laughs. "But Evan, I'm not mad at you. I've just been doing a lot of thinking."

"About what?"

"About us."

"Yeah, me, too," Evan says, wondering what she has concluded.

"I think we have to get the hell out of here," Soci says flatly. Evan holds the phone to his ear, waiting to find the courage to answer. "I'm serious, Evan," she says. "We really need to get lost."

Suzen stares at the motel and wills Kevin to come out. She wants him to come out so she can tell him to get lost. She considers her words. "Leave us alone, dammit" or "Stay the hell away from my mother." Cursing helps. It is a kind of verbal yoga, practiced silently: breathe in, breathe out, curse, relax. It is comforting forming the nasty syllables, fuming and venting. Sometimes, like now, it is a way to allay anxiety. Of course, she won't actually talk to him. She just wants to see what he looks like.

Maybe her mother simply had a flirtation, or (horrible though it might be) just a one-night stand. Maybe she acted on impulse, agreed without thinking to meet a man in a motel. Like someone in a novel, slipping from her daily life to become, for awhile, someone else. Suzen tries not to picture it but she can't help it—she sees her mother standing at the foot of a chenille-covered bed, shedding her long skirt, her sensible shoes, smiling wickedly at a man lying there, waiting. But what if it didn't end there? What if Kevin were a stalker, a crazy person who couldn't let her go and is planning to wreak havoc on their lives? Burn down their house? Abduct a pet? Just yesterday, Suzen came into the kitchen to find Hallie nervously pointing at the back door and describing a strange man who appeared and then disappeared.

"He was just there ten seconds ago," Hallie said. "I didn't imagine it."

"What did he look like?" Suzen asked, trying not to sound alarmed.

Hallie shrugged. "Tall, kind of weird. He was waving at me to open the door but I didn't know who he was. When I turned around to find Mom or someone, he was gone."

Suzen opened the back door gingerly, as if the man might jump out at her. She braced herself, but no one was there. "You never saw him before?" she asked, closing the door and bolting it.

"No. Maybe he had the wrong house?" Hallie said anxiously, waiting for Suzen to take charge, reassure her. Apparently Evan's tutorship in the absurdity of horror films had not had the desired effect; Hallie was jumpier, scared out of her wits by strange noises, dark rooms, people (real or imagined) lurking at the back door. Suzen wondered if it were just Hallie's imagination—or if the man trespassing on their porch might have been Kevin Wunderhaus. She was uneasy, but didn't know what to do about it. Then she remembered the phone number she still possessed, and the name of the motel.

Now she is sitting in her mother's van outside the Imperial Motor Lodge, which belies its title with a carpet of litter lining the sidewalk in front of the row of doors. The office has a broken window, patched with plywood and duct tape. Suzen remains in the idling car, considering. She looks at the dilapidated building, scanning the doors for the room number he offered over the phone, and she sees that it is on the end of the second floor. The balcony has an iron railing full of gaps, like broken teeth. All of the windows are draped, sealed from view. There is no sign of life in the scruffy courtyard, no cars in the parking lot. Suzen wonders if perhaps Kevin has moved on. Part of her thinks she may have overreacted—there is no proof, just a cryptic conversation that revealed nothing certain except that Kevin once knew Esme—and if Suzen simply asked her mother about it, maybe there would be a logical explanation.

As she sits, contemplating, she sees an elderly Chinese woman come out of the office and begin sweeping the sidewalk. The rain has ceased for a little while and the sidewalk is puddled and littered. Beyond the old woman, in the bleak courtyard, a concrete fountain spouts water in short, feeble bursts. The woman stops sweeping and stares at it, perhaps thinking it needs work—or remembering her other life, far away, where everything was green and lush, water bubbling from a stream behind her house. As she stands there, staring, the sky opens up again and rains down on her, though the woman doesn't move, or even appear to have noticed. Unaccountably sad, Suzen drives away.

Evan is waiting on the porch at Max's house when his friend drives up. Max is five months older than Evan and thus has his license already. He drives like an old man, however, slow and cautious, with both hands on the wheel at all times. Evan once derided him, but Max's only response was, "Just wait till you get out there—then you'll see what it's like. It's not as easy as it looks, man. People are maniacs on the road. They hardly stop at stop signs and half of them act like they're on the way to the ER. I'm serious, you really have to watch out."

The windshield wipers are flapping back and forth at full speed, and Evan laughs, thinking it looks like something out of a cartoon. Finally, Max parks the car in the driveway and gets out, after checking twice to see if he has shut the driver's door properly. Soaking wet, he joins Evan on the porch.

"Hello, Maxwell," says Evan.

"Fuck you," says Max, who loathes his given name. "Isn't my mom or anyone home?"

"I don't know," says Evan. "I didn't check."

"Why not? You could've waited inside, moron." Max tries the doorknob, finds it locked, and then bends down to fish underneath the doormat for a key. Evan wonders how many houses provide such easy access. "So, what's up?" he asks, pushing open the door and going in first. Evan follows.

"I just wanted to ask you something." He pauses. "It's personal."

Max is suddenly interested, shaking loose his book bag and coat, dripping rain all over the floor, then treading muddily through it, oblivious. He is wearing a T-shirt with a silk-screened picture of a brain, above which reads the message, *Don't make me use this.* He sits down at the kitchen table, forgoing a snack, which is highly unusual, and waits for Evan to speak. "So?"

Evan sits. "It's Soci."

"Yeah, well, I figured that much."

"She wants me to run away with her."

"Really?" Max laughs. Stops. "You're not kidding?"

"No. She wants me to go to Chicago with her for a day, maybe two, without telling anyone. Especially our parents. Or parent, in her case. She only has her dad, you know." Evan thinks the latter isn't relevant, yet somehow it is. He has never met Soci's father, and more and more he wonders what he is like, and if their relationship is as strained as she implies—or if she likes to complain for dramatic effect.

"Yeah, I know about her dad," Max says. "Pretty wild, huh." He gets up and goes to the refrigerator, rustles noisily around.

"What do you mean?"

"You know—Conrads'," Max says from behind the door.

"Yeah, so? He works at the headlight factory. So, what?" Evan says a shade defensively, thinking about Soci's comment the first time she mentioned her father, and how he knew she was right, that he judged him based on where he worked, though he didn't mean to do it.

"You mean he *owns* the headlight factory," Max says, emerging with a plate of soggy-looking chocolate cake on a platter, crowned with toothpicks and a draping of cellophane. He sets it on the table between them and uncovers the cake, digs in with his fingers.

"Owns? What are you talking about?"

"He owns the fucking factory, Ev. He's that rich guy that was in the paper a few weeks ago because he won some award for Most Altruistic Workplace or something. They live in a goddamn mansion."

"You don't know what you're talking about. Soci lives in a trailer—she told me. And when did you start swearing so much?"

Max shrugs. "Just experimenting with it, to see how it fits."

"It doesn't. You sound like a bad actor."

"Anyway, I just know what I know. And I'm sure it doesn't matter if she's rich or homeless or whatever, if you're in love. But the thing is, it's kind of weird that you're going out with her and you didn't even know that."

Evan says nothing, feels his face warm and redden. He wonders how long Max has known about Soci, and why he didn't say anything sooner. Most of all, though, he wonders why Soci lied, if she did.

Max sits quietly, his fingers slick with chocolate frosting. He licks them one by one, like a small child. "Maybe she was afraid if you found out she was rich, you'd be all weird about it," he says helpfully. "Maybe she didn't want that to matter."

"Yeah, maybe. But maybe you're wrong, maybe it's another Andersson."

Max shrugs. "So, are you going to run away with her? Is she worth it?"

Evan doesn't know how to answer either question. He keeps hoping he'll receive some sign, from God or someone, telling him what to do.

On Sunday, Suzen realizes it has been ages since she's been to church. After Aimee's accident, the family stayed close to home for a few weeks, and then it seemed they lost the habit. But Aimee is dying to go. She told Suzen she misses the organ music, and the hand-bell choir "that sounds like sleigh bells" (*Here comes Santa Claus, here comes Santa Claus, right down Santa Claus Lane!*), and Children's Worship, where Aimee sometimes gets to rearrange the flannel board for the storyteller. They drink juice in little paper cups and sing songs and praise God. *Hallelujah!* Suzen thinks how simple and clear Aimee's faith seems, pure as water, how funny that she looks forward to church. Suzen has always dreaded it, ever since she was small—Sunday mornings rushed and filled with rancor as the family argues for time in the bathroom, and then nothing is ironed, and good shoes are missing, and they are going to be late again.

There have been a few times over the years, however, that Suzen actually found herself transported at church. Sometimes it was the combination of heartfelt singing, and hushed breathing during silent prayers, and the minister pausing to sip water from a glass on the podium, earnest in his desire to tell them something that mattered. Sometimes it was simply the wind knocking bare branches against the stained-glass windows like a signal, or sunlight pouring through them, scattering shards of color across the carpeted aisles. Sometimes Suzen stared up at the impossibly vaulted ceiling and sensed something spiritual, unnameable, moving there. Rarely has she listened to an entire sermon, just fragments gathering in her consciousness, so that she is sure she possesses a very eclectic notion of faith.

This morning she does not believe the elements will work to transport her, though she is willing to try; she gets out of bed slowly and stumbles to the bathroom. No one else seems to be awake but suddenly Aimee appears at her side.

"Can you help me with this?" She is standing in her underwear and nylon slip, holding a pink dress with a scalloped collar, which is attached to her head where her curls are tangled in the buttons. Suzen gently loosens the hair, but accidentally pulls some of it from Aimee's scalp. She sees her sister's eyes water a little, but she does not yell out.

"Sorry," Suzen says.

"It's okay," Aimee says sweetly.

"You're up awfully early," Suzen says, reaching for her toothbrush.

"I want to be ready for church," Aimee says simply, smoothing her dress and plucking a fuzz from the knee of her white tights. Suzen sees her walk slowly toward their parents' closed door and knock lightly. There is a muffled response and Aimee opens the door and goes in. Suzen hears Esme saying, "Oh, honey. We aren't going to church today."

Suzen spits and rinses, relieved. She can go back to sleep.

"Again?" shouts Aimee, incredulous.

"We'll have church here at home," Esme says calmly, as if it has just occurred to her. "Won't that be kind of fun? You know, we can worship God anywhere."

"I want to go to church!" Aimee yells, apparently not caring who she wakes up.

When Evan wakes up, he is still tangled in a dream of Soci on a high wire, laughing and waving cigarettes like torches from each outstretched hand, while he looks on in horror, struggling to maintain his balance and reach for her before she falls. His heart pounds and he forces his limbs to relax. *It was just a dream,* he tells himself. He no longer knows if he is falling in love or falling down a dark hole.

In spite of the harrowing dream, he gets out of bed reluctantly. He is pretty sure that today the family will be heading dutifully to church; after all, it has been weeks, and they have always been a fairly regular churchgoing family. Evan even used to sing in the youth choir. Hallie was in the handbell choir until she dropped her bell last year and was too mortified to return. He almost wants to go to church for a change. If they were Catholics he could slip into a confessional booth and clear his conscience. *Forgive me, father, for I have sinned. It has been twelve weeks since my last confession. I have lusted after a woman in my heart. But I haven't gone very far. Yet. How much is too far? Is Chicago too far, for instance? I kind of need to know.*

They are not Catholics but Presbyterians, and Evan knows no one he could ask such questions, especially not at church. Theirs is a large, congenial congregation of mostly middle-class intellectuals raised in the faith, along with a few Born Agains. Evan likes the Born Agains, the way they come to church so shiny and scrubbed and excited, Bibles clutched in one hand, greeting everyone as if it is the best day of their lives. He has the feeling they believe that each day *is* the best, the first day of the rest, and so on.

One of these, a spindly young man named Ralphie, is a hugger. He throws his skinny arms around each person he greets in the fellowship hall, and Evan has been squeezed in his clenches more than once. It has become sort of a game between him and Suzen, to try to hide from Happy Ralphie before he ambushes them; whoever is caught and hugged first owes the other sibling a dollar. They are collecting the money to put in the offering plate, to assuage their consciences. Evan misses playing the Happy Ralphie game, and as he gets dressed, he contemplates how he will outwit him today. Just in case, though, he tucks a dollar bill into his dress pants pocket.

"We're not going," Suzen says, yawning, as they meet in the hall-way. She is still in her pajamas, oversized men's flannels, and her slept-on ponytail is sprouting like a fountain from the side of her head.

"Again?" Evan asks. "What now?" He is surprised by how disappointed he feels. Usually he groans each Sunday morning, pressing his face farther into his pillow until the third or fourth warning from his parents. And when he gets to church, he struggles to stay awake between rousing hymns and droning sermon. Reverend Milland is not exactly a bore, but it is hard to follow even his enthusiastic train of thought for twenty minutes. Yet, now that it has been four weeks since they attended a service, he is starting to worry a little. What if they get excommunicated?

"Mom says we're doing 'home church' instead," says Suzen, loping down the stairs ahead of Evan. "I think she's actually serious this time."

When they've missed the real thing due to chicken pox quarantines or blizzard conditions—or the numerous times everyone's been too tired to make the effort to go—Evan has heard his parents announce "home church" as an alternative, probably to relieve their own guilt. Rarely, however, have they followed through on the idea. Usually, Malcolm or Esme suggests they "have some quiet time," meaning spiritual meditation, but everyone simply lies about, reading the Sunday paper and eating an ongoing breakfast until an invisible deadline seems to pass and life resumes its normal secular pace.

When they get downstairs, Evan sees that, indeed, chairs have been arranged in a semicircle, festive candles lighted on the coffee table. He can smell biscuits baking and coffee brewing. In the kitchen, Aimee is prancing about in her best pink dress like a crazed fairy, her curls loose and wild. Malcolm wanders in and pours himself a cup of coffee and sips it quickly. He is dressed casually, as if he might be going out to rake leaves, though it's still raining, as it has for a week, like a plague.

"Nice outfit, Dad," Evan says.

"Thanks. I picked it out myself, from the hamper." He drains his cup, sets it down.

"When's church?" Aimee asks.

Malcolm is looking down at his stained sweatshirt. "Church?" he asks.

"I told Aimee we'd do church at home today, okay?" Esme nods toward the table, where Aimee now sits, bowed over a plate with a biscuit and a powdered donut, praying silently.

Evan understands then. They are staying home, making these elaborate concessions, just to avoid the spectacle—Aimee returned from the threshold of the pearly gates, announcing her visions to the congregation. What if Aimee leapt up during the sermon to yell, "Amen! Hallelujah!" Or during the coffee hour, accosting passersby with her amazing tale.

A imee is ringing a little silver bell, signaling that church is to commence. Suzen watches from the sofa, feeling like the living room has turned into a stage, each family member about to act out his or her usual role. Her mother will go on playing the half-present center of the household, her father the peripheral professor, Hallie the sulky preteen, Evan providing comic relief, Aimee the kindergarten-saint.

She is ringing the little silver bell again and again, and Suzen is beginning to grow annoyed. "Okay, we get it, Aim. That's enough already."

"It's the church bell," Aimee says cheerfully.

"Well, we're all here now so you can stop it, okay?" she adds more gently, trying not to lose her temper. After all, Aimee has been nothing but good-natured since she got hit on the head.

Suzen curls up on one end of the sofa, closest to the fire that has just begun to crackle. She thinks of Mary on a cold Sunday morning like this, probably sitting beside her own fireplace, drinking tea and reading the paper, breezing through a crossword, watching the storm over the lake. She has only seen Mary once in the past week, on Monday, as it has rained every day and thus, work on the maze has been postponed. There was little to do at the nursery so Mary told her to take a little time off.

"You have been such a good sport," Mary told Suzen. "I've never had such a committed apprentice." Suzen felt herself buoyed by that one comment for days.

Now she sits in the living room with her oversized family as they pretend to have church, and she resents that she has no choice in the matter. She wishes she were anywhere else. She wishes she were already grown and gone, like Mary, on her own.

Evan, sitting across from her, slyly tugs a folded dollar bill from his pocket and shows her, then tucks it back in, and Suzen laughs in spite of herself.

Aimee is now hopping up and down on one foot in a slightly deranged manner and singing, "If you're happy and you know it, clap your hands!"

"Aimee, I think we'll save that one for later," their mother says.

Aimee does not hear. She has moved on to the "stomp your feet" verse and is stomping ferociously. Malcolm grabs her hand firmly and pulls her to a seat between him and Esme. He tells Aimee something about being joyful but also reverent, though Suzen is only half-listening. She is flipping idly through the Bible, silently reading the parts she likes, the Song of Solomon in particular. The words spring from the page: *Behold, you are beautiful, my love, behold, you are beautiful . . . Your lips are like a scarlet thread, and your mouth is lovely—*

"Suzen, how about reading a psalm," her father is saying.

"All right. Fine," Suzen says. She looks down at the Bible, flips more tissuey pages, and reads, "The Twenty-third Psalm. 'The Lord is my shepherd, I shall not want. She makes me lie down in green pastures. She leads me beside still waters; she restores my soul. She leads me in the paths of righteousness for her name's sake.' "

There is a moment of silence, then Aimee says, "She changed the words."

"So?" says Suzen, defensively. "I just changed the he to she. Who says God is a man? God is just—God."

"*Is* God a man?" Hallie asks. "All the songs in church are about a he."

"Yeah, that's why it's called a hymnal," Evan says.

"Very funny," Malcolm says, smirking. Hallie laughs, getting it.

"Jesus is a man, you know," Aimee says. As if she knows first-hand—*from when she went to heaven,* Suzen thinks derisively. Suddenly she can barely tolerate her sister's strange piety.

"It doesn't really matter," her father is saying. "Let's move on. Who else wants to read? Evan?"

"I don't know if I should," Evan says drolly. "I mean, I am a *guy*."

"Come on, everyone," Esme says firmly. "Let's quit joking around here."

"Sorry," Evan says, opening the Bible Suzen eagerly has handed over. Before Evan can read, though, Aimee makes a pronouncement.

"Suzen thinks girls are better than boys."

Suzen gapes at her. "What are you talking about? I never said that!"

"Yes, you did," Aimee insists. "You told me. You like girls better. You said so."

Suzen feels her face flush. She remembers Aimee asking her the other day whom she was going to marry and answering, "No one." But when her little sister pressed her on the subject, she only said something about not needing a man; she cannot recall confessing anything else, nor how Aimee inferred such a thing.

But then, of course, her sister has only parroted what she thought she heard. It is only by accident that Aimee has guessed what Suzen herself has not seen staring her in the face. She thinks of the weeks with Mary—and Soci—and her eagerness to be near either of them. But always, it has been Mary who is in her thoughts, whom she cannot wait to see each day. And when she does, her heart flips a little, like a fish tipped from its bowl.

On Monday, when Suzen came early, before the nursery opened, Mary turned to her, beaming. "Oh good, you're here," she'd said, and Suzen felt herself go warm. "Want something to eat?" Mary asked. "I brought in some scones from home. I made them myself, believe it or not."

Suzen took the food offered and bit down, her mouth full of the cakey crumbs, and the knowledge that Mary baked it, cut it into pieces, carried it to her. *Here, have some.* As if it truly were a part of herself, a kind of sacrament. Suzen smiled shyly, wiping her mouth as if she had been kissed. *Your lips are like a scarlet thread, and your mouth is lovely.*

She can feel her family's curious eyes are on her, she can feel them without looking back. "Well, you do like girls better, don't you?" Aimee is asking, head tilted, awaiting an answer.

Suzen stands and starts out of the room, but pauses at the doorway, staring at her family, into their stunned silence. Churning with confusion she blurts it out, "So, I'm a *dyke!* So what!" She turns and runs up the stairs. A dramatic exit, surprise ending to the play. No one expected it, not even Suzen herself.

E van stares at the space in the doorway just vacated by his sister. He is stunned, and yet, strangely, not fully surprised.

The pieces fit now. The lack of boyfriends, her music only female folk singers, her door covered with quotes by women authors. Evan had attributed these to the feminist values many girls latch onto; it never occurred to him that Suzen might be—*gay.* He is not homophobic, he reminds himself. In fact, he thinks, *some of my best friends are gay.* Well, not really. He only knows one for sure, Frederick Watley, who lives with a man named Kent, and Evan has not thought much about homosexuality in terms of women or girls. Or his sister.

Maybe it is all a mistake. Maybe Aimee misunderstood and Suzen is just tired and ornery and sick of the family in general. She said what she knew would shock them—just an excuse to exit the stilted home-church atmosphere.

"What's a dyke?" Hallie asks.

"Never mind," Esme says.

Aimee rings her little bell. "What about church?" she demands.

"How about later," Malcolm says. He looks bewildered, and Evan wishes he were anywhere but here with his shell-shocked parents, his confused sisters. He watches the rain pour down the windows and wishes he had never gotten out of bed.

Suzen lies on her unmade bed, tense, fists clenched. She is mortified by what she has just done—spilled a secret she hadn't known she possessed. Now she feels she has lost something, but what? At the same time, she feels a sudden surge of relief. She thinks of the unabashed lust of *Song of Solomon,* and how it seemed meant for her, as if it were written just for her, like a sign from God Him(or Her)self: *This is who you are.* The old skin has molted away, fresh new feathers gleaming. Suzen doesn't fully recognize this other self yet. She turns over onto her stomach and breathes into her mattress.

Keeping her eyes closed, she wills herself to disappear, to slip into her imaginary landscape of Great Britain, over vales and hills and through cobbled villages. She finds a little thatched cabin, sends herself up into a soft hayloft, hidden from view. No one can find her here, in her head, she thinks, like when she was a child, covering her eyes, thinking that sufficient.

There is a knock on her door. It's her mother, she can tell by the rap, insistent yet not too loud. Suzen pictures her on the other side, like a television mother, poised to dispense her predictable wisdom and advice. Suzen does not want to let her in. She isn't ready for it. The door opens anyway. Esme stands there, holding her arms around herself, holding herself together. Suzen looks at her, looks away. What could Esme possibly know about her, what she is going through?

"May I come in?" Esme says, coming in and shutting the door without waiting for a response. She comes closer, but thankfully doesn't sit down.

"You know," she says. "When I was your age, I had a flirtation with another girl, a senior. I guess it was just an experiment, really, but I think I know how you feel. It's perfectly normal." Suzen gapes at her. "I just meant, I don't know *exactly* what is going on with you, but I just wanted you to know it's okay."

"Gee, thanks," Suzen says scornfully. "Thanks for your permission."

"Suzen," Esme says, her tone a little desperate. It occurs to Suzen that her mother doesn't really believe what Suzen said, when she announced it to the family. She obviously thinks it is just a phase. *An experiment.*

"Listen, you don't know anything about this," Suzen says. "It's my own business. And everyone can just stay out of it, okay? Besides, you have your own problems, don't you."

Esme sits on the bed beside Suzen, so that Suzen is forced to move over. "What is that supposed to mean?" Esme asks.

"Nothing," Suzen says, not looking her mother in the eyes. *What about Kevin?* she wants to demand. She wants to tell her mother that she has spoken to him on the phone, and that she knows where he is staying—all she wants to know from Esme is what, exactly, he means to her. Yet, she doesn't want to hear excuses, defensive explanations. She turns away again and says nothing, waiting for Esme to give up and leave.

When she does, finally, Suzen thinks about what her mother said, revealing that she once had a flirtation with another girl. What did that mean? Did they actually do anything? She wishes she had dared ask. She pictures her mother entwined with another girl, their tight lips pressed together.

The swimsuit model's lips are pressed into a pout as round as a Lifesaver. Her nipples are erupting from the tight fabric, and Evan squints to make the picture over his bed appear even more lifelike. He is filled with desire at the slightest provocation these days, a sudden roiling in his groin, an electrification in all of his nerve endings. Sometimes it makes him twitch, jerk his legs as with cramps. Some of his friends going through the same thing are more matter-of-fact, if not outright blunt. "I got the biggest boner yesterday," one of them will announce over lunch. They all laugh, and chime in with similar anecdotes. Except for Evan, who blushes but never confesses.

Lying on his bed, he is focusing on the model to take his mind off his warring troubles: Soci (who may not be who she seems to be) plotting their certain ruin in Chicago, and his sister metamorphosing overnight into a lesbian—not in that particular order. Soci is the last thing on his mind right now. Since Sunday's stunning revelation, Evan has avoided talking to Suzen about it—or anything else other than superficialities. He doesn't know what he should say, though he can't help thinking, *My sister is a dyke.* His family prides itself on being open-minded, tolerant, progressive—but this is more than Evan was prepared for.

He misses the way it was before he knew. Though they haven't been especially close, he and Suzen have always been able to maintain a friendly, if distant, sibling rapport. Now Evan is reluctant to be near Suzen, as if she is harboring a mysterious virus. *Maybe it is just a phase,* he tells himself again.

He thinks of how, when he first met Soci, he was entirely distracted by her every move. Soci still distracts him, no doubt about that, but he is no longer obsessed, as if it were just a phase he passed through. In fact, now he is wary. He finds fantasy a more comfortable place than reality, when it comes to girls.

He turns back to the poster girl's nipples and suddenly wonders what Suzen thinks when she passes his room. Does she pause, too, to admire the woman's perfect curves, her moist pout, the indentation of muscle at her hip, the shadow between her bikinied thighs? Does she think the same things he thinks? He swallows and stares, bewildered and overwhelmed.

Suddenly, she is there in his doorway. Suzen looks at him lying there, then points to the poster. "You really should get rid of that thing, you know," she says accusingly. "It's degrading."

"Degrading?"

"Yeah, you know. It makes women look like empty sex objects."

Evan has never spoken about sex to his sister before. He has never heard her utter the word. Nor has he ever seen her stand there that way, defiant. Like a grown woman. He wonders if she has grown taller, or if it is just the combined effect of looking at her from a horizontal position and her newly intimidating status.

"I know what you're thinking," she says then, coming into the room and shutting his door behind her. She crosses her arms over her chest, her own hidden nipples. "You think I'm a freak or something—"

"No, I don't," Evan says, sitting up and trying to look his sister in the eyes.

"Everyone thinks I'm, like, a 'lesbo' or something awful." She falters, wipes her eyes. "I don't know exactly what I am. But it's no one's fucking business, really. Not this family's or anyone else's."

Evan cannot bear to sit and watch her standing there, crying, hostile and wounded. He clears his throat. "You're right. It's no one's business." He pauses, adds gently, "I won't tell anyone."

She stares at him as if she has just been slapped. He sees then his betrayal—that he would say nothing, he would deny her; she is that strange, he is that ashamed. Before Evan can respond (*That's not what I meant*), she is gone.

Kneeling on his bed, he turns back to the model. Carefully, carefully, he peels her away from his wall. He removes the dots of blue poster putty and rolls up the paper, watching tanned skin and nippled bikini and lean legs curl over onto themselves and disappear. Then he wedges the whole thing underneath his bed and sits there, listening to the whisper of it slowly unrolling again, as if the girl will not be shoved away so easily.

• • •

Three girls and two middle-aged women sit in the salon waiting room, thumbing through oversized books of makeovers. Suzen slips into a pink chair, tucking her hair behind her ears. She sits erect, head high. A woman with a spongy perm smiles at her.

"You have very pretty hair," she says.

"Thanks," Suzen murmurs. She glances idly at a stack of magazines on the table beside her, covered with faces of beautiful women, hair shiny as paint, skin devoid of flaws, eyes bright and flat as coins. Looking at them does not stir her particularly; she is not aroused by photographs, unlike her brother, and apparently all other boys and men. But when an attractive girl walks past, Suzen looks up, swallows, wonders if she is blushing and giving herself away. She feels she has no control over her reactions, though she tries to maintain a poker face.

She imagines herself standing on the deck of a ship, heading toward a new land, full of full-bodied women and girls of every shape and size, smiling, welcoming her. She is one of Them. Boys and men on the shore are growing smaller and smaller till she no longer sees them.

Today, ironically, she is getting her hair cut short as a boy's. Like Mary's or Soci's. It is something she has wanted to do for a long time. All of the females in her family have long hair, the kind that twists into clotted little knots in the bathtub drain, nauseating her. Everything about her family nauseates her lately. She knows they look at her differently now, though little has been said. Even her brother has disappointed her, clearly disturbed by her "transformation," as if this all happened overnight, though in a way, she supposes, it has. Suzen is still grappling with her self-image, despising the labels, yet unable to separate herself from them.

The other day, her mother stopped in the hallway and attempted to say something more. Then she simply embraced Suzen awkwardly and said, "If you ever want to talk . . ." to which Suzen responded by tugging away and escaping to her room. She wants only to be alone now, away from her, from them all, ready to break free.

And she is ready to change, in every way. Starting with her long boring hair. She will look nothing like Esme now. No one will get them confused.

She has a picture to show her hair stylist exactly what she wants. Reaching into her coat pocket she pulls out a piece of newspaper. She unfolds it and examines again the front-page photograph of a girl her age with dark half-moon eyes and a sleek haircut. It is layered in such a way that it juts from behind her ears toward her jaw, and loose strands fall fetchingly into her eyes. The girl in the photograph, though it is black-and-white and grainy, clearly has skin smooth as soap and straight, movie-star teeth.

Seventeen-year-old Michelle Marie Lockheed was killed Thursday afternoon by a hit-and-run driver on her way home from Highland High School. Witnesses say she was crossing Whitman Street when a car crossed lanes unexpectedly. The driver has not been identified, although Police Chief Tom Garrison reported that his department has received several leads. Lockheed, an honors student, died en route to Highland Community Hospital.

Suzen did not know Michelle Marie Lockheed. Highland is thirty miles away, a rival high school during basketball and football season, but otherwise another planet. It is incomprehensible to think about a girl her age—a mere week ago, walking down a high school corridor just like hers, with her books pressed to her chest—lying motionless in a casket with a skull wound covered by carefully combed hair.

"Are we ready?" a voice behind her singsongs.

Suzen looks up, startled. Her hairdresser, Linda, is standing over her and smiling, holding out a black nylon robe which Suzen obediently slips into when she stands up. Linda is Suzen's mother's age, with thick hair the color of cayenne pepper. Her fingers are long, her acrylic nails painted fire engine red.

"Cute sweater," she tells Suzen as she guides her to the other room. "It reminds me of Neapolitan ice cream. So, what will it be today, a wee trim?" Linda has been cutting Suzen's hair since she was twelve, and Suzen has never let Linda cut more than half an inch at a time from the ends of her hair.

"No. Something different," Suzen says.

"Oh, goody!" Linda exclaims. She nudges Suzen into a black vinyl chair in front of a sink. "So, what are you thinking?"

"Like this," Suzen says, holding open the newspaper clipping.

Linda peers over her shoulder and gasps a little, as if her ribs have been jabbed by an elbow. "Oh, my gosh. That's that dead girl I read about." She hesitates, "You want me to cut your hair like that?"

Suzen shrugs, embarrassed. The photo she holds obviously is inappropriate, she realizes. She blurts, "I mean, I just want it shorter. It doesn't have to be exactly like that." She starts to fold up the paper.

"No, no, it's okay. We can use that. I mean, it's really cute." Linda says, overly cheerful. She fluffs Suzen's hair, lifting its ends, raking her nails over her scalp. It reminds Suzen of when she was eight, and some of the girls in her third-grade class would sit in a semicircle around her on the school steps at recess, taking turns braiding her long silken hair. She can remember how intoxicating that felt, little fingers sifting through her hair, tenderly parting it into long ribbons they wound in and out, in and out. She would sit perfectly still, sometimes with her eyes closed, soft and dreamy, the attention brushing over her in waves.

"Well," Linda says finally, her analysis complete. "You don't have the same texture, far as I can tell from that picture—hers looks thicker—but I can do something pretty close." She runs warm water over Suzen's hair and then nudges her upright, wraps her head in a towel, and leads her to another chair. Suzen stares straight ahead at her reflection, her damp, lightly tangled hair between Linda's fingers, scissors gleaming in the fluorescent light. She sits perfectly still, waiting to be transformed.

"Okay, here goes nothing," Linda singsongs.

Suzen smiles at her in the mirror, but she is thinking about Michelle Lockheed. That no matter how nice or normal you are, you might not make it through another day. You might not make it across the street. Like Aimee, nearly. It is too horrible to think about. She looks back at her own reflection, alive and glowing.

Linda grins over her head. "Well? What do you think?"

Suzen looks up from her folded hands in her lap and stares at herself. All of her long straight hair is gone, lying like dog fur at her feet. She is amazed to see how golden it looks on the linoleum. When she turns back toward the mirror, she sees a new girl there, with a swan neck and arched eyebrows. Her hair angles toward her jaw and falls in wispy bangs across her forehead.

"I love it," Suzen says finally, letting out her breath. She stands up, feeling strong and powerful. The air in the room is especially pungent, apple blossoms mixed with bubble gum conditioner mixed with musky perfume mixed with the aroma of a take out burger in a back room. The voices and music are sharp in her ears though she cannot focus on what they are saying. The mirror seems to sparkle, light ricocheting off its surface. Linda's orange hair is aflame, her smile brimming with kindness. Suzen feels her eyes water unexpectedly.

When she pushes her way outside into a gush of cold fresh air, she saunters down the sidewalk in her ice-cream sweater and dead-girl haircut. She is full of emotion and ideas and plans. She is nearly eighteen, after all. It is time for something to happen in her life.

• • •

just never expected it," Evan says to Frederick Watley, who is perched atop his desk. For some reason, he looks particularly gay today. Evan wishes he wouldn't cross his legs that way. He knows it is unfair, especially since Watley is the only person he can talk to about Suzen. Though he assumes Suzen wants it kept private for now, he also assumes the secret is safe with Watley.

He sighs. "No one expects it, Evan," Watley says kindly. "Suzen is probably still figuring it out herself."

They sit in a comradely silence for a minute, until Evan dares ask, "But is there a chance, I mean, you know, that sometimes it's just a phase? No offense," he adds quickly. "I'm just wondering."

Watley looks down from his perch and smiles benignly. He is a handsome man, tall as Malcolm and almost as lanky, but in better shape and infinitely more suave; he knows how to dress, for one thing, Evan thinks. Watley always wears softly draping trousers and V-neck sweaters layered over white shirts. His hair is graying just at the temples and he likes to joke that that is where "the smoke comes out of my head," as if he ever loses his temper, which he doesn't.

"Maybe. A phase, an experiment. Confusion." He pauses. "Well, *life* is confusing. And anyway, whether Suzen is gay or straight, so what? She just is who she happens to be. Or, is it 'whom'? I always forget."

Evan twirls a pen around on the blotter. "No, 'who' is correct. It's a relative pronoun, not an object." He sighs.

Watley laughs. "You are so much like your dad it's uncanny." He crosses his arms across his chest and assumes a grave expression. "Have you tried chicken soup?"

"Chicken soup?" Evan looks up, bewildered.

"You know, *For the Teenage Soul, For the Gay and Lesbian Soul . . .*"

"Very funny." Evan turns serious again. "What should I say to her?"

"How about, 'How're you doing?' I don't know, Evan, what do you usually say to her? Just say that." Watley glances at his silver watch. "Hey, I have a class, I better run."

"Okay," says Evan, standing and walking to the door. "And thanks."

"No problem."

After Watley dashes down the hall on his long, lean legs, Evan walks out of the sociology building, watching students flow past him. He notices how some look no older than he—some of the girls look like children, in fact, with their tiny flowered T-shirts and braided hair—while others, guys with facial hair especially, look like they should be in offices already, downing coffee and selling real estate. He sees a couple, a handsome boy of nineteen or so, and a girl with a plain face but womanly curves. She is wearing a cardigan sweater unbuttoned halfway down to her ample cleavage. Clearly she is wearing nothing underneath. The boy leans in, pressing his chest closer to hers. His mouth grazes her ear and she laughs. Evan passes by, trying not to stare, but he cannot help himself. He wonders, what if that were his sister? A week ago, he would have been appalled by the idea of a guy groping her. Now he feels vaguely sad, thinking of all she will miss.

They have no idea, Suzen thinks. No one understands what she is going through. No one, that is, except Mary—whom she hasn't dared tell yet—and her father, who at least is trying to reach out. After a few days letting her be, not bothering her or asking cloying questions, Malcolm shows up at her room like an emissary with a bag of fast food. Suzen has been skipping dinner lately, making excuses, claiming not to be hungry or that she ate a late lunch. Malcolm, she knows, does not buy it.

"You need to eat," he says, and hands her the paper bag. Suzen, in spite of herself, smiles at this simple, kind gesture, and the familiar scent of greasy French fries.

"Thanks," she says, accepting his gift, going to sit down on her bed. She holds the bag in her lap, feels it warm her thighs. Her stomach growls, but she waits.

"Are you all right?" he asks then, softly, still standing in the doorway, not coming in. She nods, trying not to cry. "Suzy, I'm always here, you know, if you want to talk."

Suzen thinks of Esme saying the same words, and what a different effect they had on her; she wanted to run away. Now she wants to run to her father, throw herself against his tall, strong frame, and have him smooth away her troubles. But she knows she cannot do it; she has to maintain her distance, she has to be an adult. The child in her is shrinking away, like the smallest of nesting dolls, buried deep down.

Whenever Suzen thinks of her childhood—not that far past, a few exits down the road—she tries to see herself as she was, not colored by her current self-knowledge. She remembers being a typical girl, jumping rope, fondling Barbies, waiting to grow up. At thirteen, her breasts beginning to emerge, her legs suddenly elongated, she felt like a strange creature, on the verge of evolving into something she wasn't sure she wanted to be. Esme seemed distant, distracted by the littler girls, and Evan, who was going through a hazardous phase, daredeviling himself into the emergency room every other month. And Malcolm seemed nervous around Suzen, as if he didn't know where she had come from. She was fast turning into a young woman, faster even than her peers. And then, unexpectedly, her father had had a kind of epiphany, apparently realizing Suzen might need some guidance. He suggested a fishing trip, just the two of them.

Early one Saturday morning they loaded the car with gear and a Thermos full of hot chocolate. The rest of the family watched from the doorway, as if Suzen were embarking on a long journey, Malcolm seeing her off. Evan, in a leg cast, waved a crutch and warned them to watch out for sharks.

On the way to the lake, they were silent, listening to classical radio, Malcolm's long fingers twitching on the steering wheel. Suzen knew he was remembering how he used to mime the violin parts when she was smaller, to make her laugh. Or he would conduct the whole orchestra from the middle of the living room rug, zigzagging a pencil in the air. In the dark car with his teenage daughter, he didn't seem sure he could still be that silly man. Suzen wanted to roll her eyes and mock him, say, "Dad, be normal." Meaning, be your old self. Play the violin. Make Donald Duck sounds with your lips. *I'll still laugh,* she promised silently.

Instead, Suzen turned to look out the window and pensively watch the dark clumps of trees whip past, the streaky colors of sky growing wider and lighter with the tinny sound of Mozart on AM radio, and her father's fingers tapping the steering wheel.

"Are we almost there?" she asked, to break the silence, to remind him she was still his impatient child. He laughed. "About two more inches," he said, pointing to the map on the seat between them.

At the lake, there were two other cars and a pickup truck parked on the slope of the sandy parking lot. Suzen could see the tiny spark of cigarettes from a boat in the middle of the lake. Men who had risen even earlier than they had, serious about their task. On shore, two lanky teenage boys stood with fishing poles outstretched, and they swiveled to look when they heard the slam of car doors. Malcolm waved at them, and they waved back, but didn't turn back around. They stared at Suzen, openly gawking. She hunched into her sweatshirt, trying to shrink into herself, standing closer to her father, who was hoisting the fishing gear out of the trunk.

"Don't worry," Malcolm said, in a voice meant to be overheard. "If anyone bothers you, I'll make sure to knock his eyes back into his head."

The skinny boys turned around quickly, focused on their lines. Suzen balked. She had never heard her father talk that way. Nor had he ever hinted at her attractiveness, implied that men might look at her *that way*.

Thinking back, Suzen doesn't know what bothered her more, the boys ogling her or her father's overreaction. Later, in the rented rowboat, he tried to apologize. Bent over the tackle box, he dug around carefully among shiny hooks and soft feathery flies, the bobble of bright-colored spinners like toys or ornaments. Without looking at her, he said, "I know they were probably harmless, but there are a lot more out there like that, and I won't be around all the time to—" He stopped.

"To what? Embarrass me?" Suzen said. He laughed a little. "I can take care of myself, anyway," she told him, crossing her arms defiantly over her chest. She felt her soft breasts there—still a surprise sometimes, as if she were touching someone else.

Malcolm sat silently in the boat, his long legs struggling to fold themselves. Then he reached for the Thermos and unscrewed the lid, handing Suzen a mug from the picnic basket. "Here," he said gently. "Hot chocolate." A moment later he held out a half-empty bag of stale marshmallows, tied with a little wire.

Remembering the thoughtfulness of the gesture—of his bothering to find them in the back of the cupboard and tuck them into the basket—brings tears suddenly to her eyes. It seems now that he was trying so hard to do the right thing—protect her, love her—and yet she was growing, changing, swimming away from him from that morning on.

When Malcolm turns to go now, still standing in her doorway, she knows he is saddened and confused, but willing to try to understand. "Remember," he says. "Above the clouds, the sun is always shining."

It is a corny thing to say, and yet it is perfect. Suzen smiles, her eyes watering again. She knows he loves her no matter what, no matter how much she changes, and the child inside her stands up a little straighter, relieved and reassured.

• • •

Evan lies on the rooftop, staring at the world, far as he can see. Ever since he followed Aimee out here, he has found that it is a pleasant refuge. Especially on nights like this when there is no moon, or only a tiny leftover sliver of one, and outer space is a bottomless black sea. If Evan stares long enough, usually he can see a shooting star, a blur of particles hundreds of miles high, looking like a mere smudge of light. He wonders if he can force himself into an out-of-body experience. He stares, unblinking, but nothing happens. Soci had said it happened to her when she looked into the clouds; perhaps it had something to do with daylight, the blankness of a pale blue sky, the mesmerizing softness of drifting clouds. He sighs.

Lately he feels all too connected to his own body, its weaknesses, its needs and desires. He cannot help thinking about his sister, and her needs and desires—not that different, apparently, from his. It is as if Suzen is a stranger now, and not because of how she behaves, which is basically the same as always, if more reticent and defensive, but the fact of *what* she is. All this time she has been living in the same house, the next room, but a different person under her skin than he'd thought. And it is not as though he blames her, or thinks her duplicitous. He simply is discovering that no one is who he or she seems to the outside world. Not even Soci, possibly, whom he has not confronted about Max's suggestion that she actually lives in a mansion. Not even Evan himself, a split personality of boy and man, clinging to his childish notions and yearning to throw them away.

He looks into the vast darkness, where stars arc over every part of the world, and he thinks idly of Italy out there somewhere, lights blinking over olive groves, stucco houses stained tomato red, boats quietly skimming down the Grand Canal. He is stunned by the clarity of his vision. It is like looking through a frosted window, wiping a clear circle with a sleeve in order to see, and it seems so real, he is sure he will be there someday.

Evan once watched *The Godfather* on late-night television, and all he remembers—besides some of the gore and the famous one-liners— were the scenes set on Sicily. The dusty roads through winding groves, and tables set outside with bottles of wine and baskets of bread, stucco houses and beautiful dark-haired girls in soft dresses. It was—is—as different a world from Whitesburg, Michigan, as Evan can imagine. And while his father keeps reminding him that *"life* is an adventure," and Soci lures him into her own kind of escapism, Evan feels certain that his destiny involves olive groves and the Mediterranean. *When you wish upon a star, makes no difference who you are . . .*

It is cold on the rooftop, the autumn night hinting of winter, and leaves swirl past his head on their downward flight. He burrows into his sweatshirt, hands in his pockets, and thinks for a moment that lying flat like this on the slope of the roof, toes pointed, he looks like a rocket prepared for takeoff. He closes his eyes and wonders when he will land.

Suzen closes her eyes and lets the afternoon sun warm her face—it feels like the last time for awhile, since the forecast is for an early cold snap. There are no more leaves on the trees, and up and down the street she can hear the *scritch scritch* of rakes, the more obnoxious hum of power leaf blowers. She has taken to sitting outside on the porch whenever possible, away from the house and its activity, away from her family.

"Hello," a voice says, a shadow falling over Suzen's face. "Is Evan around?"

She looks up to see Soci, hands on hips, as if she is exasperated. "I don't know. He might be at soccer."

It has been a few weeks since Suzen has seen Soci, and she is surprised anew by her appearance, the rakish hair, tight black clothing, a lime green scarf the only color on her body. She is looking at Suzen, too, and Suzen wonders how much she knows about her. All she says, though, is, "Cute haircut."

"Thanks." Suzen touches it self-consciously, but she is happy with it, with the loss of its weight on her neck and shoulders.

Soci sits down beside Suzen, sighing. She lets her legs fall open slightly, dropping her arms between them. For a long time she says nothing, just sits there fingering a dried leaf, as if deeply interested in its veins, then crumpling the papery fragments into dust.

"Is he seeing someone else?" she asks, turning her head slightly to look at Suzen.

Suzen laughs. "Evan? I mean, I guess I don't know, but I seriously doubt it. You're the first girl I have ever seen him with, you know."

Soci stares at her. "Really? The first?" She seems so surprised that Suzen wonders if she should not have told her. Maybe a crucial part of Evan's—or any boy's—self-esteem is maintaining an air of worldliness. "I just wondered," Soci is saying, "because I wonder if he's avoiding me or something."

Suzen feels a little sorry for her. "No," she tells her, though she has no idea what her brother is thinking. "I think he's just preoccupied. They're unpredictable, you know. Guys."

"Yeah, you're right," Soci says, relieved. "You are so right." She takes out a pack of cigarettes and offers one to Suzen, who impulsively accepts. While they sit smoking, Suzen turning around to make sure no one inside the house can see her, Soci says, "I haven't seen you around lately at the 'amazing maze.' Did you quit?"

"No, but with all the rain, you know—Mary says we'll be going back next week, before it gets too cold. Though that's hard to imagine now."

"Yeah, it feels like summer. I skipped school yesterday and went to the beach."

"Really? Aren't you afraid of getting in trouble?"

Soci laughs. "Trouble is my middle name." She shrugs then, fiddles with her cigarette, turning it between her fingers. "I don't know. I hate school, really. It's hard to see the point."

"I know. I can hardly wait to finish," Suzen says. "To be out on my own."

Soci asks then, "So, are you seeing someone yet?"

Suzen presses out her cigarette, though she has smoked only a third of it. "Sort of." She pictures Mary in her white T-shirt, smiling winsomely.

"Younger? Older?"

"Older," Suzen says, blushing. "Quite a lot older."

"Ah," Soci says, grinning. "Married?" She seems keenly interested.

Suzen does not know her well enough to trust her yet, but she blurts out, "Divorced."

Soci's eyebrows raise a notch. She blows a ring of smoke up toward the bare oak tree that faces the porch. She smiles. "Well, well," she says, appreciatively. "You really are something. Maybe I should find me an older man. Not that your brother isn't great, don't get me wrong. He's just—reluctant."

"What do you mean?" Suzen asks, pretty sure she knows what she means.

"We haven't gone very far yet. You know, just kissing." Soci shrugs. "It's all right, I mean, I like kissing. I *love* kissing, actually." Soci sits musing for a few moments, then stubs out her cigarette and begins digging in her backpack for something. She pulls out a piece of paper, dimpled all over with tiny bumps. She holds it up to show Suzen, smiling. "Isn't this great? It's Braille. I'm learning to type it."

"Really? How?" Suzen takes the paper and runs her fingertips over it.

"I have a Braille typewriter. My aunt bought it for me. She's blind. And she needs magazine articles and things like that translated to

Braille. She can get some books at the library or special order, but sometimes she's impatient and wants to read other things, or write letters to friends. She's very independent."

Suzen looks at Soci with new admiration. "I wonder what it's like," she says, closing her eyes.

"Like this," Soci says, taking Suzen's hands and guiding them to her face. "See? This is how you would get to know me, touching my face." Suzen's fingers explore the soft terrain of nose, cheek, flat cool forehead. She lingers over Soci's brows, feeling the tiny hairs, the curved bone, then the bristled lashes of her eyes. She does not want to take her hands away.

"Have you ever kissed a girl?" Soci is asking. Suzen opens her eyes, jerks her hands away. She is so stunned by the question, she cannot speak. Evan must have told her and Soci is teasing her, taunting. But her expression is completely guileless; the question seems pure coincidence. Suzen shakes her head no.

"Have you?" she manages to whisper back.

"Come here," Soci says, stubbing out her cigarette and pulling Suzen by the wrist toward the garage. Suzen, in a daze, follows. Inside the shadowy garage, a jumble of bicycles and yard tools, Soci wastes no time. She leans in to kiss her full on the mouth. Suzen's senses are bristling, alert; she almost can hear the slender muscles of Soci's neck as they bend, hairs on her head realigning themselves, soft as a paintbrush. It is exactly as she had imagined it. Soci seems to be willing Suzen to comply, and finally she does, parting her lips a little, amazed at how soft the other girl's mouth is. It lasts less than fifteen seconds but seems enough time has lapsed for the earth to rotate once around.

"There," Soci says quietly, triumphantly. "Now you've kissed a girl. Not so weird, is it? I used to do it with my best friend back home. That's how I got so good at it." She laughs, her soft, musical laugh. She seems to read Suzen's mind then, watching her face turn pink in the dimly lit garage. "Don't worry about Evan. I would never tell him.

Anyway, it's no big deal, right? Just a harmless experiment." She smiles again. "Well, tell Ev I stopped by," she adds nonchalantly, pushing open the side door and stepping back out into the sunlight as if nothing unusual has happened.

The sun is in Evan's eyes and he squints. After the deluge of the past week, the skies are clearer than ever, wiped clean, and it is unusually mild for late October. Evan pulls off his sweatshirt and waits to be called to the field. The game is just a practice scrimmage, junior varsity against the seniors, as the coach has informed the latter that they'd better watch out; the younger members are fast encroaching on the seniors' reputation as stellar players. Evan has been a little wary of the comparison, knowing it only invites feuding, grandstanding, swaggering, and eventually, smaller guys like him being pummeled in the locker room by sausage-limbed seniors. He wishes the coach wouldn't taunt athletes just to get them to try harder. After all, it isn't the Olympics. It's small-town soccer.

Evan has never much liked competition. It brings out the anxious underdog in him, fearing winning as much as losing—losing one gets over with healthy doses of self-pity, but winning only prompts others to expect more and more.

Out of the corner of his eye, he can see the coach waving him onto the field. It's his turn, and he takes a deep breath. He is playing offense, which he hates—again, the expectations to win, to get the ball downfield and to the goal, or at least, to someone nearer the goal. Evan has never actually made a goal himself, only assisted plenty of times. He is regarded as a good team player, ready to pass or help defend, but no one ever passes him the ball at the crucial moments.

He watches Brett Miller, the two-hundred-twenty-pound senior, heading downfield. Not a graceful bone in his body, but he moves like a giant appliance set loose, careening toward any and every body in his path. He often gets the ball, and surprisingly, the goal, and he is always deeply elated, bowing to the applause and swatting high-fives all around. Miller never seems to consider the possibility of failure, and even if he does stumble, he is so quick to divert attention or blame elsewhere, that he remains on top—the hero.

Evan has entertained hero fantasies, of course, but they are always cinematic, unrealistic, inspired not by the desire to win anything, but only to feel a little power. To laugh in the face of danger, to be the outsider, the hero, James Bond. In fact, other than *Breathless* and other foreign films, his favorite movies feature 007. Evan finds such movies strangely soothing; he can relax watching Bond dispatch a dozen potential attackers with his wit and savvy and cleverly hidden weaponry: an exploding shoe, a poisonous fountain pen, little bombs that shoot out of his taillights. Evan sometimes nods off during the peak action scenes because he already is assured the hero will make it through unscathed; there is no cause for alarm or tension, and so he falls asleep to the sound of explosions and dying screams.

The coach is screaming at Evan to move his butt, and he does, running fast, dodging two seniors to catch up with Larry, one of his sophomore classmates who is trying desperately to dribble the ball. Larry is a fairly agile kid, though smaller than Evan, and Evan can see he moves now out of fear, shuffling his feet around the ball like a maniac. He glances for just a second at Evan and says, "All yours." Suddenly Larry drops back, self-dismissed, and the ball is Evan's. He nearly trips over it and his own feet, but he moves on pure adrenaline, fueled mostly by the grunting sounds of Miller approaching.

Evan runs and runs, no longer thinking, simply moving, his feet and the ball somehow connected as if by an elastic band. It is revolving around him like the earth around the sun, in perfect synchronicity. The other players dart in close, but he manages to weave away easily. Miller's huge face comes into full view—he is right there, ready to knock the ball out of Evan's grasp—sometimes he seems to forget it is soccer and not football—and Evan almost lets him. But then, miraculously, he is watching himself kick the ball with all his might, the ball soaring over heads and straight to the back of the netted goal. There is an uproar. His own teammates whooping and descending on him, several seniors joining in.

As Evan is clapped on the back, his hair ruffled by admirers, it occurs to him that he is invincible, he can do anything he puts his mind to.

Suzen used to believe she could read minds; now she is not so sure. She never has any idea what Mary is thinking. When she arrives at Strohman's nursery one afternoon, she watches Mary for clues, wondering what to say, how to open the conversation she desperately wants to have.

Mary is standing behind the cash register, winding a roll of white tape through the machine. "No one seems to know how to do this," she laments. "Like changing the toilet paper roll. I mean, how hard can it be?"

Suzen laughs. She busies herself with rearranging a stack of decorative gourds and miniature pumpkins that a toddler bumped into. He had shrieked with delight at the tumbling fruit, until his mother scolded him and yanked him out of the store. "It's okay— really!" Mary had called after her, but the mother was already gone. Now Suzen piles the gourds and squash carefully atop the display table, trying to make them less prone to toppling.

She wonders what would happen if she told Mary what has been throbbing through her: *I kissed a girl. I think I'm in love—with you.* She has been thinking of Soci's startling encounter as a trial run, a kind of dress rehearsal for Mary. Now she is ready for anything. She teeters on the soles of her tennis shoes, clears her throat, searching for something to say.

Before she can, Mary turns to the sound of the bell jingling over the door. A customer has walked in, and Mary clearly recognizes him because she leaves Suzen to go to him. He touches her arm, then her hair, as if admiring changes in her. Mary looks him in the eye, puts her hands on her hips and looks away. He says something and she bows her head. Suzen cannot help staring at them, wondering who he is, what he is saying.

"Suzen, can you keep an eye on the front for me?" Mary asks, her voice an octave higher than usual. Suzen nods. She wonders if she should be concerned, if the man is a threat somehow. He doesn't look menacing, however. He looks like a middle-aged businessman with an expensive suit and longish hair too young for his face, which is lined and slightly ashen. Beyond the front door, Suzen sees a brown sedan in the parking lot, a BMW, and deduces that the man is the infamous ex husband, Philip. He follows Mary into her office and closes the door.

Twenty-five minutes elapse, during which Suzen reads and rereads the front page of the local newspaper at the counter, waits on three customers, and doodles a winged fairy on a receipt. She idly counts seed packets on a little stand nearby. Forget-me-nots, black-eyed Susans and bleeding hearts. The apt titles make her laugh. There are also miscellaneous wildflower seed packets—"Toss them into your yard or field and watch a kaleidoscope of color come to life!" She slips them back into place, rearranges them alphabetically and then back again, worried that Mary has some system she is not aware of. She watches the closed door of the office, but no one comes out. It is nearly closing time and Suzen has to get home for a family event, an art award ceremony at the high school for area students, one of whom happens to be Hallie. Suzen does not want to be late, for Hallie's sake, and finally she finds the courage to knock on the office door.

"Mary?" she says through the door. "I need to get going, okay?"

The door opens, and Mary smiles at her through tears. "Fine, okay. Sorry to keep you so long. Can you just lock the front door for me, and turn the sign around?"

Suzen nods, then says softly, "Are you all right? Should I stay or something?"

"Everything's fine. It's just—my mother-in-law died."

"Oh, I'm sorry." Suzen is surprised yet relieved; there is no threat to Mary, except sorrow. Beyond Mary, sitting in her desk chair, is her ex-husband, also crying, or just finished. He wipes his eyes with a handkerchief and sighs. When Suzen turns to go, she sees that Mary has gone to Philip and put her arms around him, half sitting in his lap. They resume talking in low, familiar tones, and it strikes Suzen that they were a couple once, and that anyone observing them would think they still were. She is oddly envious—of their physical closeness, of their history and rapport. For not the first time Suzen feels desperately out of her depth, like a child in the shallow water watching the big kids dive and plunge, fearless and capable.

S he looks scared to death," Evan notes.

"I know," Malcolm says. "She said she hopes she doesn't win so she doesn't have to go up on the stage." He hands Evan a program and he looks it over, sees his sister's name listed underneath the elementary school entrants in the countywide art contest. The auditorium is full to the brim with parents and siblings and friends, waiting for the prizes to be awarded. The VanderZee family has arrived at the last minute, Malcolm shouldering his way down the aisle and procuring a row for the five of them, vexing another family who was attempting to save seats with draped coats. Malcolm persevered, convincing the other father (lightweight, prone to reddening) that *surely* they could move down a few seats, even though it placed them partially behind a support post.

Evan searches the front-row seats for Hallie, and spies her craning around, looking for them. He waves encouragingly, and she sees him, waves back and smiles with open relief, then turns back around, slumped down. She is dressed in her Sunday best, Evan knows, down to the patent leather shoes Esme made a fuss polishing at the last minute. He noticed Esme seemed particularly fluttery during the preparations, making much of the event that Hallie seemed sheepish about, if not downright blasé. It occurred to Evan that perhaps his mother was projecting success onto her daughter. It has been years since anyone noticed Esme's art, and until today, no one even knew that any of her offspring had inherited her talent. Apparently, Hallie has been painting prolifically, at school and in the privacy of her room. A regular child prodigy, according to her art teacher, Mrs. Francis. Evan heard her telling his parents how proud she was of Hallie, and Esme registering surprise.

The first awards are given out to two high school students for sculpture. The boy is clad in black with carefully wild hair and a row of earrings dotting his floppy ears. He walks like a marionette across the stage, his limbs independent of the rest of his body. The other winner is called Erin Nin, and Evan entertains himself by repeating her name under his breath—*erinnin, errinin*—until his father lightly whacks his arm.

The junior high winners are a conglomeration of budding confidence and abject awkwardness; the three girls tower over the lone boy, who is acne-speckled with pipe-cleaner limbs. Two of the girls hunch over as if to appear shorter, but one, a bright-eyed redhead, grins merrily and waves to the audience like a beauty pageant contestant.

Lastly, the winners are announced for elementary school, which is the largest group, an interminably long list of kindergarten through fifth-graders. Evan's feet are nearly asleep, yet he waits patiently to hear his sister's name. After all the names are read, the fresh-scrubbed children trotted across the stage with their little fake-metal trophies, Evan realizes Hallie has been overlooked. The applause is dwindling; the show is nearly over and people are beginning to gather coats, making motions to leave. Evan looks down the row at his parents, brows raised in a question. He wants them to do something; even if Hallie wanted to avert attention, he is sure she would be devastated to be ignored altogether.

"It must be a mistake," Esme is whispering, turning over her program.

"Shoot," Malcolm mutters. "Poor Hal."

There is a small commotion at the front of the auditorium, the squawk of a microphone being adjusted, then a voice calling, "Please, if we could just have your attention for one more moment." Ms. Montella, the director of the area Arts Council, is tilting the microphone toward her face as she beams at the audience.

"In all of these categories," she says grandly, "we have seen a tremendous response of creativity and hard work. So many gifted and worthy young artists are represented here tonight . . ." *Blah, blah, blah,* thinks Evan. ". . . and I am delighted to present the final award, a new one, for Best of Show, because we have a most remarkable student this year. Someone who has demonstrated an unusual talent rarely seen at such a young age."

Evan is about to bolt out of his chair, go find his little sister and rescue her from this horrendous travesty, when he hears Ms. Montella call, "Hallie VanderZee? Are you here tonight?" Far up front, Evan can see her, tiny in blue velvet, nearly swaying on her feet, being led to the stage by her art teacher.

Afterwards, when they go to find her, she is leaning against a wall for support and holding her trophy like a doll in her arms.

"Way to go, munchkin," Evan says.

"Thanks."

Aimee begs to look at the trophy, then to hold it; Suzen squeezes Hallie's hand, and Malcolm beams. Esme, however, stands slightly apart, a puzzling expression on her face. She is saying, "Hallie, we're so proud of you. This is so wonderful," but continues to look bewildered.

"Someone called you the next Kandinsky," Malcolm says proudly.

"What's a Kandinsky?" Aimee asks.

"A famous abstract painter," her father says. "Like your sister will be."

"Let's go home and celebrate, have some ice cream," Esme says brightly.

"Hey, we have to go see Hal's art first," Malcolm reminds her.

"Oh. Right!"

As they walk down the hallway to the display area, Evan glances at his mother and sees that she is staring straight ahead, a smile frozen on her face.

The ice cream has melted and congealed in the bowls. Suzen helps clear them away, watching her mother rinse methodically. They are alone, everyone else gone up to bed. The two of them are rarely in the same room together anymore, and when they are, like now, there is only cautious small talk, or silence. The light over the sink illuminates the sudsy water and Esme's long fingers. Her hands, Suzen notices, are starting to look old and veiny. She almost feels sorry for her, upstaged by her nine-year-old daughter, the *wunderkind*.

In the school corridor, where all of the winning students' artwork was hanging, the biggest cluster of onlookers was positioned before Hallie's four paintings. Each was distinct, but equally rich and alive, with strange swirls and fanciful strokes, the colors deeper than any watercolors Suzen had ever seen. Mrs. Francis, standing nearby, had remarked to Esme and Malcolm, "I want to get her into oils next. Think what she could do!" and Esme had nodded politely. Was she envious? Suzen wondered. How could she envy her own child, a little girl? Yet, she could. She did. Suzen can see it in her face now, as she leans over the sink, saying nothing, humming a nameless tune.

When she was eight, Suzen went along with her parents to an opening of her mother's work at a gallery an hour's drive away. Evan, with pinkeye, and Hallie, an infant, had stayed home with a sitter. There were clusters of well-dressed people congratulating Esme and studying her paintings—large confusing oils of elongated people with disproportional limbs and features. Suzen remembers thinking, *A little kid could do that.* She wandered around the room, sneaking bits of bread and cheese from the white-draped tables and even sipping someone's leftover red wine when no one was looking. It was so awful, she gagged, then ate two pieces of a spongy chocolate cake to take away the flavor. The cake, though, was saturated with liqueur, and Suzen had spent the drive home vomiting in the back seat. She never went to another opening. Not that there have been any in a long time.

Suzen thinks how Hallie astounded all of them. Always so quiet, reserved, holding her secrets close to her chest; it just never occurred to anyone that she might actually *have* a secret.

"It was really great, wasn't it? Hallie's art?" Suzen says finally. She wants to force a reaction from her mother, something that isn't false or feigned. She is startled to see Esme's cheeks are wet with tears. Her mother dries her hands on a towel and then wipes her eyes.

"Yes," she says. "I really am proud of her, she is extremely gifted." She picks up the trophy from the table, looks at her daughter's name (Halliwell, Esme's maiden name) etched above *Best of Show.* Then Esme looks at Suzen and says, "I know you think what I do is a waste of time. That I am just this boring person and I *used* to be an artist. That I can't even come close to the talent Hallie has. That I am a fraud." Her words are bitter, and Suzen swallows, unprepared. "Well, maybe I am a fraud, as an artist—derivative, unoriginal, whatever. But I will have you know, Suzen, that there is nothing false about who I *am.* No matter what you might think you know about me."

Suzen stands there, dumbfounded. *Where did this come from?* she wonders.

"Let me show you something," Esme says. She leaves the room and returns a moment later, holding a large piece of paper. It is a collage of images, some drawn, some obviously cut from magazines and old picture books. It takes awhile to take it all in. Suzen notices immediately, however, that there is a theme—a deceptively flat but three-dimensional painting of an elaborate hedge maze. The coincidence startles her; Suzen has never told Esme about her work at the Anderssons' and she is sure no one else knows about it. Mr. Andersson made it clear he wanted his maze kept secret until it was complete. But then she remembers that Hallie has a children's book of mazes she loaned Suzen weeks ago; it was left out on the coffee table and Esme probably found it there.

Suzen looks over her mother's artwork, curious now. In various corners of the paper maze are pasted photographs of the VanderZees, school pictures of the four children, and Kodaks from holidays and vacations. There are also random bits of domestic imagery—a spoon, a washtub, a lawnmower, a wineglass—and other things, apparently symbolic: a clock, a cloud, a rabbit, a tiny house on fire with the words, *stop, drop, and roll* stuck to the flames.

"This is my life," Esme says matter-of-factly. "Sometimes I feel like I am running in circles and there is no way out." Suzen looks at Esme and has an awful thought. Is her mother considering leaving? Is that what she is trying to say? Is that why Kevin keeps calling, to try to convince her?

"Mom—" she says, suddenly wanting to clear the air once and for all.

"Forget it," Esme says. "I think we both need to get some sleep. It's been a long day." Her tears have dried and her mouth is firm now, a closed door. Suzen thinks that perhaps Esme is punishing her for her long and silent grudge.

Before Suzen can try to apologize—or demand more information, as she is torn between the warring emotions—her mother turns out the light and walks out, leaving Suzen alone in the dark, silently begging, *Don't leave.*

Suzen starts walking home from school, silently counting down the months, weeks, until she will graduate, walk one last time from the confining walls of high school. *The end.* Her own beginning.

"Hi," a voice says, and she turns to see find Eduardo there, beaming at her. She had almost forgotten about him. He is wearing a red sweater with blue jeans and green shoes. He looks like a child's drawing—bright clothing, warm brown skin, inky hair.

"I like it," he says, pointing to her newly shorn hair, and then gingerly touching it. "Looks nice. Like a boy, but nice." He laughs a little, all of his pearly *tooths* showing.

"Thanks," Suzen says, resuming her gait. Eduardo follows.

"Before, you are Rapunzel," he says, pronouncing the name with an *s* instead of a *z*, motioning down her back to where her hair used to end. " 'Rapunsel, Rapunsel, let down you long hair,' " he sings out. Suzen laughs.

"Where did you learn that?"

He shrugs, his dark eyes shining. "I learn English from—fairy tale?—yes, fairy tales. My teacher read them to us, so we can learn. We have to rememorize stories. I not forget them still."

"Well, that's good," she says, not knowing how else to respond.

"Susannah," he says, still getting her name wrong, though endearingly, she has to admit. "Can I ask you something?" She nods, braced for the inevitable. She knows when she is being pursued; though she hasn't spoken to him since the afternoon in the auditorium, every time he sees her, he smiles ecstatically.

"I want to call you . . ." he says, faltering. He pulls a scrap of paper out of his pocket. It is well-worn, but Suzen sees her name and phone number scribbled on it. He smiles. "I like talking in person, it is better. You know?" Suzen nods again. There is something irresistibly captivating about Eduardo, even now. His hair falls across his brow in shining dark curls. Suzen realizes that part of his appeal is his dogged infatuation with her.

"I will be going home to Peru in six weeks' time," he says sadly, still holding her phone number in his hand. *I'm a lost cause*, she wants to say, to spare him the trouble.

They have reached the corner near her house, hidden from view by the neighbors' tall hedgerow. Suzen feels her heart pounding, as she contemplates a course of action that never crossed her mind till now. She wants to run away, yet part of her does not. She thinks of Soci, drawing her into the garage. Perhaps Soci enjoys shocking people—perhaps her audacity was what had scared Evan away—and she just wanted to toy with Suzen, test her. But maybe she simply felt like kissing Suzen and she did it without any forethought. Eduardo is standing so near, Suzen can smell the piney cologne and faint, nervous sweat.

"Come here," she whispers, pulling Eduardo by the wrist to a secret place between the house and the shrubs. Without taking her eyes off him, Suzen tilts her head and kisses Eduardo. He does not hesitate to meet her, pulling her in close to his body, pressing her lips open with his warm tongue the way Suzen used to dream he would. Something tingles inside her, deep down, but a part of her is pulling away, as if she is merely experiencing the kiss, as if outside herself watching. It is like a carnival ride where you wait and see where the dips and curves are going to happen; sometimes it thrills you and sometimes you just watch the scenery fly past. Suzen feels alternately dizzy and detached from the experience. She cannot form words for what she feels. But when Eduardo reaches up with one hand to graze her breast, she pulls away.

"I have to go," she says, wiping her mouth on her sleeve.

"I am sorry," he says, halting. "I want to ask you the—uh, there is Halloween party? On Friday night? I want to ask would you like—"

"I can't," Suzen says, her voice high and apologetic.

"You have boyfriend?" he asks, his brow furrowing.

"Yes," Suzen lies. "No. I mean—I'm sorry." Then she brushes past Eduardo and runs toward her house.

"Wait—Susannah!" he calls, but she does not look back. Once inside she leans against the door for a long time, just feeling her heart beating until it slows to a natural rhythm. He got what he wanted, she tells herself. Back in Peru, he can tell his friends whatever he wants to about her. That they kissed, that she started it, that they made love underneath a hedgerow. She doesn't care if he embellishes. Leaning against the door, she almost hopes that he does.

On Friday night, Evan is at the front door, waiting for the monsters to come begging. "Trick or treat!" they yell through the heavy oak. He opens the door a few inches, and erupts in ghoulish moans. A little girl in orange lipstick and an ambiguous costume starts to cry. Evan quickly pulls off his mask, removes the bloody stake from his head.

"See, it's just pretend!" he assures her. The parents are glaring at him, or at least the mother is. The father merely looks a little embarrassed, perhaps at his own child's wimpiness.

"It's just a regular guy," the dad says in an adenoidal tone used to placating. "See? And he has lots of candy."

Evan takes this as a hint to give the crying girl extra. He reaches into the bowl and drops candy bars into each child's open bag. After the others mutter thanks and turn away, Evan tosses an extra piece to the girl, who has smeared her orange lips with her hand and now looks a little crazed.

He closes the door and sets the bowl down. "Mom!" he yells through the empty hallway. "I don't want to do door duty all night!" Although there are still two more hours till the party at Max's house, Evan is eager to escape. He knows Soci will be there, and after a few weeks of cooling toward her, something inside him has heated again. *From freezer to microwave!* he thinks, remembering a commercial on television. Lately, this is how his mind works—a jumble of mismatched thoughts popping in and out. He wonders what insanity feels like, if it comes on suddenly or in little innocuous bursts, and if anyone, on any given day, could be a poster child for madness. He thinks of Soci, unpredictable, erratic, yet generally good-natured. When he called to invite her to the party, she seemed delighted.

"I've missed you," she said, never alluding to or explaining her own aloofness.

"Me, too."

"Let's forget about Chicago," she said. "I don't think you're ready for that, are you." Evan let his silence answer.

The next day at school, she smiled coyly and said, "You won't recognize me."

"Yes, I will," he said, coming close as he dared, almost touching her.

All day Evan has imagined her in various getups—small breasts pushing against a tight stripper's costume/maid's uniform/scuba gear/low-cut witch's gown. He is sweaty with suspense and lust. The suspense outweighs the lust, however; he isn't sure it's a positive feeling.

Max asked him when he was ever going to "explore the scenery," and Evan said, "What makes you think I haven't already?"

"Because it would be written all over your face, dude. No one can hide it, not the 'first time,' " Max said knowingly.

"Then I suppose it's safe to say that you haven't been anywhere yet, either?"

Max chortled. "I might have tickets, though. I'll let you know after tonight."

Sometimes Evan was tired of their showy intelligence, their clever insinuations. He wished Max would just blurt out, "Nailed her yet?" and Evan would retort, "Damn straight." Other guys communicated like this. It was direct and devoid of irritating analysis. Even if it was bullshit. Evan resolved to begin living his life deliberately, no longer stopping to think things through so carefully.

Evan pours another bag of miniature candy bars into the bowl beside the door and waits for the bell to ring again. He is just biding his time, waiting for the pieces to come together; tonight, he is sure, is the night.

Suzen walks into the family room to find her mother trying to piece together a costume, which is funny, since she knows Esme hates to sew. She blames it on her own mother, Suzen's grandmother, Eleanor. According to Esme, Eleanor's solution to slipping hemlines was Scotch tape or staples. She has told of going to school with little scratches on her knees from the staple teeth biting through her skirt when she sat down. Suzen misses her and her grandfather; they died five years ago from cancer, one after the other like old trees toppling together in a storm.

Suzen watches her mother pinning the hem along Aimee's dress, teeth gritted, and she feels momentarily sympathetic. "Too bad Grandma's not here to help, huh," she says.

Esme looks up, startled. Then she laughs a little. "Yeah, she would be a *lot* of help." She sits back on her haunches and says, "Once I called her and told her it was all her fault I couldn't even fix a hem, and she said, 'Hell's bells. What did you expect? I was too busy fixing gourmet snacks for you brats.'"

Suzen smiles and Aimee blurts, "You said a bad word, Mom. You said the H word."

"Sorry, I shouldn't have."

Aimee looks in the mirror and asks, "Do you think I'm beautiful?"

Esme laughs. "Yes, of course. But don't let it go to your head, gorgeous."

"What does that mean?" Aimee asks.

"It means, get over yourself," Suzen says.

"Are you going to dress up?" Esme asks, turning to Suzen.

"I doubt it."

"Isn't there a party, at Jenna's house?" Esme asks. Always trying.

She sounds so eager for Suzen to be normal, to do normal teenage things; Suzen is appalled. She considers telling her mother that it is a drinking party, that there will be no adult supervision, but decides there is no point. She decides to change the subject.

"You had another phone call," Suzen says levelly. "Kevin."

Esme, not looking at her, says, "What did he say?"

"He wants to talk to you. 'It's important.' The same thing he *always* says."

Esme says nothing in response, apparently deciding that no answer will satisfy Suzen, which reinforces Suzen's belief in her mother's guilt. Suzen grits her teeth, fuming. Her mother has become an easy and habitual target at which to rage. Yet, as Suzen watches her turn back to Aimee, tight-lipped, pins trembling in her fingers, the small, childish part of her feels ashamed. And she misses the way things used to be. She wants her mother back, but isn't willing to go to her. Esme gently turns Aimee in front of the mirror, and Suzen feels a pang, remembering what it was like to be held in her grip, literally and figuratively.

When she was Aimee's age, she would run to Esme after school, throwing her arms around her mother, who hugged her as if she were the best thing, her most valuable treasure. At night Esme would lie stretched beside Suzen on her little twin bed and read her lengthy passages from *The Little Princess* and *Robinson Crusoe, Little Women* and *The Adventures of Sinbad*. She claimed there was no such thing as "girl" or "boy" stories; her daughter would have access to them all. When she turned off the light, she'd lean down to kiss Suzen, and Suzen would kiss her cheek; she still remembers the velvety roundness of her mother's cheek. Now she cannot remember the last exchange of affection between them. It has been a long, long time.

Aimee, in front of the mirror, waves her iridescent wings made of nylon mesh and wire. Oblivious to the conversation, she twirls and sings, "I can fly! I can fly!"

"No, you can't," Suzen snaps. Aimee stops and looks at her, offended.

"There," Esme says dully. "You can take it off now, Aim."

Aimee sighs. "Do I have to? I like it."

"I know you like it. But you can't wear it to Eliza's party unless I finish sewing it, okay? I'm starting to feel like a broken record." Aimee shrugs, then yanks the dress over her head and stands there for a moment in her flowered underpants. "Okay, go," Esme says wearily to Aimee. When she is gone, Esme turns back to Suzen. "You obviously have something you want to say, so just say it."

"No, I want *you* to say it."

"It's complicated, Suzen. And I don't think it's your business anyway, but if you really want to know, I want to tell you." Esme looks up at Suzen, pushing a strand of long hair out of her face. Most of her hair is held back by a wide headband, into a style Suzen thinks of as Aging Sorority Girl.

"You should cut it," Suzen says coldly. "It's too long for your age." And she turns to leave without bothering to let her mother finish.

Hallie enters the foyer and announces to Evan, "Mom says to quit yelling. She'll be right back. She's taking Aimee to the party."

"Yeah, okay," Evan says mindlessly, opening a third candy bar and eating it in two bites. "But I have places to go. I can't stand here all night."

"What does 'Halloween' mean?" Hallie asks.

Evan, with his mouth full, says, "I think it means 'hallowed' or 'holy' night. It probably comes from Latin, but you'd have to ask Dad."

"That doesn't make sense. *Holy*," Hallie says. "It's just kids getting candy, or getting in trouble."

"It used to mean something else, I think," Evan says. "You know, like a night to scare away evil spirits. That's why kids dress up in scary costumes."

"Like this?" she asks.

Evan turns to have a good look at his sister, who is dressed in a green jumbo-sized plastic trash bag with the letters "M & M" taped to the front. He laughs. "Yeah, that's pretty scary, Hal." She is still pinning it on, and runs off as the doorbell rings again, not wanting to be seen. Evan yanks the door open and is surprised to find not a group of children, but a man standing in the dim light of the jack-o'-lanterns that ring the flagstone entry.

"Hello. Is your mother here? Esme?"

"No," says Evan. "She'll be back in a little while. Do you want to wait?" He has no idea who the man is, nor if it would be a good idea to invite a stranger in, just because he knows his mother's name. Also, there is something a little odd about his demeanor, distracted and slightly agitated.

"Yeah. I mean, okay. I'll wait out in my car," the man says a shade tersely, and Evan watches him walk back down the front path and to his car, a rusted and banged-up Ford that looks held together by string. He gets in and sits in the driver's seat, shoulders hunched. While Evan continues to study him warily, the sky thunders and pours rain again. Children up and down the block squeal and scatter, clutching their bags of loot and running for cover. A few of them run straight toward the VanderZees' open front door, huddling underneath the arched entryway.

There are twin boys dressed as ninjas, dripping wet, and a girl wearing a homemade black costume that probably once looked like a cat, but her makeup is smeared so it's hard to tell. In spite of the rain and accompanying cold, they hold open their soggy bags, while their parents wait patiently on the sidewalk underneath a golf umbrella.

"Well, you guys are good sports," Evan says, dropping candy into each of their bags.

"No, we're ninjas," one of the boys pipes up.

"Oh, right," Evan says, trying not to laugh. When the children have thanked him and run off, Evan glances back at the Ford parked in front of the house. The rain is so heavy now, Evan cannot see the driver inside the car.

Suzen watches the rain pouring down the kitchen window, so steadily it is like a thick sheet of water, pressed to the glass. She thinks of Mary, who has been pensive at work lately, ever since she returned from the funeral of her former mother-in-law in Milwaukee. Suzen has refrained from asking about her relationship with Philip and his family, though she is curious about how the ties remain attached, if loosely, and if she still has feelings for him—for men in general. After she kissed Eduardo, Suzen began to wonder if she were divided in her own loyalties. He wasn't bad; in fact, he was quite wonderful, and a kiss was a kiss, in a way, as long as the two people kissing were interested in each other—out of mutual curiosity if nothing else. Sometimes Suzen doesn't know what or who she is at all, as if she is outside herself looking in, trying to see something beyond gauzy curtains. But longing pours through her like rain; she actually shivers, standing there alone.

Hallie comes in, startling her. "Who left the lid off?" she shrieks, running to the glass cage in the corner of the room. "Where is Cupcake?" She is ruffling through the cedar chips, panicked. Suzen wanders over to her side and looks in. There is no sign of the rat, who is so large she couldn't possibly hide in the shallow layer of bedding.

"Calm down, Hal, I'm sure she's around here somewhere. Don't have a heart attack." Suzen gets on her hands and knees and begins searching the room, and is crawling near the back door when she hears someone knocking. She looks up, squints through the darkened window, the screen door behind it.

"It's him," Hallie is saying in a very low, scared whisper.

"Who?" Suzen asks, still crouched on the floor.

"The man I told you I saw before, it's him."

Suzen stands up and stares directly into the man's face on the other side of the door, and sees that he is motioning to her and saying something she cannot hear. Then she sees that he is holding something white in his other hand. Hallie sees it, too, and grinning, yanks open the door. She seems to have instantly forgotten her terror of the man, as if now he is a saint, the deliverer of rodents.

He pulls back his hand, swiveling his body away from her. "Uh, no, sweetheart, you don't want to touch this thing. It's a rat. It's a good thing I got it when I did, because it was heading right for the door when I walked up."

Suzen understands then. She looks again at the animal in his hand and sees that it is not moving. Cupcake is dead. And the man at the back door killed her. "Oh, my gosh," Suzen says. She turns to Hallie, to protect her from the bad tidings. The man, whoever he is, clearly thought he was doing them a service. Hallie, unfortunately, has seen the twisted little neck, the terrible angle of Cupcake's white head in the stranger's outstretched palm. Recoiling, she screams. She screams and screams, and apparently cannot stop.

Evan hears Hallie screaming and runs toward the back door. He can see through the open doorway that the man is on the porch—he must have gotten out of his car when Evan was distracted by the children—and he's just standing there staring, with something in his hand. It clearly isn't a gun or a weapon by the way he holds it, his palm flat as a serving tray. When Evan gets near the door, he sees that at the same moment, Malcolm has rushed up the porch steps behind the man.

"What the hell are you doing?" Malcolm asks in a high, agitated voice that Evan has never heard before.

The man turns and looks Malcolm over, then smiles testily. "I swear I didn't do anything, man, I was just stopping by—and when I saw the rat, I did what any decent guy would do, I got rid of it. I'm sorry if it upset your kid. I swear."

Evan sees now that the thing he is holding is a dead Cupcake. Malcolm has started to push past the stranger toward his daughter, saying, "Hallie, Hal, it's okay, it was an accident, he didn't know—"

Evan is still standing inside, wondering again who the strange man is, when his mother comes up from behind him. She puts her arms around Hallie, to comfort her, and Hallie leans into her, now weeping softly. By the look on Esme's face, Evan suspects she knows the man, and isn't happy to see him.

"Kevin," she says. "What are you doing here?"

Evan vaguely remembers messages left for his mother, Kevin Wonder-something, though he never paid much attention to it. To Evan's amazement, Malcolm now turns furiously to the man and says under his breath, "You *sonofa*—" And then, without warning, Malcolm rushes him, and slugs him so hard both men land on the porch floor. The dead rat flies through the air and lands somewhere in the dark slushy grass. The rain gushes into the porch at a slant and Evan stands by, helpless, wondering if he should dive in, too, but he is frozen. Esme is yelling at them to stop, Hallie has resumed screaming, and Edgar, the old silent dog, has found his bark again.

"Get *off!*" Kevin Whoever is yelling into Malcolm's ear.

Malcolm hits him again. "I want you to stay away from my family," he says fiercely, still pinning the man to the ground. "And stop calling my wife."

"Malcolm, let him go," Esme says. She has stepped out onto the porch and is leaning down. "Kevin?" She speaks calmly now, as if to a child. "I told you I was sorry." There is a long suspended silence, just the sound of breathing and rain.

"I know," Kevin says finally, helplessly. "I know." He hardly seems to notice Malcolm still on top of him. "I just came back to make amends. I just needed to see you—"

"I know. It's okay. It's all over now. Ancient history. You need to let it go."

Evan notices that Suzen has joined his side and she is staring, stricken and very pale. "*That's* Kevin Wunderhaus?"

"What the hell is this?" Evan whispers back.

Suzen shakes her head. "Never mind," she says finally.

"I just thought," Kevin is saying dully. "I mean, when you called me back I thought I should try—"

"When *I* called *you?*" Esme says, bewildered.

"Oh, my gosh," Suzen says softly, then turns and slips away.

Evan feels like he is watching a play, having missed the first act, and he struggles to make sense of it. Malcolm loosens his grip then, apparently feeling sorry for the man. Suddenly Kevin shoves Malcolm off and struggles to his feet. Malcolm attempts to help him up, but Kevin jerks away.

"Yeah, well, whatever," he says, his jaw set as he pulls a slender cell phone out of his jacket pocket, breathing heavily, blood streaming from his nose. He calmly dials, repeating aloud, "Nine-one-one." He pauses. "Hello? Yes, I've just been attacked, and I would like to press charges." Then he gives the VanderZees' address and snaps his phone closed.

"Kevin, don't be ridiculous," Esme is saying, but apparently Kevin has chosen to ignore her now. He sits down to wait. He doesn't have to wait long, though, because—as everyone stands there, wondering what to do, and Malcolm starts to try to reason with Kevin—sirens are already wailing in the distance. With all the screaming and barking, Evan thinks, a helpful neighbor like Mrs. Sedgewick must have called, too.

•   •   •

n the midst of the screaming and barking Suzen backs away, takes off running. She doesn't even know where she is going, but she doesn't stop, though she is soaked through all the layers of her clothing.

She is so grieved by the events of the evening that she cannot catch her breath, even when she slows to a walk. She thinks of her father slugging Kevin. And Esme, terse yet calm. At one point she turned to Suzen and said, "Don't worry, things will be fine. It's just a terrible misunderstanding." *It's complicated.* She is besotted with rain and fatigue and emotion. What now? She can't go back; she might never go back.

Straightening up, Suzen sees orange jack-o'-lantern faces grinning at her from every doorstep, every porch down the block. Bedraggled clusters of children and parents stomp past, persevering in spite of the downpour. She sees that she is half a block from Strohman's nursery, the parking lot glowing from its lamplight at the end of the street where residential fades into commercial property. The trick-or-treaters have turned the corner, in search of more orange-lit houses, and Suzen continues on to the nursery as if she has been drawn there by an insistent, invisible hand. It is where she belongs. She has her own key now, a sign of Mary's faith in her.

Stepping inside, she is engulfed in the earthy dampness, the watery scent of wet soil and ephemeral floral, some already drooping in the darkness, as if giving up. Suzen realizes she is shaking, standing in the entryway of the nursery, familiar and consuming. It is so completely quiet, like standing on an island, waiting for the ship to come take her home. No one is going to come for her, though, she knows. She has to be the one to go. Suzen slips back through the door and locks it behind her, wasting no time.

The lock turns and there she is, Soci staring at Evan from her front doorway. "What are you doing here?" she asks, taken aback. "I thought I was going to meet you at the party." She is wearing a bathrobe and her hair is covered in a dark wig of snaky coils atop her head. Green glitter eye shadow glows in the porch light, and Evan stands looking at her for a moment, speechless.

"I'm not going to the party," he mutters.

"Why not?" Soci is incredulous, slightly annoyed. "You have to go! And where's your costume?"

"I don't have one," Evan shrugs. "My dad's in jail."

Soci gasps and steps out onto the threshold, shivering in the cold. The rain has ceased, but an Arctic wind has taken its place. "Jail! What happened?"

Evan isn't sure he appreciates her *schadenfreude*. At the same time, he is strangely turned on by the situation—danger, disruption, a girl in a bathrobe and green glitter. He has grown accustomed—or finally succumbed—to the effect Soci has on him. On impulse, he grabs her arm, thick in the soft chenille. "Let's get out of here, okay?"

"Now? Where?" Soci asks him.

"Chicago," he says firmly. It's about time. He has waited too long to give in to his urges, and her seductions. "You said we needed to get the hell out of here, right?"

She looks past him. "Is that your car?"

"No. Max's. I called him and he said he'd drive us."

"To Chicago?"

"No, he can't. But he said Greyhound runs at night. He'll take us there."

"Just a minute," she says. Soci turns and goes inside.

Evan leans against an enormous column to wait. He looks around at the grand facade, the gleaming marble floor through the glass panels on either side of the door. So, Max was right about her, after all. He turns and sees Max leaning down in the driver's seat to watch him. Evan wonders, for not the first time, if he has lost his mind coming here, doing this. But when Soci comes back outside, closing the door behind her and taking his hand, he feels more sure of himself. She is wearing tight blue jeans and a nearly translucent ivory sweater. Her hair and makeup are the same though, a weird juxtaposition, as if she has come from a stage and neglected to finish changing out of her wig, or wants to remain incognito.

"So, what were you going to be?" he asks, as they walk to Max's car.

She grins. "Medusa," she says, pointing to her fake hair. "See? Snakes—or that's what these were going to be, but I hadn't finished putting in the green gel when you came."

"Sorry," Evan says automatically.

She laughs. "About what? I didn't really give a damn about the party. I just wanted to show off for you."

Evan smiles, blushing. He puts his arm around her, claiming, or reclaiming, her.

"So, now you know where I live," she says, a shade uneasily.

"Yeah. It's pretty nice for a trailer," Evan says, glancing back at the house.

Soci laughs. "I don't know why I said that." Evan shrugs, no longer caring. Soci climbs into the front seat as Evan squeezes in beside her. "Hey, Max," she says.

"Hi. Soci, right?"

"Yeah."

"What's it short for?" Max asks as he pulls out of the long driveway. Evan wonders why he never thought to ask that himself.

"Antisocial," she says, and laughs.

When they arrive at the Greyhound bus station, which is really just a convenience store on the highway, Max waits for them to get out and then calls Evan back to his window. "Be careful," he says, sounding like a father.

"I am," Evan says, trying to sound cavalier. "You better go, or you'll be late for your own party."

"I'm serious, man," Max says gravely. "You're all wound up and I don't want you to go do something you might regret. Okay?"

"Okay," Evan says. "I'm coming back tomorrow," he promises, realizing as he says it that he has planned no further than getting on the bus.

When Max drives away, back toward town, Evan is awash in guilt. It's true, he is all wound up, and he left home without permission or explanation, simply reacting and fleeing.

He was aghast at his father's behavior. He had never seen Malcolm that mad before, never seen him hit another person. He remembers how last year, on Martin Luther King, Jr. Day, Malcolm had sat at the kitchen table trying to help Hallie answer some difficult questions for her third-grade social studies assignment. *Why did Dr. King preach nonviolence? Does any good ever come from violence?* Malcolm tried offering hints, until finally Hallie answered simply, "Violence is stupid. People only get hurt and Martin Luther King wasn't stupid." Malcolm nodded in agreement—*that's right*—smiling at Evan and then turning back to watch his daughter writing in a careful scrawl the word "violence" in a happy tilt, the "i" dotted with a little heart.

Yet, tonight, when he first saw the stranger there with Hallie's beloved, dead rat, acting strange and claiming to be there for Esme, Evan didn't blame his father for pummeling him, even as he stood by in disbelief. He heard Malcolm mutter to Esme afterward, "I'm sorry. I couldn't help it." Was the man his mother's lover? Evan didn't want to know. After the police left with Malcolm, Esme assured them— Evan and Hallie, the only ones left—that it was all a mistake and Malcolm would be free within an hour. Professor Watley was going to go take care of things. Evan had to go then, he couldn't help it. He felt like a pot left too long to simmer, the edges burned, in danger of exploding.

Evan takes a deep breath and clenches an arm tighter around Soci as they climb aboard the idling bus with their tickets in hand.

"Ow!" she pulls away a little. "You're squeezing the hell out of me, Ev."

"Sorry."

The bus is only half full of passengers who are quietly reading or staring out of the windows, so Evan and Soci have the back half of the bus to themselves. They could get away with quite a lot, he thinks, sliding a hand toward her breast. His fingers dangle there for a moment, considering. Her sweater is so tight and sheer, her entire bra line is visible. He can see the lacy scallop along the top rim of each cup, the little bump of clasp in the back when she leans over to reach into her purse. It would be relatively easy to reach underneath and unhook it, he thinks. He wishes she had worn a skirt instead of jeans; they are like armor, he has no idea how to discreetly do anything down there. His father, ever unhelpful, always advised him to stick to hand-holding because it was "safe, yet satisfying." This, Evan thinks, from a man who got his girlfriend pregnant in college. Ever preaching, never practicing. On the other hand, perhaps that was why he wanted Evan to go slowly, to avoid making the same mistakes; perhaps Malcolm was not being exasperatingly ignorant, after all. And there was Mara Torelli from Tuscany, too. Evan remembers the description in his father's journal—*her belly flat but soft, her legs opening like a flower . . . what it was like to be inside her.*

Evan looks through the window and tries to see the sky, the moody clouds, wishing he could float free from his body. But there he remains, pressed into a warm seat as the bus rattles along the highway, Soci's hand on his thigh. And all he can see in the window is his own scared reflection.

Suzen squints though the windshield of her mother's van. She knows the turn is around here, a mile or so ahead, but the road is not well marked. Though she feels remorseful for all of her misguided malice toward her mother, and now for taking her car without permission, Suzen felt she had no choice. She had to go, and once she went, she had to keep going. It is as if all of her life has been pointing to this moment, to this place.

The cottage is lit up like a little Chinese lantern in the woods. It is just as she imagined it would be. Something out of a fairy tale. In fact, at the very moment Suzen turns into the winding gravel driveway, it begins to snow. Big, fat snow-shaker flakes, out of nowhere. First the downpour of rain, then the sudden freezing temperature, so strange on Halloween, and now this. Suzen parks away from the house where there are a few other cars lining the dirt shoulder of the road. She fixes her short hair in the rearview mirror, puts on a coat of Vixen lipstick. Then she watches the snow through the window for a minute, taking deep breaths as she gets out of the car.

She watches her footprints melting into the thin layer of snow like sugar dissolving. Closer to the door she can hear music. She hesitates, steps around the side of the cottage and sees the lake, dark and churning. Tiny whitecaps edge the surface like bits of lace. When she took off in the car, Suzen had it all worked out how she might surprise Mary, showing up at her house. She'd reread part of *Tess*, and it seemed a sign: ". . . neither having the clue to the other's secret, they were respectively puzzled at what each revealed, and awaited new knowledge of each other's character and moods without attempting to pry into each other's history." Suzen imagines that Mary has spent time, as has she, trying to decipher the hints along the way, the crumbs Suzen has left in the path of the woods, waiting for Mary to follow—or to lead.

Now, however, standing outside her door, in front of a knocker the size of a dinner plate—oddly out of proportion to the elfish house— Suzen is nervous. Even so, she unbuttons her shirt a little, exposing cleavage, and raises her hand to knock. The door suddenly swings wide open.

"Oh!" says a voice, not Mary's. It belongs to a man around thirty-five, with buzzed black hair and tidy goatee. He is holding a glass of wine in one hand and the door handle gripped in the other. He grins at Suzen with a look of bemusement. Then he turns back toward the living room and calls out, "Hey, Mary, do you have any candy? Looks like the kids have found your house after all!" Then he looks back at Suzen, smiling, peering beyond her. "Are you alone?"

Suzen, mortified at being mistaken for a child, nods. She sees the man's gaze then drop from her face to her breasts; he is clearly surprised. She pulls her coat closed, finds her voice, "Is Mary here? I'm a friend of hers."

There are others, she sees, sitting in the small warm living room. Two women in front of a roaring fire, perched on the edge of a coffee table and sharing a joint, passed back and forth. They are laughing and leaning on each other. Another couple, a man and a woman, are looking out of the big windows that face the lake. Mary appears then out of the kitchen, a yellow bowl in one hand.

"Sorry," she is saying, sifting through the bowl with one hand and not looking up. "All I have is Jolly Ranchers. I kind of forgot it was Halloween, plus I never get any trick-or-treat—" She breaks off when she sees who is in the doorway. "*Suzy!* What on earth are you doing all the way out here?" Suzen, against her will, begins to cry. Mary reaches for her. "Oh, hey. Suzy. Come here."

And just like that, after all this time, she is in Mary's arms. She never expected a party, though. A houseful of strangers, watching. Thankfully, Mary leads Suzen into another room—her bedroom—and shuts the door behind them. The room, at least, is just as Suzen imagined it. The spare furnishings, the swept wooden floor, the bed covered in white, the window overlooking dark waves.

But Mary is not standing before her removing her shirt or pulling her close. She stands apart like a mother waiting for an explanation. "What is it, Suz, what's wrong?" she is asking.

Suzen shrugs, feeling small for the first time in Mary's presence. She can only say, "It's, I don't know, it's—everything." Mary guides her to the edge of the bed and sits beside her, solicitous. She puts an arm around her. Suzen feels her fingers on her shoulder like a jolt.

"What?" asks Mary, gently prodding.

"I'm just confused and I've made a mess of everything—"

"I'm sure that's not true," Mary says, patting Suzen's hand lightly. They sit together for a long moment and then Suzen blurts out what she can no longer contain.

"I love you," she says. The words come out so softly, at first she isn't even sure she has spoken aloud. Mary looks into her face, her gaze flickering, then she sits back, discreetly removing her arm from Suzen's shoulder.

"Suzen," she says warily. "I'm not sure you should be here. Do your parents know you're here?"

"No, but I just needed to see you."

"Well, I just wonder if—" Mary stands up again and goes to the window, running her fingers through her own short hair. She sighs heavily, puts her hands on her hips, then crosses her arms over her chest, paces a little. She doesn't look directly at Suzen when she speaks again, "I've had a feeling you have a crush on me. Is that it? I mean, I don't want you to think, to get the wrong idea—"

The air in the room suddenly seems to have disappeared. Suzen feels herself growing faintly dizzy, breathing a little harder. She is like one of the plants on the end of the greenhouse table, listing toward the water that isn't quite reaching its leaves, desperate for a drink. She is so full of longing and confusion and disappointment, she fears she might topple over.

"—I just know a lot of girls your age go through phases when they think they might be gay, or they experiment and they aren't really sure," Mary is saying, echoing Esme, and Suzen is having a hard time focusing on her words. "You probably are just feeling mixed up, it's normal, it's perfectly normal."

"It's not a phase," Suzen blurts. "I know the difference. I *know*."

"But you can't love me, Suzen. We're too different. You're a girl, a minor, and I'm much older than you. If I were a man, think how wrong it would be."

Suzen is trying not to cry again, it is childish, but she can't help it. She is a *minor,* Latin for "small", or "less." She is withering, bent over and weeping into her hands, bobbing like a flower. And Mary comes and puts her arms all the way around her, holds Suzen's face against her flat belly. The red lipstick is now smeared across Mary's clean white blouse, through which Suzen can hear her heart beating. Mary is as close as she has ever been to Suzen at the same time she is pulling further and further away.

But Suzen is the one to pull away first, standing up and wiping her eyes again.

"Suzen," Mary says helplessly. "I'm not sure—I mean, it *can* just be a crush. People have them all the time, with the opposite sex, the same sex, movie stars. Attraction is a powerful thing, I know. Sometimes you can't help it and you think it's something more than it is."

Suzen looks out the window at the black lake and the snow swirling into it and disappearing. Mary's words swirl around her, then disappear. Mary is a stranger, with a houseful of strangers. Outside the familiar realm of the nursery, she is a different sort of person, someone who does not know who Suzen is at all.

"Someday this will all make sense," Mary says gently. "Someday you'll understand."

Suzen already does. She walks out of the bedroom, finds a back door as if by instinct, and trudges through the muddy snow to her car. And by the time she has backed down the driveway, hearing nothing but her own breathing and the crush of gravel beneath the tires, she has crossed over into "someday"; she is years older.

The bus is going too fast. Things are happening light-years too fast.

"Well?" Soci is laughing, holding something. She presents both fists to Evan, smiling wickedly. "Pick one," she says.

He points to her left hand. She opens it. "Good guess," she says, revealing a shiny square packet. *Trojan.*

Evan stares at it as if he has never seen one before, though as Soci once guessed, like most boys his age, he does have one of his own, never used, never opened, just a little badge of manhood. He even has memorized the tiny blue lettering: *If used properly, latex condoms will help to reduce the risk of transmission of HIV infection (AIDS) and many other sexually transmitted diseases. Also highly effective against pregnancy. Caution: This product contains natural rubber latex which may cause allergic reactions.*

The last line is what gets him. Allergic reactions. How would he know? He never uses anything latex, and if he were allergic, what would happen? Hives? Grotesque, elephantine swelling? He doesn't want to find out. Also he can't quite believe Soci has planned ahead in this way. He only wanted to touch her breasts. Evan wants to will the bus driver to turn around and head back home. He should never have come, it was a mistake. He should have stayed at home; he should have gone to his father's aid. It seems clear to him now that being a man means being where you are most needed, not proving yourself to a girl. And running away with Soci is nothing like he'd imagined anyway. It's like the difference between watching Tarzan swinging from a rope and trying it yourself, feeling the burn in your palms and cursing. Life really isn't like the movies.

"I need to go back," he says daring himself to look into Soci's eyes. "I shouldn't have left."

"Yes, you should have. We both had to," she tells him firmly.

"Why?" Evan is bewildered.

"Because I've been trying to find a way out of here for ages, and you're it. You were meant to happen to me, Evan. You're restless, just like me. It's fate, don't you see?" A long black curl has fallen loose from her wig. She pushes it away and Evan can see tears on her cheeks. "Damn, I wish you could smoke on a bus."

Evan looks at the girl beside him—at her eyes, not her breasts, and sees a tormented depth he had never noticed before. How could he have missed it? It frightens him. "What?" he asks her softly. "What is it?"

"You don't want to know," she says, looking past him at the darkness. It's true, he doesn't. But he can tell she is going to tell him anyway.

The reason she lied about her background, she says, composing herself, is because she hates being the rich girl. It was how she was identified in her last school, and when she moved, she thought it would be the perfect time to metamorphose into someone else.

"Plus, I had a reputation," she says, running her finger along the back of the headrest in front of her.

"I don't want to know about that," Evan says. "I don't care."

She ignores him and continues, "I had a lot of boyfriends, Evan. A *lot*. And one of them worked for my dad. He was twenty-eight. My father wanted to have him arrested but I told him nothing happened. He said he believed me, but then all of a sudden he decided to move here—I think he thought if we went somewhere else it would be like it never happened, and I could lead this innocent midwestern girl's life." She sighs, looks out the window. "We never talk about it. We never talk, *period*. He thinks I'm going to turn out just like my mother, or that I already have, a lost cause." She makes a bitter face at her reflection in the window. "I'm a lost fucking cause, Ev."

"No, you're not," he says, wholly unprepared to comfort her, to take in what she has told him, and to go on from here. He knows nothing about her mother, as she has never told him, and now he doesn't want to ask. He knows more than he wanted to hear. And yet, there's still more.

"I've had other boyfriends here, too," Soci is saying, as if talking to herself. "Like Eddie, that jerk at the Esquire, and Eduardo—I guess I'm drawn to the E's for some reason." She continues musing but Evan cannot hear any of the words.

The bus is no longer careening down the highway, but has, in fact, slowed to a near-halt. The driver is pulling over at its first stop outside a diner. None of the passengers are getting off, apparently all in for the long haul to Chicago, but a few people are waiting to board. Evan seizes the opportunity and stands up. So does Soci, sighing.

At the front of the bus, the driver tells them to "take care, now." He looks at them with a kind, fatherly smile, as if he understands what has transpired.

Evan and Soci push through the cluster of new passengers climbing the steps and land on the wet pavement beside the bus. Evan looks at the sky, at the thick snowflakes falling. Soci says nothing, not even about the strange weather. She tugs at her coiled wig.

"So, I guess this means we aren't going," she says simply, as if unfazed, after the bus has left and they are alone on the side of the road. "Now what?" Soci glances at the warm lights of the diner behind them as if hoping Evan will suggest they go in.

"I guess we walk," Evan says, striding on without looking to see if she is following.

She drives to where she should have in the first place; though, of course, it never occurred to her until now. Suzen feels her life has been a maze she has been wandering through, blindly feeling her way, bumping into walls and backing out again. Now, as she walks to the door, past rows of cars crowding the driveway and the grass, she thinks, *Why not?* Her jaw is set, she is numb. Everything inside has tumbled, crashed. There is too much debris to sift through; like a stunned survivor, she wants to walk away from it all and not look back. She needs to be held, comforted. She needs someone to lick her wounds.

When the door opens, music pours over her like waves, thunderous, pulsing. She pushes her way past the drunken boy at the door and wanders through the crowd. A few girls from school greet her, others are too distracted with drinking and smoking and flirting to take notice.

"Hey, Suzen," a soft voice calls from a corner of the living room. It's Melissa, from English, who borrowed Suzen's copy of *Jude the Obscure* and never returned it, though she promised she would, as soon as she finished. "It's really hard to read," she had said. "I mean, I don't get it." Suzen advised her to stick with it, that it was worth it, but she knew she would never see the book again. Suzen waves a halfhearted hello to Melissa, and walks past the kitchen where the host, Jenna, is serving gin and tonics and rum and Cokes, slicing lemons with a long knife, her midriff bare beneath a tight T-shirt. Some of the revelers are wearing costumes, but most have not bothered, so it is not difficult to scan the rooms and find him.

"Susannah! You come!" he says, and his smile is so enormous and full of joy that Suzen blushes and actually smiles herself for the first time in what seems like days.

"Yes," she says. "I had nothing else to do."

Eduardo is leaning against a wall beside a bookshelf; it is obvious he feels out of place, though he has many friends and acquaintances from his semester at the school. Suzen knows that sometimes an exchange student is like someone's pet brought for show-and-tell; everyone finds him fascinating and adorable at first, but eventually they return to their own concerns. Suzen knows how he feels—smiling, lost.

She takes his hand. It is large and soft and it curls around hers without hesitation. This time he is the one who pulls her away, not into a hedgerow, but along the rows of books (she runs her fingers over their spines) and past the drunken boys and girls, a few kissing, most talking and laughing too hard, tossing pretzels at each others' heads. They walk up the carpeted stairs, stepping over coats tossed there, and stop when they find an empty room, dark, scented by vanilla and expensive perfume.

When he kisses her, it doesn't seem to matter that he is Eduardo, not Mary, not Soci, that he is practically a stranger, a man, a foreigner in every sense of the word. But when he holds her, he means it. It is like before, yet not at all. As he kisses her again and again, the tears roll down her face; he brushes them away with his fingers, licks them with his tongue. She doesn't even know what she feels anymore. She feels like she is wearing someone else's skin.

His hands travel down her neck, bump over her collarbone, hesitate at her breasts. He turns loose the buttons of her blouse, like tiny keys—*Let me in, let me in*—and she does not stop him. When his warm hands envelop her, slide down her sides, slip underneath her clothing, he stops kissing for a moment, his mouth open in a small gasp. Time stands still as they stand pressed together in someone's mother's bedroom. Eduardo's fingers find a hidden place and Suzen's mind races, though she is frozen. She knows that they cannot go further, this cannot be happening; even so, she isn't sure she wants him to stop. His fingers are so soft, they are moving so slowly, she could just let him . . .

"Just kiss me," she orders in a whisper. She pulls his hands back up and places them on her face, spreading his fingers over her from ear to nose. Like a blind man, he obeys, eyes closed, hands finding her there. His mouth covers hers again, and Suzen thinks it is enough, being absorbed in his kiss, losing herself in his large embrace. And then, it isn't enough. Somehow she keeps breathing. She keeps her eyes open, so she can see what Eduardo is thinking, can see him falling in love with her, even if it is for a few minutes; for now, it is all that matters. It is more than enough.

Soci has had enough. For the first two miles, Evan has led the way on the slushy shoulder of the highway, following the path of tail-lights leading back toward town. Suddenly, Soci stops in front of a brightly lit gas station and says, "I just want to go home," as if she has run out of energy and will. "I'm going to call my dad, and tell him we got lost on the way to the party."

"Why don't you just tell him the truth?"

Soci laughs. Then she looks at Evan as lights from passing cars flicker across her face. "You really don't understand how we function, my dad and I. I told you—*we don't talk.*"

"So. Maybe you should start," Evan says impatiently.

"Yeah, easy for you to say, with the perfect, nuclear family."

Now Evan laughs. "Very funny. You should have been there to-night."

Soci shrugs. "Well, that sounds like it was just a little drama. An aberration."

Aberration, Evan thinks, *from Latin, meaning "to go astray."* He'll miss that about Soci; she does have a way with words. In spite of every-thing, he finds he cannot easily dismiss her, and he won't forget her. Right now, however, he is sopping wet and angry and hurt; he just wants to leave her.

However, after she phones her father, Evan waits with her on a bench outside the gas station, too much a gentleman to leave her alone. Fortunately, it doesn't take long; Mr. Andersson shows up just ten min-utes later, in a black Mercedes splattered with snow. He peers at his daughter through the windshield with a look of consternation, and Evan expects him to jump out of the car and start screaming at them, at him. Instead, Mr. Andersson pulls the car to a parking space beside the building and gets out slowly. Evan automatically stands, out of a deeply ingrained sense of propriety and good manners.

Mr. Andersson nods at him. "Are you kids all right?"

"Yeah, fine," Soci says, sounding bored and annoyed. She does not look at her father.

"You must be Evan," Mr. Andersson says, holding out a hand.

Evan shakes it. "Yes, sir. Sorry about—" He stops, not sure what to say by way of explanation, nor what it is he is sorry for. Everything, he supposes.

"Don't mention it. I'm glad you're both all right. Do you want me to drive you to the party? Do you have an address?"

"No. We aren't going," Soci says flatly, finally standing up. "We're going home." She walks past her father and gets into the passenger seat of his car, slams the door.

"All right, then," Mr. Andersson says, apparently trying to maintain his composure. Though he is clearly unhappy about his daughter's attitude, he seems used to enduring it. "So, where do you live, Evan?" he asks, motioning him toward the rear door of his car.

"It's not far," Evan says, deciding then that he wants to be on his own, needs to be alone to think. "I can walk. But thanks, anyway."

"Well, okay. Are you sure? It's a nasty night."

"Yeah, sure."

Mr. Andersson gets into the driver's seat. Soci looks at Evan once, and waves sadly. Her expression tells him everything he needs to know, which is that she is letting him go.

He walks on, eighteen more blocks, his hair plastered to his head from rain and snow, his jacket sodden, dead weight. With each step he relives the previous hours, days, months. It is like watching a movie after knowing the outcome; everything is colored by the knowledge

that Soci is not really who he thought she was. Nor is he, for that matter. He is not a cavalier, hormone-driven boy but a person with a conscience, large and ticking like the Tin Man's heart. He found out
tonight that he cannot ignore it, nor does he want to.

When he arrives at the police station—a small unassuming brick
building next to a hair salon and an accounting firm—Evan opens the
door slowly, as if afraid he might be arrested on the spot; his guilt
engulfs him, though he hasn't committed a crime. And he has a pocket
full of cash (which he'd stored up for Chicago), prepared to use it if
need be.

He is relieved, however, to find Frederick Watley leaning against
the receptionist's desk as if simply waiting for coffee. As usual, Watley
is immaculately dressed, though there are hints of Halloween makeup
hastily wiped off his face.

"Evan!" he says cheerfully. "Have you come to help spring your old
man?"

"Is he okay?" Evan asks.

"Oh, yeah. Just a matter of a little paperwork," Watley says. "Come
with me. He could use some company."

As they walk down a corridor to the jail cells, Evan swallows. He
can see his father sitting on a narrow bed, looking dejected, then smiling meekly when he sees them coming, like a kid in detention. He
stands up.

"Hang in there, buddy," Watley says, grinning through the bars.
Evan shuffles awkwardly beside him, looking around. It's not as bad as
he'd had imagined it, from years of police dramas on television and B
movies. It is not particularly cold or dank; there are sheets and a blanket tucked neatly on the bed, even a pillow. The toilet looks recently
cleaned—its water is blue—and (the little touch Evan likes best) there
is a roll of flowered toilet paper.

"Hi, Dad. You all right?"

"Yeah, fine. But can you believe this?" Malcolm says. He runs a hand through his own messy hair and tries not to appear upset. "I just don't understand why they didn't arrest *him*."

"I know," Evan agrees. "He was a lunatic."

"It was a long time ago," Malcolm says.

"What was?"

Malcolm sighs. "Never mind. I'll tell you about it later."

From his tone, Evan gathers that whatever happened between his mother and Kevin Wunderhaus doesn't affect anything now. He is relieved—and he really doesn't want to know the details. He's had enough surprises for one night.

"Anyway," Malcolm says, coming close to the bars so that his face is divided in two neat halves, "that guy seems to have some problems with managing his anger."

Watley grins. "Right. If that isn't the kettle—"

"I know, I know," Malcolm says, exasperated, though more with himself than his friend, Evan suspects. "I realize I'm culpable. I lost it. But he did start it, in a way."

"The thing is, he didn't hit anyone," Watley says, but without reproach. "And apparently he hadn't actually trespassed because he never entered your house."

"Hallie was hysterical," Malcolm says quietly. "It all happened so fast."

"It's true," Evan says.

"I know," Watley says.

Then Malcolm says, "What if I lose my job?" His black-inked fingers grip the bars.

"Don't worry. You aren't going to get fired over slugging some idiot."

"Well, look at Pincer, last year. Remember?"

"That was a whole different can of worms," Watley says. "Besides, the administration doesn't look too kindly on sex, but they are sort of fond of violence." Evan laughs and Malcolm does, too. Then Watley comes closer to the cell, conspiratorially. "Hey, by the way, I just heard through the grapevine that you're in for a little rest anyway."

"What?"

"Your sabbatical. It was approved this afternoon."

Evan grins, looks down at his feet. He can't believe Malcolm went through with it. He feels he has been given a reprieve himself; finally, he can *go*.

"How did *you* hear?" Malcolm says. "Why didn't anyone tell me first?"

"You don't sleep with the right people." Watley winks at him and laughs. "Don't worry—I'm kidding. Not about the sabbatical, though. I just happened to have been in the right place and nosing around at the right time. It was on the dean's desk. I think he probably tried to call you, but you were—tied up."

Malcolm laughs again, giddy this time. "I can't believe it!" Then he sobers. "But now, when they find out—"

"This is nothing." Watley waves an arm. "I talked to one of the arresting officers. Dick, I think? He said this falls into the category of domestic dispute and, really, he says he's seen a *lot* worse."

There is a sound behind them and they all turn to see an officer bearing keys. Evan steps back as the gate is unlocked. The officer, an overweight man with a swirl of thinning hair, announces cheerily, "Okay, Mr. VanderZee, you are free to go. I hope you enjoyed your stay with us. But please don't drop in again." Then he turns and ambles down the hallway.

"Looks like you were the only one here, Dad," Evan notes as they walk out, passing four empty cells.

"Slow night in Mayberry," Watley says.

"So, when do we leave?" Evan asks, barely able to contain his excitement as they push through the double doors.

"Leave?"

"For Italy! Your sabbatical."

Malcolm stops walking. They are on the steps outside the station house. Snow is falling again, collecting on their heads like dandruff.

"Um, Evan, I did apply for a sabbatical—six months. But we aren't going to Italy. Your mother and I decided you and your sisters need to stay in school. I mean, since Suzen is graduating this spring, and you only have two more years, and well, we need to simplify our life a bit. I'm taking time off to work on a little writing. A novel, a sort of coming-of-age-story about a young man falling in love in Italy." He grins and bows his head sheepishly. Watley pats his back encouragingly.

Evan cannot speak, first as he absorbs this information (and the pages of the ancient notebook flutter once again, colored by a new meaning) then the blow of disappointment, throbbing like a headache (*We're staying*). He begins to walk on ahead.

"Hey, Ev, my car is right over here," Watley calls.

Evan waves a hand. "I'll walk. Thanks anyway." He goes on trudging through the night by himself, deconstructing and reconstructing his plans.

Suzen arrives home late, pulling into the driveway as if in a dream; in one night, it seems, everything has changed. She walks up the path in a daze, her coat flapping open in the cold wind, her heart still thumping. Before she opens the door, she checks to make sure that her blouse is buttoned, that nothing is revealed. She wants to tell someone, and yet she doesn't. It is too big, all of it.

She opens the back door slowly, unsure of what to expect, what has happened in her absence—startled to find her mother sitting in the kitchen, alone.

"Some night," Esme says, turning to look at her. There is only one light on in the room, over the sink, and in its dim glow, she looks girlish—and tired.

"Is everything all right?" Suzen asks, quavering.

Esme nods. "It will be." She motions to the chair opposite her and Suzen sits, wrapping her coat around her.

"I still think you need something warmer," Esme says. "Something wool." She smiles, as if to say, *No hard feelings.*

"Yeah, you're probably right," Suzen says.

While they sit at the table, two cups of hot tea between them, Esme explains what happened. Anticipating the worst, she had sent Hallie next door to Lily's, picked up Aimee from the party and delivered her to Mrs. Sedgewick, then rushed to the police station—where Malcolm was taken when Kevin insisted on pressing assault charges. Esme assumed that she had to post bail, but had neglected to take her purse with her, so Frederick Watley promised to pay it himself, though it wasn't necessary after all.

"They're coming home any minute," Esme tells Suzen, though she looks shaken. "Evan's there, too, thank goodness," she adds, looking at her fingers as if she has been counting her family members and now they are all accounted for. She looks up. "Listen, I know I should have just told you before about—"

"It's okay," Suzen says quickly. "It was mostly my fault."

Esme does not comment on this, just says, "I guess I was sort of ashamed."

"Why?"

Esme laughs. "I don't know. It was a mistake, that's all. I was young. You know, your dad didn't even know until a few weeks ago. I had to tell him. All those phone calls—even *he* was beginning to wonder." She lifts her arm, then drops it, helplessly. "I was engaged to Kevin," Esme says then, looking at Suzen, her eyes wide as if she can't quite believe it herself, "before your father, twenty years ago. It lasted about a month and then I broke it off. I was actually in a bridal store, looking at veils, and I realized—it was like being hit by lightning and I had no choice but to back out. I thought he took it pretty well, considering, and to tell you the truth, I got over it pretty fast; I always thought back then that there were plenty of fish in the sea." She shakes her head. "Funny how you think what you do doesn't really affect anyone that much, and then you find out that it can, it does."

"It's not your fault," Suzen says. She knows, deep down, that it is her mother's fault—for being beautiful and desirable, and oblivious to the power that holds. Yet, she can't blame her, either. "You can't help how he reacted," she adds, gently.

"That's true," Esme says. "He has a lot of things to deal with, I guess, and it isn't really about me." She drops her gaze, picks at her cuticles. "You know, a secret is sort of like an egg. You carry it around so carefully, and after awhile you forget about it. But it's still there, and it's fragile, and eventually, you're going to drop it."

They sit in silence for a few minutes. Then Esme takes Suzen's hand, folds her fingers into her own. Esme says finally, "I know you think I don't understand what you are going through. But I try—" She pauses, sighs. "Sometimes, I wish I could just keep you small and innocent."

Suzen smiles sadly. *When was that?* she thinks. She feels so tired she wants to sleep for days and days. She holds all of her secrets—each kiss, each touch, each word—like little eggs, robin's eggs. They nestle inside her and she holds them tenderly, protectively.

Her mother reaches across the table and smoothes Suzen's hair with her hand. She smiles. "Why don't you go get some sleep? I'll stay up till everyone gets home."

Suzen nods and rises. When she gets to her room, it seems years since she was there, a girl in her boudoir, wrapped in blankets and dreaming. She lies down on the bed, lets the tears roll all the way down the sides of her face, into her ears in tiny pools. She weeps for the girl she is, and was, the pain she has endured and inflicted, the loss of someone she wanted but hardly knew, the loss of one she now knows deeply.

She didn't plan it, but at the time, she needed him—someone she knew wanted her. And then it just happened, and she let it; she let him touch her in the dark, scented room, let him enter her body. At the same time, she felt lost, and in a strange way, departed—a piece of her breaking loose and flying away. So she held onto him, and he took her with him to wherever he was going. Her face was pressed into his chest and she thought of Mary; she couldn't help it. It was as if Mary were part of him, etched onto his skin, and perhaps that was why she wept.

She still can't help thinking it. It is the bruise she needs to press, the scab she can't resist nicking at with her fingernail. She wants to look at what happened and think about it even if she cannot bear it, until she can bear it, and then it will be over—then it will all make sense.

EARLY SUMMER

On the drive to the airport, Evan's family keeps up a constant flow of chatter, either to distract him and themselves, or simply because that is how they are; they can't help it. He realizes then that he will be away from it all for a whole year—the sound of their voices, the chorus of too many people talking out of turn, the singular tones of each one he knows by heart. He tries to concentrate on what is being said, but he only hears bits and pieces, Hallie pointing out a Beetle on the road ("Slug Bug!") and Aimee retorting that she's seen "a hundred" already, and Malcolm and Esme talking together in the front seat, and Suzen leaning up to ask them about customs requirements.

"Not when you're going overseas," Malcolm tells her. "You only have to declare what you're bringing back into the country."

"You better bring something good," Suzen says then, turning to Evan, smiling. "And I don't mean ashtrays with the Coliseum printed on them."

"Okay," he says amiably. But he finds he can't say any more. He remains almost silent the rest of the way to the airport, only responding when spoken to, trying to control his mounting anxiety.

For months he has been preparing. After sending applications to an exchange-student program, enduring lengthy (but benevolent) interviews, and undergoing a physical, Evan received a letter from his host family, the Castellis of Spoleto, a hill town in Umbria. He has written them back, in carefully translated Italian, using words that are now familiar. He finds that everything sounds better in Italian anyway, and he has memorized vocabulary from his father's cassette tapes: *la valigia* (suitcase); *l'uovo sodo* (hard-boiled egg); *il cappello* (hat); *il pane bianco* (white bread). It is pure poetry; it falls through his head like confetti.

His father offered plenty of advice for travel, including how to pack. "Whatever you set out to take, cut that in half. You'll need less than you think you do, trust me. On the other hand, you never know what the weather is going to be like, or if you will be able to get things like unscented deodorant or fluoride toothpaste." He paused, looking around at Evan's belongings. "Maybe you should take bigger bags. These won't hold nearly enough."

His mother's advice was simple: "Just come back in one piece, okay?"

When Soci found out he was leaving, she said she was happy for him. She said she understood the desire to "get the hell out of Dodge." But this time she smiled. She told Evan she was seeing a psychologist and it was helping. Yet, she seemed strangely shrunken, as if she'd been deflated. Evan feared she was turning anorexic. Girls her age under stress often did, it seemed. Just as they neared adulthood, they began to shrink to their childish selves as if to ward off the inevitable burden of growing up.

"You need to eat more," he said gently.

"Yeah," she said. "My doctor says so, too. So, how long will you be gone?"

"Nine months. Maybe for good." When he saw her large eyes widen, he relented. "Just kidding. I'll be back in April."

She leaned over and kissed him lightly on the cheek. "*Arrivederci, baby,*" she said.

Funny, how he was the one leaving, after all.

Outside the enormous airport windows, the summer sky is dark but streaked with the bruised watercolors of sunset. Evan watches the sky, the sparking lights of planes taking off and landing, the row of runway torches and the constantly shifting reflection in the glass of people rushing toward their gates. He is one of them, though at the moment he is not rushing, but standing still, heart pounding. He can see wing lights blinking in the purple sky, and soon he will be up there, all alone. On his way to the *Castellis de Spoleto*. What if they don't like him? What if he doesn't like them? What if he forgets every word of Italian he has memorized over the past nine months? Hours of cassette tapes, columns of vocabulary, notes on tense and rules for articles and gender of nouns. He takes deep breaths and tries to remember, repeating them like mantras. *La luna, la stanza, la strada, la banca. Il Gatto, il cane, la casa, il treno.*

He watches his parents, now a little tense and edgy, Malcolm hustling his bags onto the scale for the attendant to weigh, Esme nervously checking the departure times on the monitors. Suzen and Hallie are sitting together, whispering and laughing, obviously playing the people-watching game, inventing stories and maladies for passersby. Aimee is sitting cross-legged, quickly going through a bag of snacks Esme had packed for Evan. He is glad; he wouldn't be able to eat anything anyway.

"There won't be anything left for Evan," Suzen snaps, snatching the bag away from Aimee. Still a little of the mother in her, Evan notes.

Aimee looks up, chewing. She shrugs. "They have food on the plane, you know."

"Yeah, but it's gross," Hallie says.

"It is?" Aimee asks, uneasy. Then, more skeptical, "How do you know?"

"Everyone says airline food is gross," Hallie says. "It's freeze-dried eggs and stuff like that. Lily told me."

"Hey, Ev, come sit down," Suzen is calling, patting the chair on the other side of her, and he obeys. "Nervous?" she asks, and he shrugs, then nods.

To distract himself, Evan watches airline attendants strolling past, pulling their navy blue carry-on bags behind them like pets on leashes. One of them is regally tall, brunette, with bright eyes and impossibly long legs. She bends slightly to adjust her stocking. "Look at that," Evan whispers to Suzen. "I bet she's from Europe, you can tell."

"How?"

"The posture. Definitely un-American. And look at her teeth—perfect, but not from braces. Only Swedes have teeth like that. Or the Irish. Or Germans."

"Well, pick one," Suzen says impatiently. "I'd say British."

"*British?*"

Suzen shrugs. "I'll bet you ten bucks—or is it lire? Ten lire wouldn't get you much, would it? How about ten thousand?"

"Okay. How are you going to prove it?"

To his astonishment, Suzen stands up and walks directly to the flight attendant in question, asking her an apparently innocent question; Evan sees the woman pointing down the corridor. Suzen smiles at her, then turns and grins at Evan as she returns to her seat beside him. "She told me the *loo* was directly down there, to the left of the *kiosk*," Suzen says in an exaggerated English accent.

"Really?"

"Really. Go ask her yourself, Romeo."

"Maybe I will," Evan says. "You saw how she was looking at me. Lustily."

"Actually, I think the correct word is 'lustfully,'" Suzen says, musing. "Though in this case, it probably isn't a reality."

Evan looks at her. "When did you get so smart?"

Suzen shrugs. "I always have been. You just never notice."

"So, what's her name?"

"Who?"

"The English stewardess! Didn't you get her name—and phone number?" Evan asks. Suzen laughs, but then looks away, clearly uncomfortable. They haven't spoken much lately, not about anything important, anyway. Their sibling relationship has been strained, edgy, a dance of avoidance. Now Suzen reaches across her seat to take Evan's hand. He lets her, turning to look out of the window for a moment to let the moment be, knowing they don't need to say any more.

"It's time to board," Esme says, suddenly standing over them. Evan rises and his sisters follow, getting in line beside him like bridesmaids. They smile at Evan, teary-eyed. He has not thought much about leaving his sisters behind; he has been looking and charging ahead. Now, it seems there is a part of his heart that is contracting. He can barely look at Hallie's sharp little chin, or Aimee's new overlarge front teeth, or Suzen's burnished hair, growing out like soft straw. They hug him, one by one, Suzen whispering, "Be good—and call me, okay?" and her tears wet the rim of his ear. Esme can say nothing, just holds and holds him as if he is going off to war. When she lets go, she turns halfway around, as if she cannot watch him go. Malcolm is last, embracing him heartily, also clearly emotional, but determined to keep the mood light. He slaps Evan one last time on the back and hands him his boarding pass and ticket, asks again about his passport, phone numbers, allergy medicine, reading material.

"Got it," Evan says, smiling. "I think I have everything—and then some."

Malcolm laughs. He needlessly adjusts Evan's backpack strap over his shoulder, an oddly tender gesture. Evan has to swallow hard.

"Grazie," Evan finally says.

"Prego," Malcolm answers automatically. Evan stares at him appreciatively and grins. There is nothing left to do but go forward. He backs slowly away from his family, smiling bravely, finally turning when it is his turn at the gate. He hands his boarding pass to the ticket agent, and allows himself a last glance back at his family. They are still gathered in the same spot, as if unwilling to take a step until he is safely on

board. Evan smiles and waves, and they all wave back, vigorously, grinning through their tears. Evan hoists his bag, clears his throat, and saunters down the corridor to his plane.

When he takes his seat, he slides in beside the window and looks out. The sky is black now, and he can't see anything but his own blurry face in the scratched oval pane. All around him passengers are settling in, slipping off shoes, unpacking paperbacks, talking quietly. Evan looks around the cabin and feels strangely at home among them. A million emotions collide inside him, and he knows there are no words for what he feels or what he wants, not in any language. It doesn't matter. He smiles, mute, sublimely happy. He is ready for anything and everything.

Suzen is ready, with all of her belongings—at least those that fit— heaped into the back of her secondhand car. She goes back inside the house and walks through every room one last time. Stopping at her bedroom door, she notices how small it looks without her things in it. The flowered wallpaper looks girlish, the curtains white and ruffled, the carpet Hoover-striped. She feels like a realtor gazing at it through a new buyer's eyes—there is no sign of chaos anywhere, no dried tears or recorded rantings, no hard feelings nestled between wallboards or grudges behind closed doors. It amazes Suzen sometimes how a person is like a room, containing all of life in a single body, in a headful of memories and experiences no one else can tap into. Just as she could scream obscenities in a room and the room would look the same as before, she can be thinking anything at all while her face remains placid, revealing nothing.

"When are you leaving?" Aimee asks from behind her. Suzen turns, startled from her thoughts.

"In the morning, first thing." Suzen looks at her sister, who has grown a little; her front baby teeth are gone and two wide tips of new teeth are wedging into place. Her hair is braided tightly, making her look somehow older, sturdier. She has all but forgotten about her brief stint in the afterlife. All she cares about now is gymnastics—at which she excels—and getting her own room, which will happen momentarily; she greedily eyes Suzen's empty room.

"I'm going to miss you," she says suddenly, as if it has only just occurred to her.

Suzen laughs. "No, you won't."

"Yes, I will!" Aimee says emphatically. She throws her arms around Suzen.

"I'm not going that far, you know," Suzen says. "Just about five miles. That means you can visit me anytime. Okay?"

Aimee nods against Suzen's hip, then lets go. "Can I sleep over?"

"Sure. You and Hallie both."

"When—tomorrow?"

Suzen smiles at her. "Well, probably not tomorrow, I'm just moving in. But soon, okay?"

"Okay. Wanna see my back flip?"

Suzen follows her downstairs and out into the backyard, where Aimee tosses her lithe little body across the grass, toes pointed, a nearly perfect X tumbling over and over. Suzen applauds. When Aimee has exhausted herself, she stands upright and wanders over to the garden where a hose has been left to trickle water into the ivy. Aimee picks it up and begins to wave it around, shaking droplets of water in the air and spraying erratically until the water reaches a white wooden marker. She stops and stares at it for a moment, reverently. It is where Edgar lies buried beside Cupcake. The old dog simply lay down one afternoon a few weeks earlier and never woke up. Malcolm wrapped him in an old blanket that the dog had chewed, and buried him, surrounded by marigolds and impatiens. Suzen watches Aimee watering Edgar's grave and knows she is hoping that he feels the cool water, can taste it on his long ribbon tongue. He is probably cavorting with giant rabbits even now.

Suzen sits down on the back porch and waits for her parents to return home. They are running errands—together, part of a new routine. Like newlyweds, they have begun spending more time together, and more time at home, as if they have decided that it is time to start over, as a nuclear family. It is a decidedly smaller one now. Yesterday, Evan left for Italy for a school year and tomorrow her parents will accompany Suzen across town to her new apartment.

Frederick Watley found it for her, through a friend of a friend—the whole top floor of a sprawling white Victorian house with its own balcony in the treetops. Suzen fell in love with it; she knew it was meant to be hers.

A month ago, right after her eighteenth birthday, she walked through the three sunlit rooms, the roomy bathroom—all hers—and had to take a breath. Outside the windows was, amazingly, a farm visible just a half a mile away, a wide swath of land divided into quilts of soybeans and corn, and bordered by small woods. Just like England, or close enough, for now. Suzen handed the landlady a month's rent for a deposit (from her college fund, raided a little with her parents' blessing), and was told she could move in after the apartment was repainted. She roamed around, picturing just where she would put her bed, her books, the dented secondhand table unearthed from the basement. She looked at the sky through her new windows and thought that it was a color she had never quite noticed before.

Now that she is on her own—or nearly—everything seems different. She thinks of the end of *Jane Eyre,* when the lonely and lovestruck governess finally finds herself. "I am independent," she tells her former employer, the tormented Mr. Rochester, "I am my own mistress."

Having learned all she was going to from her own employer, Suzen has also found another job; she told Mary she needed to move on. Mary said, of course, she understood. Suzen scoured the classified ads for weeks after graduation, until she found a tiny advertisement for the right thing—a florist's assistant (not apprentice). She still will handle flowers, inhaling the earthy aroma clinging to cut stems, as she wraps them in tissue paper and delivers them to the arms of surprised and delighted recipients. Not a bad way to spend her days, she thinks. She is rethinking everything. And perhaps gardening will be her salvation after all, her oasis on the weekends. Her landlady told her to "feel free" to take over the neglected backyard and Suzen already has visions for a transformation, something small and manageable, where a person could get lost, but only if she wanted to. Not like the Anderssons' maze, designed to confuse.

Suzen recently visited the nearly finished project one last time, secretly; after she left Strohman's, she resolved never to look back, but she couldn't resist. When she happened to spy Soci and her father eating dinner at a restaurant downtown, Suzen drove on past and kept driving until she reached their house. She parked out of sight and walked quickly round to the back, half expecting guard dogs to run barking at her heels. Of course, she knew there weren't any, and she felt immediately at home, just as she used to. She strolled through the hedges, neat row upon row, winding her way easily, as she knew the plans by heart. This time, however, her imagination didn't soar, and she didn't find herself turning into a fictional English girl lost in the grandeur of the landscape. Instead, she felt disappointed, misled. The maze was pedestrian, midwestern. There was no magic, no surprise, just order and contrivance, and she couldn't wait to escape—back out, not in deeper, as she once wanted.

The afternoon sun is pulling away from the treetops, slipping lazily down. Aimee continues to vault across the grass, and Hallie, who has left Lily's house to come home, joins her. Suzen watches her sisters, confidently flinging their bodies into the air. Then she looks up at the sky and imagines their brother in it, flying away. She envies him a little, yet she knows she is flying, too, just closer to home, a fledgling leaping from the nest.